PARADING THE COWBOY BILLIONAIRE

A CHAPPELL BROTHERS NOVEL: BLUEGRASS RANCH ROMANCE BOOK 4

EMMY EUGENE

Copyright © 2020 by Emmy Eugene

All rights reserved.

No part of this book may be reproduced in any form or by any electronic or mechanical means, including information storage and retrieval systems, without written permission from the author, except for the use of brief quotations in a book review.

ISBN-13: 979-8583202577

1

Cayden Chappell pulled up to the farmhouse where his brother lived now. The new sign had weathered its first rainstorm, and the whole state of Kentucky had come through the weekend's downpour just fine.

Cayden felt like he'd had that storm cloud raining on him for almost three months now. The invisible weight he carried on his shoulders made him sigh as he got out of his truck. He knew where it came from, but he didn't know how to shrug off Virginia Winters.

She'd captured him completely, and while their relationship hadn't been traditional before, it was better than none at all.

He pushed her out of his mind, though he knew she'd just come back. She always did, and Cayden had lost way too much sleep to thoughts of the woman he'd only kissed once.

Once.

She shouldn't have such sway over him, and yet, she did.

He obviously hadn't made that big of an impression on her, because she'd never called him after she'd returned from her Caribbean vacation two months ago.

He went up the steps and rang the doorbell at the farmhouse, listening to it ring on the other side of the door. It sang through the country stillness too, and Cayden gazed out over the pasture that sat in the front left corner of the ranch. The grass was starting to green now that it was almost April, and Beth had two horses there, their heads down as they grazed.

There was something peaceful and serene about it that called to Cayden's soul. As the public relations manager, he didn't spend nearly enough time with the horses at Bluegrass Ranch. He could spend whole days in his office, in the administration building where few people normally came.

The only time the administration building was busy was during one of their events—the yearlings sale or their auctions. Then, the whole ranch bustled with activity, and Cayden was the one responsible for all of that.

He needed to get outside more, and he wandered away from the door and toward the railing on the far side of the porch. He'd just leaned against the railing when Beth said, "Cayden?"

"Mm." He continued to gaze at the pasture for another moment before he turned to his sister-in-law. Beth wore a denim skirt that narrowed at her knees and a black blouse with brightly colored flowers on it. She was exactly the kind of woman Trey should be with, and Cayden smiled at her.

"Sorry. I got lost looking at your horses. I need to get outside more." He'd finally finished wrapping up the horses-of-all-ages sale that had taken place at the ranch last month, and he was ready for a tropical vacation now too. It would be hot in Kentucky soon enough, and then he'd be wishing for cooler mornings like this one, with plenty of breezy afternoons.

"Those are actually Trey's," she said. "He brought them over last night."

Cayden crossed the distance between them. "You told him I don't want to go to this, right?"

"Repeatedly," she murmured without looking at him. "He has it in his head that if you two will just get yourself into the same room together, you'll remember why you liked each other so much."

"I don't need a reminder," Cayden said darkly. He'd never thought of himself as a growling, moody man, but since Ginny's disappearance from his life, he'd certainly become exactly that.

"Maybe she does," Beth said. "There's nothing wrong with reminding her of certain things."

Cayden pressed his teeth together and kept the words he wanted to bark at her contained. He'd told two people what Wendy Winters had said to him. Exactly two—Lawrence and Trey. Neither had bothered him much about calling Ginny or trying to breathe new life into a relationship that had gone quiet.

Until now. Now, Trey seemed to think it was his job to make sure Cayden embarrassed himself at every turn.

"If I'm so forgettable," Cayden said. "Will the reminder really matter?"

"You're not forgettable," Beth said. "Come on in now. TJ wants to ask you somethin' before we go." She turned and went into the house, and Cayden had no choice but to follow her. He wouldn't disappoint TJ if he could avoid doing so. The child had some sort of magic about him that made everyone bend to his will.

"He's here," she called as she went past the comfortable couches in the living room. The farmhouse had huge windows flanking both sides of the front door, letting in plenty of light. Cayden had never given much thought to where he lived, but as he'd gotten to know Ginny and seen her house, he'd been stewing on it more and more.

He wasn't even sure why.

She hadn't called him. He'd been very busy with the horses-of-all-ages sale, sure. He hadn't asked her to stay away, though. He hadn't given her any indication that he didn't have time for her.

Not only that, but another month had passed since that event, and she still hadn't called. He hadn't called her, because she'd been prepping for the Sweet Rose Gems & Gin event.

His mind seized on that thought, but he couldn't examine it before TJ yelled, "Cayden!" from the kitchen.

The little boy came running through the doorway Beth had just gone through, and Cayden braced himself to receive the kid. He had a battery that never seemed to run out, and Cayden had seen him trailing behind Trey several times. He'd think TJ had gotten tired, but it was never true. He'd pick up the pace a moment later or see a dog and go chasing after it. Or Trey would say something to him, and he'd perk right up, running to catch Trey and get swung up onto a horse, where his face would glow like a lantern.

The little boy had a bright personality and a shock of dark hair that made him look like Trey's son, even though he wasn't.

"Heya, boy," Cayden said, his soul warming with the hug of the smaller human. "Your momma said you had something to ask me."

"Yeah." TJ released the tight grip around Cayden's neck and pulled back. "My teacher asked if anyone had a mom or daddy who knew how to make banners, and I was talkin' to Trey and he says you do."

"Said," Beth said from a few feet away. "Trey *said* you do."

Cayden grinned at TJ and then Beth. "I do know how to make banners," he said. "I know lots of people who make banners, actually."

"She wants to talk to you, then," TJ said. "I guess she needs some help with it."

"Okay," Cayden said, not sure what he should do here. He looked at Beth, who rolled her eyes.

"Trey can give her your phone number," Beth said. "If that's okay."

"Is it okay?" TJ asked, his eyes bright. He started playing with Cayden's collar, a hint of nerves in his movement.

"Sure," Cayden said. "Why not? What's her name?"

"Miss Robertson," TJ said. He wiggled, and Cayden put him on the ground just as Trey came in the back door.

"You're late," Beth said, and Trey just smiled at her, grabbed her around the waist, and kissed her. She giggled and made a lame attempt to push him away. Cayden couldn't help staring, and he felt bad for doing so once his brother looked at him.

Cayden was three years older than Trey, and three years younger than Spur. They were both cut from similar cloth—a rough, scratchy cloth. They didn't speak as often as the younger brothers. They held their emotions tight.

Blaine had the biggest heart and showed the most emotion. Duke, Ian, and Conrad were the loudest, always jockeying for a position of attention in the family. Lawrence was a mix of Cayden, Trey, and the younger boys, and Cayden got along really well with him.

Cayden felt like a black sheep in the Chappell family. He wasn't overly emotional, but he did feel things deeply. He didn't have to be the center of attention, but he didn't mind speaking his opinions either. He wasn't a natural-born leader, but he did possess a level of charisma that made him the natural choice for the public face of the ranch, something he'd been doing for twenty years now.

Trey had told him that he was the brother TJ talked about the most. He asked when Cayden could come over, and whenever Beth and Trey were going out, TJ asked if Cayden could watch him.

Cayden wasn't sure if that made him likable or pathetic.

"Do you have the invite?" Trey asked, stepping around Beth to the fridge.

"You need to go change," she said. "We're eating there."

"I have the invitation," Cayden said, reaching into his inside jacket pocket. "You guys can just take it."

"It says right on it that the person it was sent to has to be there. Guests are encouraged, *with* that person."

Cayden had read it a hundred times. He knew what the postcard said. When he'd gotten it at the homestead, he'd been two seconds away from tossing it in the trash.

Trey had seen it, and since it had a glinting diamond taking up the entire front, he'd grabbed it.

He and Beth were in the market for new wedding rings. Rather, he and Beth were going to buy their *first* wedding rings. Since they'd gotten married last fall in an unconventional way, they didn't have a lot of the same things a more traditional couple would.

Cayden could see how much they loved each other, though. He wanted that same kind of giggling, doe-eyed woman in his life. He'd used to not care if he had a girlfriend or not. He was focused on his career, and as one of the only brothers with a college education, he was determined to prove to everyone that it mattered. *He* wanted to matter.

"Maybe once this is over, you two will be able to get your schedule to line up," Beth said, and Cayden's mind returned to that thought he'd stalled on before TJ had distracted him.

"I don't know," he said. "Is texting hard?"

"Have you texted her?" Trey challenged.

"Go change your clothes," Beth said, her irritation plain on her face. Trey nodded and headed down the hall, leaving Cayden alone with Beth and TJ.

He didn't want to hear more about what could maybe happen with Ginny at the event. He met Beth's eye and said, "I'll go wait outside," he said. They'd asked him to drive and everything, and somehow Cayden had said yes.

He went back the way he'd come while Beth said

something to TJ. Several minutes later, everyone was in the truck and Cayden was following his map to her father's house. She ran TJ inside and returned to the truck less than a minute later.

"Ready," she said, exhaling heavily.

"Let's do it," Trey said.

Cayden could make the drive to Sweet Rose Whiskey in his sleep, and he let Trey and Beth talk amongst themselves as he navigated them across town. The parking lot was fairly full already, as the event had started about ten minutes ago. It was an open house, so it wasn't like they'd needed to be there exactly on time.

He turned right and went toward the huge field adjacent to the lot, as he drove a big truck and could handle the rougher road. He parked and handed the postcard to Trey, who promptly pushed it right back at him.

"You're coming in," he said. "Just get us through the door."

"No," Beth said. "He's coming in, and he's staying. He's our ride."

Cayden wanted to argue with her, but he said nothing. He got out of the truck and took a deep breath. The evening had started to darken and cool, and Cayden loved the slower, quieter evenings in the country.

He knew what the event inside would be like, and he inhaled the calm before the storm. Before he knew it, he was stepping up to a gentleman at the door and handing him his postcard.

"Evening, Mister Chappell," the man said. He looked up and met Cayden's eyes, and Cayden's breath stuck in his throat. He knew this man. He'd parked his truck at Ginny's New Year's Eve party.

"Evening," he managed to say.

"Two guests?" he asked, glancing at Trey and Beth.

"Yes, please," Cayden said, slipping into his more formal personality. He hated that, and he pulled himself right back to his cowboy roots. If Wendy Winters was going to think him unworthy of her daughter, he might as well act like the heathen she thought he was.

Cayden had never been much of a rule-breaker, though, and his natural instinct was to please people. His mother. His teachers. Spur. Ginny.

Wendy.

He wondered if Ginny's mother had said anything to her, and he almost laughed. Of course she had. Wendy wasn't the type of woman who would hold back.

"We have drinks straight ahead," the man said, and Cayden blinked to focus back on the conversation. "Once in the first room, you'll find the food. Beyond that are the gems. Have a great evening."

"Thank you," Cayden murmured, and he went first into the building. He hadn't been inside this one, and the hallway in front of him was long and dark. It opened up into a cozy room with a western theme. Dark brown leather couches dotted the room, with black and white cow-patterned rugs in front of them. A longhorn skull sat above the fireplace, and all of the tables looked handmade from hewn logs. A pair of cowboy boots acted as a lamp base on the light fixture closest to him, and Cayden reached out to touch it.

Cowboy boots. He wore a pair right now, and he was actually surprised Ginny's mother would allow such décor anywhere on her property.

"Sir," someone said, and he turned toward a man who held a long tray with several glasses on it. "Would you like to try one of our gins?"

"I would," Beth said, stepping to Cayden's side. "Tell me what you've got."

He smiled at her like he was the happiest man on earth. "Down here is our classic gin," he said. "It's got that juniper taste you associate with gin. Next to it is our orange blossom gin. It's got the strongest citrus flavor out of any of our fruit-flavored gins." He continued to outline the alcohol on the tray, and as Cayden wasn't a fan of whiskey or gin or any alcohol really, he declined them all.

Beth selected the orange blossom, and Trey picked up the one with more anise in it. He took one sip and made a face. "This is why I don't drink."

The waiter had already moved away, thankfully, and Trey simply put his glass on the table next to those cowboy boots. Beth nursed hers as they looked around the room and then went through the doorway and into the next one.

This room was twice as big as the one with the cocktails, and there were far less people. Apparently, the drinks were more alluring than the food. Not to Cayden, and he took whatever the first man had on his tray and popped the whole thing into his mouth. Something salty and vinegary mixed with the beef, and then a bright pop of cilantro exploded in his mouth.

"Tartar," he said. "That was *good*."

"The chef made it with farm-raised cattle right here in Kentucky," the man said, beaming as if he personally owned the farm.

Cayden wanted to pull him aside and ask him if he really was that happy to be working here tonight. He suspected the Winters paid very well, and that they insisted their people wear smiles for miles.

Instead, he picked up another wafer with the beef tartar on it and threw it back as if he was eating oysters.

He hadn't seen Ginny yet, and some of the tension he'd been harboring in his chest and shoulders dissipated. She'd likely be in the gem room, where all the goods were. Sweet Rose had partnered with Down Home Jewelry for the event, as both were local Dreamsville corporations that had expanded to worldwide giants while maintaining their Kentucky roots.

Cayden drifted away from Beth and Trey and toward another tray of food. Then another. If he ate enough, coming here tonight would be worth the risk to his heart. As if on cue, it skipped a beat, and he reached for another Southwest eggroll.

Ginny had pulled out all the stops for tonight's event. Low music played in this room, and there were multiple places to sit and relax. Talk and get food and order additional drinks. Nothing ever ran out and while Cayden had seen behind the curtain at an event like this, he suspected most of the people here had not.

Trey appeared in front of him. "We're going in. You'll be okay here?"

"Yes," Cayden said, biting back on the sarcastic remark that popped into his head. He watched Trey and Beth duck through the door at the back of the room, and he took another crab cake when the tray came around again.

He'd just finished it when Ginny exited the room where Trey had gone.

Cayden got to his feet without even knowing that he had. He soaked in the sight of Virginia Winters, sparks flying through his whole body.

Beth had been wrong; the reminder wasn't for Ginny. It was for him.

Go talk to her, he commanded himself. He had to talk to her tonight. He had to explain that he'd gone silent because of her mother.

He couldn't believe he'd cared what Wendy Winters thought of him. He couldn't believe he'd given up the curvy, gorgeous woman currently smiling at a couple of men. Ginny wore an elegant off-white dress with plenty of lace everywhere. Her dark hair had been piled up on top of her head and secured with glinting gems that probably cost more than most people made in their entire lifetimes.

Her heels made her legs tight and slender, and Cayden's mouth turned dry.

It was her eyes that always captured him, and as she laughed and looked his way, he caught sight of those navy blue pools that pulled him in every time.

He knew the moment she saw and recognized him. The smile slipped from her face, and her eyes widened.

One hand flew to her mouth, which had dropped open, and then lowered to press against her chest. Her dress had wide straps that went over her shoulders and left a lot of skin to be observed.

Cayden couldn't move, though he wanted to. He could at least wave or something to indicate to her that he'd seen her. If he could just get his blood to stop burning him up from the inside out, he'd go talk to her.

Ginny had frozen too, and then she seemed to shake herself. Her masks flew into place, and she took a step toward him—and collided with a waiter carrying a full tray of sea bass and tomato canapés.

2

Virginia Winters had ruined many dresses in her lifetime. None as spectacularly and as publicly as the Victoria James gown she currently wore. She never wore a formal dress more than once, but that didn't mean she wanted tomatoes, balsamic, and fish juice embedded in the lace.

She certainly didn't want it to happen in front of anyone, least of all Cayden Chappell, who now loomed above her as if he'd sprinted across the drawing room to be there for her when she first opened her eyes and realized what had happened.

What had happened was that she'd been so entranced by his presence that she hadn't looked at anyone or anything but him. She'd run into a waiter carrying a full tray of canapés, causing both of them to tumble to the floor. She'd shown too much leg to everyone within the near vicinity, and she'd ruined her twenty-thousand-dollar dress.

Her hair brushed her face, and she realized she'd ruined that too. Embarrassment heated her whole body, and she watched Cayden's mouth move but no sound come out. Around her, everyone seemed to be looking at her with equally alarmed expressions, and Ginny wanted to tell them to back up and let her breathe.

Cayden reached out and touched her face, brushing that errant hair back. "...can you hear me?" Cayden's voice finally broke through the haze in her mind.

"Yes," she said, and sound rushed at her from every side. She couldn't grasp onto any one thought, and her mind raced through what she should do now. Change her clothes and come back to the party? Call it a night?

Just get out of here, she thought, and when Cayden asked, "Can I help you up, Ginny?" she put her hand in his, sparks flying up her arm and into her shoulder.

She looked at him, and so much was said between them. Her chest pinched, though, because he hadn't called.

She managed to get to her feet, pull down her dress, and wipe back her hair.

"Which door?" Cayden asked her, his voice low and meant only for her. She could still hear her name coming from his mouth, and he'd spoken it with a great deal of care.

"Straight ahead," she said, nodding to the door dozens

of paces away. If she could just make it there, she could figure out what to do. "I'm sorry," she tossed over her shoulder to the waiter still trying to clean up the things she'd spilled.

Cayden kept the pace brisk, and Ginny pushed to keep up with him. "I feel so stupid," she muttered, the feeling intensifying when he didn't answer. Maybe he hadn't heard her.

Yeah, she thought dryly. *Like all those times you thought that maybe he'd forgotten your phone number.*

Or that he'd gotten a new phone.

Then had a complete memory lapse and couldn't remember where she lived and worked.

In her most desperate moments, she'd even started to think he'd been in a terrible accident and was in a coma in a nearby hospital.

Anything to not have to face the fact that he'd kissed her, wished her well on vacation, and then dropped her without another word.

He twisted the doorknob and let her go through first. Ginny immediately kicked off her heels, because one of her ankles was throbbing from her fall. Her palms stung, and everything felt out of place.

She made it to a small settee from the 1600s that had been reupholstered in the ugliest fabric on the planet. Her mother loved it, but Ginny did not, so it got stuck in here. If Mother wanted it, she should take it to the mansion where she lived alone.

Ginny was so tired of being alone.

Her emotions stormed, and before she could contain it, a sob wrenched itself from her throat. She lifted her foot to her knee and started massaging her ankle, though it wasn't hurt that badly.

"Ginny," Cayden said. "Can I get you anything? A drink. Some medication." He actually looked around like this storage room would have anything like that. It didn't look like a storage room, so she could understand his desire, she supposed.

"No," she said, looking down at her stained dress. The scent of fish hit her squarely in the nose, and a fresh wave of tears got triggered.

"Sweetheart," he said softly, coming closer to her.

"Don't you dare call me that," she said, lifting her eyes to his. She was so tired of being so proper all the time. She wanted to rage and scream. She wanted to tell him what she really thought of his behavior. Then, she wanted to eat ice cream and tell her dogs all about it, probably while she cried.

She stood, raising herself to her full height, though she was nowhere near as tall as him. "You have a lot of nerve, Mister Chappell, coming here."

"I got an invitation for this event."

"You never called." She folded her arms and fixed him with a hard stare.

He glared right back at her. "Last time I checked,

phones make outbound calls too." He took a step toward her.

"I wasn't going to call someone who wasn't interested," she said.

"Neither was I."

They stared at one another, and Ginny's anger started to ebb away. "What happened?" she asked.

Cayden opened his mouth to say something, then promptly bit it closed again. She'd never known him to keep his mouth shut when he had something to say. He'd told her multiple times that he was interested in her, and that he wanted their relationship to be more than him escorting her to fancy parties.

He looked away, the indecision plain on his face despite the low lighting in the room. Watching him, she could feel his tender heart and his sexy vulnerability. She tasted him on her lips again, something that had been haunting her since their New Year's kiss.

"Let me tell you how it looks from my end," she said, her voice powerful but not loud. "You came to my New Year's Eve party. We danced and laughed. We kissed, and it was amazing. Then you left, and I went on vacation. When I got back, you didn't call. The one time we spoke, you said you were worried about Trey, the Sweetheart Classic, and the horses-of-all-ages sale at the ranch."

She stopped and took a long breath, blowing it out slowly as if she were doing one of her yoga exercises. "I figured you were quite busy, so I left you alone, thinking you'd call when things wrapped up. You didn't."

Familiar nerves ran through her. Ginny had grown up with a cruel father and a proper mother, and she knew what inadequacy felt like. She'd been inadequate since the moment of her birth, and it was something she had not overcome yet.

With Cayden, though...he'd always made her feel like royalty, like her life was a gift to him personally. She hadn't realized how much she'd needed that—needed *him*—until he was suddenly gone.

"I apologize," he said stiffly, still not looking at her.

"You apologize?" She took several quick steps toward him and touched his chest. "Look at me."

He swung his head toward her, but ducked it, not truly meeting her gaze.

"You don't say, 'I apologize.' That's something *I* say."

"I don't know what you want from me," he said.

"I want the truth." She pressed her palm against his chest again, not really pushing him, but needing to get his attention somehow. "Tell me what happened."

He lifted his eyes to hers, anger and danger there. "I don't want to tell you."

"If you met someone else, just say so."

"I didn't."

"You broke your phone, then."

"No."

Ginny's desperation spiraled out of control, and she

couldn't stop herself from looking at his mouth. Oh, that mouth. It had claimed her so completely, and she couldn't comprehend what could've happened to drive him away.

He'd kissed her like no man ever had, and Ginny wanted him to do it again right now.

Without thinking or second-guessing herself, Ginny put her hands on his shoulders and tipped up onto her toes. She pressed her mouth to his and kissed him, a sob working its way through her stomach.

He stood very still for a moment, then two, then his hands ran up her arms and into her hair. A growl started somewhere in his throat, and his mouth softened, receiving hers and kissing her back.

The rough version of Cayden disappeared after a few seconds, and he turned the kiss sweet and sensual, dragging it on and on until he finally pulled away, his chest heaving as he breathed hard.

Her heartbeat sprinted in her chest, and she couldn't open her eyes and look at him. If this was all she got of Cayden Chappell, she wanted it to end with a kiss like this. One filled with passion and yet respect, with love and desire, and with all the tenderness of a man who cared about her.

She dropped her hands from his face and opened her eyes, and he cleared his throat and stepped back. She wasn't going to apologize, because she wasn't sorry for what had just happened.

"The only other thing I could come up with was that

you'd been in a terrible accident and had been in a coma the last few months." Her voice hardly sounded like hers, especially at the end when her emotions got the best of her.

"Ginny," he whispered, stepping into her personal space again and gathering her right against his chest.

"Here you are," she said. "Obviously not in a coma." She wanted to push him again, but instead, she sank into him. He smelled like leather and horses, sunshine and freshly laundered cotton. Blast Olli for her perfect male scents.

"If I tell you, you have to promise not to do anything."

"Do anything?" She pulled back enough to look up at him. "What does that mean?"

"You're going to be very angry."

Ginny's pulse pounded, and she needed a clear head to hear what he was going to say.

"Because you obviously don't know." He pressed the tips of his fingers together and turned around. "Dear Lord, is this a mistake?" he prayed right out loud.

Ginny watched him with wide eyes, fear running through her now. "Just tell me," she said. "Because no, I don't know."

He took his sweet time turning back to her, and it should be illegal for a man to look as good as he did. Long legs clad in black slacks. Bright blue dress shirt, open at the throat. Dark leather jacket, black cowboy hat, with a little scruff on his face since he hadn't shaved since that morning.

He wasn't wearing a tuxedo, but this look was so much better.

He ground his voice in his throat as he removed his hat and put it back on. "Your mother asked me to stay away from you." He nodded once, like that was that.

Instant fury roared to life within Ginny. "She did *what*? When?"

"At the New Year's Eve party," he said. "After we kissed. She said horses and whiskey don't mix, and that if I respected you at all, I'd break things off between us."

"I am going to kill her." Ginny had never felt such rage.

"That's not quite right," he said, frowning. "She said if I respected you at all, I'd make sure that that night was the last time we were seen together."

Ginny didn't care what wording her mother had used. She'd overstepped her bounds—again. Ginny stepped around Cayden, her destination the mansion in the middle of the family land.

"Whoa, whoa," he said, darting in front of her and blocking the door. "You're not going back out there."

"Yes, I am," she said calmly. "Get out of my way."

"I said you couldn't do anything if I told you."

"I didn't promise," she said, stepping right into him but not for a good reason this time. "You don't get to tell me what to do."

"I—don't," he said, his eyes wide and alarmed. "Of course I don't."

Ginny took a step back, refocusing her anger on the right person. Mother. "*No one* is going to tell me what to do," she said, her teeth gritting. "I'm forty-six years old, and if I want to go out with Cayden Chappell, I'm going to."

She needed to find her core again, because she didn't like this wild feeling coursing through her.

"Ginny," he said, his fingertips landing lightly against her forearm.

That grounded her, and she looked at his hand and then up into his eyes. "Yes?"

"What are you going to do?"

"I'm going to go find my mother," she said. "I'm going to tell her she was right—I should always pack a second outfit for formal events. I don't do it, because well, because she said I should. Then I'm going to tell her she had no right to speak to you about our relationship. Once that's ironed out, I'm going to call you and ask you to dinner."

A small smile touched his mouth. "You're scary when you're mad," he whispered. He bent his head and trailed a line of fire up the side of her face with his lips. "You don't need to ask me, sweetheart. Just tell me when and where, and I'll be there."

"You're still interested?" she asked, her voice breathy now.

"Was that not obvious from that kiss?"

"Maybe I need you to show me again."

"Mm...I can do that." Cayden took her fully into his arms and kissed her again, every stroke a reminder of how much she liked him and how much he liked her. Every touch became fuel for the courage she needed to talk to her mother. Every pulse of her heart beat only for him, and while she'd have to deal with that and what it meant later, right now, it sure felt nice to be in his arms again.

Ginny didn't ring the doorbell or knock. She didn't even use the front door. Her mother lived in ten percent of the house, the bulk of that at the back, away from the public face of Sweet Rose Whiskey.

She'd parked five feet from the servant entrance, and she'd used her key to get through the door. To her right sat the kitchen, and to her left a set of stairs that went up. Harvey and Elliot had tried to get Mother to live on the first floor, but there was only one bedroom on the main level, and it was in the front corner of the house.

Mother wouldn't even go in that room, as Daddy had lived there. There had been little love left between them, and by the time he'd left Sweet Rose in an advanced stage of heart failure, they hadn't been speaking.

Ginny knew exactly how her father felt as she turned and marched up the steps. She went right at the top and down a hallway that had been torn out and rebuilt to accommodate Mother's flowing ball gowns. She owned more than anyone else on Earth, it seemed, and she always had a back-up plan for her back-up plan.

"Mother," Ginny called as the sound of the television met her ears. Her step almost faltered, but she kept going. Things had been building and frothing between her and her mother for months now. This was just icing on a poisoned cake that needed to be thrown away.

"Mother," she said again, pushing into the room where her mother spent her evenings at home. She sat in the recliner, gently toeing herself back and forth, a crochet needle working on the outer edge of a baby blanket.

"Ginny, dear." Mother looked up from her work, a smile soft and easy on her face.

Secrets, Ginny thought, her gaze stuck to that blanket. They both had plenty of those.

"I thought it was the Gin and Gems event tonight?" Mother phrased it like a question when it wasn't. She knew exactly what happened on the two-thousand-acre farm that was a distillery.

"It is," Ginny said, tearing her eyes from that blanket. Why couldn't Mother be wearing a black dress and stirring something nefarious over a fire? To find her crocheting a border on a handmade baby blanket while a cooking show droned on made her so...normal.

"Did you tell Cayden Chappell that horses and whiskey don't mix?" Ginny asked, making her voice as strong as she could.

Mother's fingers stumbled, and that was all the answer Ginny needed.

"Mother, you do not get to dictate to me who I will see and who I won't."

"He is all wrong for you."

"*You* are wrong about that," Ginny said. If there was one thing Mother hated, it was being told she was wrong. "I'm not sixteen anymore, Mother. I'm not even twenty-six. I'm almost fifty years old, and I've been doing everything you've told me to for my entire life."

Her frustration and annoyance blossomed and bloomed, expanding rapidly as her breathing increased. "I'm done, Mother. I like him, and you have *no right* to boss him around."

"Ginny, do think rationally," Mother said in a disdainful voice. She set her crocheting aside and sighed as if Ginny had interrupted the most wonderful moment of her life. "You're always over-reacting."

"I am *not* over-reacting," Ginny said. "I've lost almost three months of my life, wondering what I did to drive him away, only to find out it was *you!*" She advanced on her mother as she pushed herself up out of the chair.

She took a moment to steady herself on her feet, but when she looked at Ginny, the fire in her eyes was just as prevalent as it always had been. "He does not fit at Sweet Rose."

"He doesn't need to," Ginny said. "He owns and operates a hugely successful horse farm."

"Spur does that," Mother said, shaking her head. "I don't know what the Chappells are worth, dear, but there are eight of them. I doubt he could keep you in your current state of comfort." She turned away from Ginny and started for the small kitchen in the back corner.

"I don't need any of that comfort," Ginny spat back. "I hate that house. It's fifty times too big, and I hate coming home to it all by myself."

Mother paused and twisted back to Ginny, her eyes wide. "Your ingratitude is unbecoming."

"I am not ungrateful," Ginny said. "I'm *lonely*. I'm tired, Mother." She laughed, but it wasn't a happy sound.

Mother turned fully toward her, a malicious glint in her dark eyes now. "Of course I can't forbid you from seeing him. Go see him. Go to dinner with him. Fall in love with him. See if he has anywhere for you to live on that cattle ranch he shares with seven brothers."

"It's a racehorse operation, Mother."

"Whatever," Mother said, her appraising eyes sliding down to Ginny's feet. She'd left her heels in the car, and suddenly, all the smells and stains leapt out from where they'd been hiding. "Good Lord," Mother said, pressing her hand to her pulse. "Did anyone see you like this?" She reached out as if she'd touch the gown, but she yanked her fingers back before she did.

"Yes," Ginny said. "Everyone at the Gin and Gems event."

Mother's eyes flashed again, probably because of

Ginny's blunt tone. She lifted her chin, not a tremble or tremor in sight. "If you choose him, you'll be choosing to walk away from Sweet Rose."

Ginny's eyes widened and she pulled in a breath. "I can have a husband and run the distillery."

"Not *him* as a husband."

"Why not?" Ginny asked, desperate to see Cayden through her mother's eyes. A horrible thought entered her mind. "Did Daddy... He's not a Winters, is he?"

"No," Mother said quickly. "But not for lack of trying."

Ginny watched the agony and betrayal roll across her mother's face, though Daddy had died years ago. "Him and Julie Chappell?"

"They even dated in high school," Mother said, her voice pitching up a little. "I won him, of course. Julie is a beautiful woman, but she failed to understand your father on a level I always did."

Ginny had no idea what that meant. "Mother?"

"You knew your father, dear. You'll put it together." She continued into the kitchen and began filling a teapot with water. Ginny didn't want to think about her father and his many affairs. No other illegitimate children had come forth, but Ginny and Mother had already agreed not to tell the boys if they did.

Harvey had taken Theo Lange's existence particularly hard, which Ginny could understand, as they were only one month apart in age.

She watched her mother in the kitchen, unable to

move. She was so used to siding with her. Mother and Ginny. Ginny and Mother. They'd been two peas in a pod as Ginny learned the whiskey business from her mother.

Daddy had always handled the business side of the distillery, while Mother tended to the fields, the flavors, the people, and the events. She was the public face of Sweet Rose, and she'd built it from a small regional operation to a global powerhouse in the world of whiskey.

"Money," Ginny said.

"Bingo," Mother said, not bothering to turn or look at Ginny. "Your father valued money above almost anything. Julie had nothing to offer him." She turned around then and leaned into the counter behind her. "I, of course, had all of this." She swept her hand toward the ceiling as if the room she'd converted into a living room and kitchenette was a grand ballroom. The smile she wore almost felt predatory, and Ginny wanted to run back to her house and lock herself in her bedroom until things made sense.

"Cayden is not related to me," she said slowly. "Daddy didn't cheat with Julie. Your objection to my relationship to him is because of…because his mother dated Daddy in high school?"

"She kissed him the day before we got married," Mother said, lifting her teacup to her lips as if she'd just said it would rain tomorrow. She lowered it a moment later, her eyes hard, dark marbles.

Mother did not like Julie Chappell, plain and simple. Mother could hold a grudge for a lifetime, something

Ginny had always known and joked about with her brothers. To see it manifest itself as reality, though, was a much harder pill to swallow.

"I do not want that woman anywhere near my life," Mother said. "She will get nothing from me, certainly not my only daughter. She will not ever be welcome on my property." She set down her cup with hardly a clink, despite the venom and power in her voice.

"So, Ginny, dear. If you want to be with Cayden Chappell, you will need to walk away from Sweet Rose. From your family. From me." She folded her arms, a knowing glint in her eyes, as if she knew such a thing was impossible.

It *was* impossible.

Ginny's fury roared again, and her fingers curled into fists. "I'll think about it." She spun and stalked toward the exit.

"You'll think about it?" Mother called after her.

Ginny didn't answer. She had to get out of there before she started sobbing. She made it back to her SUV, everything clenched tight. She peeled out, spitting gravel behind her as she tore away from the mansion she hated.

"I hate this," she said aloud, pounding her palm against the steering wheel. "I hate whiskey. I hate Sweet Rose. I hate this dress, and this car, and I hate my mother."

Tears rained down her face and she put her car on the highway leading south from Sweet Rose, and she just drove as the storm inside her swirled and brewed, blew and raged.

When she'd calmed, she only had one thought left: Her mother owned her. She'd been wrapping Ginny in thin bands of barely-there control for almost five decades. She couldn't break free, even if she wanted to.

She was stuck. Trapped. Subject to her mother's whims and wishes—at least if she wanted to be part of her family and take over the whiskey business.

Her car started to slow down, and Ginny looked down at the speedometer. "No," she said, pressing harder on the accelerator.

It was no use—she was out of gas.

With the late hour, there wasn't anyone on the stretch of Kentucky road, and Ginny was able to easily maneuver to the shoulder and ease onto it as her car continued to decelerate. When she finally came to a stop, it was as if everything in her life now existed on a hinge.

Her next decision would decide the rest of her life.

She didn't have shoes she could walk very far in.

She wore a stained and stinky designer gown.

She had no food or water in her car.

She closed her eyes, everything burning inside her. "Time to be reborn from the ashes," she whispered, and she reached for her phone.

After dialing, she held the device to her ear and exhaled one long stream of apprehension and nerves.

"Ginny?"

"Cayden," she said. "I know it's late, but I'm stranded on the side of the road, and I'm wondering if you could come get me."

He started chuckling, of all things. "Is this going to be a pattern with you?"

"Probably," she said, trying to tame her crying into laughter and failing. "You should know that upfront, I suppose."

"You sound upset," he said.

"Yes." She could admit it. "I also have no idea where I am. I'm going to have to look at my map and send you a pin."

"How long have you been driving?" he asked quietly, the slight jangle of keys in the background.

She pressed her eyes closed, because he was going to be her knight in shining armor again. "What time is it?" she asked.

"Almost eleven."

"A while," she admitted.

He didn't sigh or huff. He didn't press for more information. All he said was, "Send me the pin, sweetheart."

3

Cayden pulled up behind Ginny's SUV after driving through the blackness of Kentucky for over an hour. Her car was dark, and a trickle of nerves ran down his spine as he picked up his phone. Even he didn't want to get out of his truck out here.

He dialed Ginny, glad when he saw a white-blue light in her car. A moment later, she said, "Hey, is that you behind me?"

"Yes, ma'am," he said. "I'm getting out now. I just didn't want to startle you."

Everything about tonight had startled him. First, watching Ginny stumble and fall. Second, the kissing. His bloodstream heated with the mere thought of the two kisses they'd shared that evening.

He wanted more, but one of the biggest regrets of tonight was actually the kissing. He didn't know Ginny very well, despite escorting her to parties and events. He knew a fake version of her. A plastic cutout. He wanted to know the real woman behind the makeup, the perfect Southern accent, and layers of lace.

He'd already told himself he wasn't going to kiss her again until he knew the real her.

He got out of his truck and left the door open as he approached her SUV. She opened her door too and got out, shoeless but still wearing that stained gown. She would steal his breath if she wore a burlap sack, and he managed to put a small smile on his face despite the distress he saw in her eyes.

"I take it the conversation with your mother didn't go well," he said.

She shook her head, handed him her purse, and started toward his truck. He went in her wake, reaching past her to open the door and staying close until she was settled on the passenger seat. He handed her the purse and went around the truck to retake his seat behind the wheel.

He had a feeling they weren't going to be doing much talking tonight. He wasn't sure how he felt about that.

Be her friend, he thought, and a friend wouldn't push for answers the other person didn't want to give.

"Where to?" he asked.

She swung her head toward him and blinked.

"Did you want me to help you find gas?" he asked. "Fill your car up so you can drive it back? Did you want...to just go home?" He swallowed and looked away. He didn't want to admit that he'd bring her back here to retrieve her car, but the truth was, he would.

"Get a hotel?" he asked. "Then you can get gas in the morning? Tell me what to do."

"What would you do?" she asked.

Cayden wasn't expecting that question, and it took him a moment to think through the situation. "If it were me, I'd probably either get a hotel nearby and call a tow truck in the morning to bring me my car—full of gas, of course. Then I'd drive home tomorrow. Or, since I have a friend here, I'd go home now and call a tow service to bring the car all the way back to Dreamsville."

"That's the one I want," she said, turning back to her window and leaning her head against it.

"Home it is," Cayden said, easing back onto the road. He went past her car and flipped around, getting them headed in the right direction.

"Cayden?" she asked a few minutes later.

"Hmm?" He'd need coffee or a caffeinated soda to make this drive in silence. He'd also need to put the radio on loud, because he was exhausted, and the steady rhythm of the road was going to lure him right to sleep.

"Can I stay at Bluegrass Ranch tonight?"

He jerked his attention toward her. "Why?"

"I don't want to go back to my house," she said simply. "Just for a few nights. Do you think Blaine would care?"

"I don't think he would," Cayden said. He hadn't

minded last time Ginny had stayed a few nights in the homestead.

"Then if it's okay with you, that's where I'd like to go."

"Okay," he said, focusing his eyes back on the lonely road in front of him. "Can I ask what your mother said?"

"It's a long story," she said with a sigh.

"We have a long drive."

She didn't say anything for several minutes, but Cayden was now too keyed up to think about sleeping. Ginny just needed some time to get the words right.

"She does not approve of you," she said.

"I got that."

"Because my father dated your mother in high school."

Cayden took a breath and then started laughing. "You're kidding."

"I wish I was," she said. "Mother can hold a grudge for a lifetime."

Cayden quieted, because Ginny had not joined him in his laughter. "That's insane."

"Apparently, your mother kissed Daddy the night before he married Mother. And, uh." She cleared her throat. "My father stepped out on Mother several times. Apparently, one of those times was with your mother."

Cayden's fingers tightened on the wheel. "No," he said harshly. "I don't believe that. My mom didn't cheat on my dad." He looked at Ginny, pure shock moving through him. That couldn't be true. It just couldn't.

Ginny rubbed her eyes with one hand. "Mother said... you're probably right. She said 'not for lack of trying.' Perhaps my dad just wanted to have an affair with your mom, and she said no." She sighed, the sound full of exhaustion. "Either way, she refuses to budge on this. She does not like your mother, and she will not concede her only daughter to her."

Cayden's mind raced now. He needed to talk to his mother immediately. He hadn't spoken with her much recently, and his guilt ate at him. He'd been meaning to get over there and make amends the way Spur had advised them all to do.

Cayden had enough experience with his mother to know that his feelings would be dismissed. He'd gone to her after college, after he'd finished his degree in business management with a minor in public relations. He was the only Chappell to go to and graduate from college, and she'd dismissed his accomplishments.

Later, he'd made the mistake of telling her that he wanted his life to matter. He wanted to be someone important, to someone. She'd said, "You are important, Cayden."

"To who?" he'd asked. Spur and Ian had been married at the time. Blaine and Trey engaged. Cayden had always felt two steps behind, and two degrees away from truly belonging in his family.

His mother had said, "To me," and waved her hand like his concerns and ambitions were frivolous. "Now, come on," she'd said. "Let's get over to Marianne before she buys the wrong horse."

That had been that.

Cayden hadn't ever gone to his mother for advice or comfort again. She didn't even listen to him, let alone try to help him through his thoughts to a place of clarity.

He lost the drive to his thoughts, and before he knew it, he drove down the lane that led to the homestead. It came into view, lights winking in the darkness from the porch and along the garage. He parked next to Blaine and got out of the truck.

He helped Ginny down and walked at her side into the house. Down the hall they went, and he stayed in the doorway of the master suite where she'd stayed last time. "You know where the towels and everything are," he said. "Right?"

"I can manage," she said, her voice little more than a whisper. "Thank you, Cayden." She came toward him, and he received her into his arms.

He held her tight, breathing in the soft, floral scent of her hair. "What are you going to do?"

"I don't know." She sniffed and stepped back, averting her eyes. "She said if I chose you, I'd be walking away from Sweet Rose. Everything at Sweet Rose."

A new brand of horror filled Cayden, and he suddenly understood why Ginny had been out on that road, driving away from Dreamsville.

He didn't want to challenge her, so he took another

breath and made his voice as kind as possible. "I suppose this is it for us, then."

Ginny shrugged, nodded, then shook her head. "I don't know."

"You need some rest," he said. "We can talk more in the morning."

She nodded again, and Cayden backed out of the doorway. "Good-night, Ginny." He wasn't sure if she said it back, because he closed the door and walked away quickly. His bedroom was upstairs, and he went that way, his cowboy boots making a lot of noise on the stairs.

Only he and Blaine lived here now, and come the first weekend in June, Blaine and Tam would get married, and then Blaine would be gone too. Cayden couldn't imagine living in this homestead alone, and he had no idea how Ginny had managed to exist in her mansion all by herself for as long as she had.

Upstairs, Cayden stripped off his clothes, brushed his teeth, and got in bed. He closed his eyes, but sleep would not come. All he could think about was the woman downstairs and what the morning would bring—heartache when she said she couldn't see him again? Or happiness if she said she didn't care about her mother's threats?

∼

THE NEXT MORNING, CAYDEN SMELLED COFFEE AS HE WENT into the bathroom to shower. Twenty minutes later, he looked somewhat presentable, and he went downstairs to the kitchen, where the scent of bacon now filled the air too.

Ginny stood in the kitchen, removing strips of crispy bacon from a pan and laying them on a plate covered with a paper towel. She wore a gray T-shirt that was easily two sizes too big for her, the fabric billowing around her like a tent.

The jeans she had on were also not the right size, sagging in some places, but clinging to her legs in others. Her hair was a mess on top of her head, wisps of it falling out of the half-ponytail, half-bun she'd put them in.

She looked absolutely amazing.

He cleared his throat and continued toward the bar, where Blaine sat nursing a cup of coffee and eating a plate of scrambled eggs. "Morning," he said.

"There you are," Blaine said pleasantly. "You're up late."

"Yeah," Cayden said, his eyes never really leaving Ginny.

She turned toward him too, and the electricity between them made the hair on his arms stand up. "Good morning," she said in a somewhat formal voice. She wore no makeup, and she was like a goddess straight from heaven.

"Morning." He cleared his throat. "Are you making eggs to order?"

A smile touched her lips. "Yes, sir. Scrambled or over-easy?"

"Scrambled is fine," he said, holding out the I in the word for an extra beat.

"Coffee?" she asked.

"Yes, ma'am."

Blaine shook his head, but Cayden just ignored him. He couldn't talk about everything right now anyway. Instead, he took the mug Ginny handed him and he poured plenty of cream and sugar into the dark liquid while she went back to the stove to make scrambled eggs.

"Ginny says she'll be here for a few days," Blaine said. "I told her that's fine."

Cayden grunted, not sure what else to say.

"She's going to send Melanie to get her clothes."

"What's she wearing right now?" Cayden couldn't help looking at her again.

"Some of my stuff," Blaine said with a chuckle. "Ridiculous, right?"

"I couldn't wear that dress," Ginny said, smiling over her shoulder. "These are fine."

Cayden's phone rang, and he glanced at it. Lawrence. His pulse skipped and he swiped on the call. "Lawrence, you're on speaker with me, Blaine, and Ginny Winters."

"Ginny Winters?" he asked.

Ginny didn't turn around, and Blaine said, "What's up, Lawrence?"

"Just wondering where you are," he said. "Cayden.

Where Cayden is. We have a meeting in half an hour with Georgia Cartwright."

"Right," Cayden said. "I'll be there." He hadn't exactly forgotten. He had everything in his calendar anyway, and it would've alerted him with enough time to get to the conference room in the administration building.

"Okay," Lawrence said. "I guess we'll go over the stuff you want me to send to the second publicity firm after the meeting with her?"

Cayden closed his eyes, his memory firing yesterday morning's conversation at him. "Yes," he said anyway. "Sorry, Lawrence. I had a late night and got up late this morning. I should've texted." They were supposed to go over the split between firms before the meeting. He should've been in the admin building fifteen minutes ago.

"It's okay," he said. "If Ginny's there, something must've happened."

Something had happened all right, but Cayden couldn't say what. Ginny turned from the stove and slid his breakfast out of the pan and onto a plate. She brought it over to the counter, interest in her eyes as she set the plate in front of him.

"See you in a bit," Cayden said, tapping to end the call. "Thank you, sweetheart." He picked up a fork lying there and positioning the plate closer to him.

"So...are we a thing again?" Blaine waved his fork between Ginny and Cayden.

Cayden scooped up a bite of eggs and put them in his

mouth. He glared at Blaine. While he hadn't told him what Wendy Winters had said to him at New Year's, the two of them lived together. He knew Cayden hadn't been seeing Ginny for a while now. He just didn't know why.

"Yes," Ginny said, her voice that quiet kind of powerful that got Cayden's blood moving at a quick clip. What she'd said helped too.

He looked at her, his eyebrows sky high.

"Yes," she said again, this time to him. "If he'll have me, we're a thing again."

4

"Oh, I think he'll have you," Blaine said with a laugh. Cayden hadn't said anything, and that lit Ginny's nerves on fire. "He's been moping around here for months. If he's not doing that, he's throwing things and yelling."

"Neither of those are completely true," Cayden said, shooting another sharp look at his brother. "You're finished eating. Don't you have work to do somewhere?"

Blaine burst out laughing, and Ginny wished it would cut the tension in the kitchen. It didn't, at least for her. She turned around and started cleaning up, her stomach tight though she hadn't eaten anything at all. She supposed that could've been why her stomach hurt, but she wasn't sure.

She wasn't sure of anything anymore.

She wanted Cayden in her life.

She wanted Sweet Rose.

She felt like everything had just been divided down the middle and she was trying to walk with one foot on both sides of the line. She needed to make a columned list of everything, just to get it out of her head and somewhere she could examine it rationally.

"I know when I'm not wanted," Blaine said. "See you two later." He got up from the barstool where he'd been sitting for the past half-hour, picked up his cowboy hat, and put it on his head as he walked down the hall and out the door that led into the garage.

Ginny finished washing the pan she'd made eggs in and set it in the dish drainer.

"Ginny," Cayden said, and she turned toward him. At least fifteen feet separated them, and Ginny made no effort to close that distance. She needed it right now.

"If you don't want—"

"You know I do," he said. "I just don't want you to lose Sweet Rose. That's your core. That's everything you've worked for throughout your entire life." He wore an anguished look on his face.

Her chin started to quiver, but she pressed her lips and teeth together to get it to stop.

"I don't think I'm worth that," he said, looking down into his coffee cup. "That's all."

"That's not your decision to make," she said. "I know what I want." She took a step toward him and then another until only the counter where he sat to eat separated them. "I want my own life. I don't want that house. I want to make my own decisions. I don't want to wear another formal gown for a year. I want to wear jeans and sweats and learn to ride a horse."

She wasn't sure what he saw on her face, but his eyes widened with every sentence she said.

"I want Sweet Rose," she said. "I'd be lying if I said I didn't. But Cayden, I want you too. There is no *good* reason why I can't have both."

"Your mother—"

"Won't live forever," she interrupted. "I've already spoken to Harvey and Elliot, and we're meeting tonight for dinner." She turned her back on him and picked up the pan she'd fried the bacon in. Washing it with the hottest water that would come out of the sink and then using the garbage disposal to make sure the grease wouldn't sit in the trap gave her a few minutes to gather her emotions back into the tight ball she needed them to be in.

She faced him again, finding him in the same position as before. "Will you come to dinner at my brother's house?"

"Tonight?"

"No," she said. "Sorry. I'm thinking Tuesday."

He cocked his head to the side, and Ginny knew he was thinking through things. He was very, very smart, and he'd know Tuesday meant something to her. Otherwise, why not dinner tomorrow night? It was Saturday, and many couples went out on the weekend.

"Let me check." He picked up his phone. He tapped and swiped and said, "Tuesday is fine. Which brother?"

"Drake," she said. "It will be at his country house."

"His country house?"

"I'm going to live there for a while," she said, picking up the sugar bowl and turning around to put it back in the cupboard where she'd found it.

"In your brother's country house, because the mansion he lives in *out in the country* on the family block is...not his country house." Cayden sounded confused, and a sigh pulled through her. She had too much to explain and no desire to explain it.

Cayden got up and came around the peninsula and into the kitchen. "Ginny," he said softly, and it was that two-syllable name in that luxurious voice that solidified her decision to walk away from Sweet Rose—at least for now.

His hand trailed along her waist, and Ginny leaned into him. He didn't say anything else, and Ginny simply breathed in and out with him, the silence in the house absolutely wonderful.

She finally took a long breath and said, "You're about to be late, I think."

"That's true." He still didn't leave her side.

"I'm going to have Mel bring my dogs out here," she

said. "Blaine said it was okay, and that you love dogs." She looked up at him. "Is that really okay?"

"Yes," he said, gazing down at her.

"I'm going to go live in Drake's house, because he rarely uses it, and I don't want to be on the family block."

"Okay."

"I *am* choosing you, Cayden. I don't care what my mother thinks or says or does, but I'm going to talk to my brothers and see if we can find a way for me to have you and pacify Mother."

He nodded, his jaw tight and his eyes blazing. She wasn't sure if he was angry or not.

"We might have to keep things...secret," she said. "How do you feel about that?"

"I'll do what you want," he said. "Okay, Ginny?"

She smiled and stretched up to kiss his cheek. "It might be kind of exciting to have a forbidden relationship, don't you think?"

That got him to smile, but an alarm on his phone sounded, and he stepped away from her. "I'll see you... when?" he asked.

"Probably tomorrow morning," she said.

He nodded, swiped the alarm off, and said, "Okay, sweetheart. See you then." He swept a kiss along her forehead and left. Ginny stood in a kitchen that was not hers, wearing men's clothes, all alone.

She was happier here than she'd been in years, and a smile stretched across her face. Now, she had to figure out how to have this life combined with the work at Sweet Rose that she loved.

"What Mother doesn't know won't hurt her," she murmured to the horizon out the window above the kitchen sink. She turned away from the sink and went to get her phone so she could give Mel the go-ahead to pack up the trio of dogs when she stopped by the house to get Ginny's clothes.

∼

GINNY COULD SCARCELY LOOK AT HER BROTHERS AS SHE approached the booth at Old Ember's, an upscale, ritzy restaurant in downtown Lexington the four of them had been dining in for decades now. Their standing dinner date normally fell on Tuesday evening at nine p.m., but anyone could call an emergency dinner at any time.

In the past, an emergency dinner had only been initiated twice, once by Harvey when he'd found out about their father's philandering, and once by Drake when he'd panicked over asking Darcey to marry him.

Not everyone made it to every dinner every Tuesday, but the majority of them were attended by all four Winters siblings each week. Ginny only missed when she had social events for Sweet Rose drawing her away.

The past several months, she'd purposely scheduled other dinners and get-togethers on Tuesdays to avoid this meeting, as Harvey and Elliot had started down a road to modify the budget for employee salaries that Ginny did not like.

As the current majority shareholder in Sweet Rose, she ran the board meetings each Thursday morning, and a lot of the final say on things fell on her shoulders. She'd blocked their attempts to pay their full-time people less over time, despite the grandfathering they'd outlined.

Ginny wanted Sweet Rose to be the premier whiskey distillery, farm, shop, and event venue in Kentucky. She wanted their whiskey to continue to top the charts in flavor and style around the world. She wanted to attract the very best employees, and keep them in their jobs for their entire careers, not constantly be re-training people as others left due to harsh working conditions and low pay.

They had the money in the company, and she didn't need any more lining her pockets. Harvey and Elliot had cited looking ahead to the future and needing a reserve, but Ginny didn't understand why the eighty-seven million dollars they had in their reserve wasn't already enough.

They had not been happy with her; she was not happy with them. They hadn't spoken outside of business meetings in a while—until she'd returned from her trip to the Caymans in mid-January.

Then, Ginny had finally broken down her exterior walls and gone to Old Ember's. She'd repaired some of their bridges, and while she'd always been talking to

Drake, she now spoke to Harvey and Elliot about their families as well.

Standing in the hallway at her house on New Year's Eve and looking at the cards and notes from her nieces and nephews had reminded her of what was most important. Family. Loved ones.

Her heart pinched as she slid into the booth next to Harvey. "Evening," she said, barely looking at him. Across from him Elliot sat against the wall, and they were still waiting for Drake, who'd take the spot directly across from Ginny.

"Evening," Harvey said just as formally.

Elliot nodded at her, his dark eyes missing nothing. "You look tired, Ginny."

"Yes," she said, and that was all. She hated that even within her own family she struggled to let her guard down. She picked up her silverware and unwrapped it, carefully laying the dark blue napkin over her lap.

A waitress arrived, offering wine or whiskey, and Ginny waved her away with, "I'll take a club soda with lime, please."

"Do either of you want another drink?" she asked Harvey and Elliot, and they both ordered another shot of Dark Horse, which was their preferred brandy. She almost found it comical that none of them drank whiskey.

Her father had been notorious for his consumption of the stuff, and Ginny hurried to lock the door on those memories before they could stain her mind again.

"How's Janice?" she asked Harvey, who smiled.

"She's doing well," he said. "The surgery is complete, finally, and she should be back to eating solid foods fairly quickly."

"That's wonderful," Ginny said. "Did you get the soup I sent a few days ago?"

"Yes."

She could feel the weight of his eyes on the side of her face, and she turned toward him. "I'm glad."

"She didn't text you?" Harvey's eyes flashed so much like Daddy's had. He was the spitting image of their father, and Ginny had a hard time looking at him sometimes.

Ginny shook her head. "It's okay. I'm sure she was in a lot of pain." Ginny would've been had she just gotten dental implants, after three other mouth surgeries to get her to the point of being able to get the implants.

"She said she would. I apologize," he said. "I would have had I known she didn't. It was delicious. Even Carlisle ate it." He smiled, and Ginny felt something crack inside her. She wasn't even sure what it was.

"I'm glad," she said again, her voice dropping in both pitch and volume. She cleared her throat as she let her gaze fall to the tabletop too. "I'd love to see Carlisle. How is he enjoying his new teacher?"

"I'll bring him by tomorrow," Harvey said, grinding his voice through his own throat. "Elizabeth's been dying to show you how she can make crepes now too."

Ginny's eyes filled with tears. She didn't know how to

walk away from her family. She didn't know how to cut them out of her life completely.

"What's wrong, Ginny?" Elliot asked, his hand coming across the table and covering both of hers. She hadn't even realized she'd knotted her fingers together until the warmth from her brother touched her skin.

Elliot was taller than all of them, and he'd inherited more of Mother's slanted nose and high forehead. He had long limbs and keen eyes, and his children were polite and personable. She missed them too, and she hated that she'd let business come between her and her brothers for so long.

"Let's wait until Drake gets here," Harvey said. "She obviously won't want to explain it twice."

Ginny didn't even want to explain it once. At the same time, she had things to say to the two of them that Drake didn't need to hear. He'd sided with her on the employee salaries, and they'd been getting along fine all this time.

"I want to apologize to the two of you," she said. "We shouldn't let business come between us the way we did these past several months." She looked up, her tears miraculously staying in her eyes. "You're my brothers, and I love you. I'm sorry."

Ginny had never been one for long speeches, and none of the Winters were either.

"It's okay," Harvey said, glancing at Elliot. "We're to blame too. We should've come to you before unilaterally trying to take the company in a new direction."

"I understand your position," Elliot said. "In the end, Ginny, you were right." He gave her a smile that turned wry quickly. "As usual."

"I am not always right," she said quickly, glancing from him to Harvey.

"No, but you think differently than we do," Harvey said. "It's not always about numbers on a paper. It's about people too."

She nodded, grateful for their acceptance of her views and feelings. "We can add to the reserve in other ways."

"I thought the increased venue rent was a good idea," Elliot said. "We've not seen a drop in bookings at all."

"None whatsoever," Harvey agreed.

"I'm glad." Ginny looked up as her drink arrived. She stirred it with the straw and took a tiny sip. The bitterness of the soda and the lime made her pucker slightly, and she looked over as Drake slid into the booth across from her with a loud sigh.

"Sorry," he drawled, his voice the most Kentuckian and the loudest in the family.

She smiled at him, and he grinned around at everyone else. "Y'all been here long?" He signaled to the waitress, and she came bustling over to take his drink order.

"Yes," Harvey said dryly as the woman went to get Drake his bourbon. "Since nine, like we agreed."

Drake just smiled at him and all three of them turned their eyes on Ginny. She'd called the emergency meeting, and none of them liked to waste time.

She took another sip of her club soda and put the glass down. "Mother's given me an ultimatum," she said, deciding to go right for the heart of the issue. "Sweet Rose Whiskey, or my new boyfriend."

No one said anything, and Ginny couldn't read their expressions. Growing up in the Winters household, one learned to hide everything behind a mask from an early age. Mother hadn't had a problem with any of their wives, but Harvey's came from a proper Southern society family with millions in real estate and agriculture.

Elliot's wife came from old money in the South as well, and Drake's wife came from the rich and famous out of Georgia. Ginny liked all of their wives just fine. They fit in the family.

She wasn't even sure Cayden would.

She didn't care. There was something about him that filled all the empty places in her heart and soul, and she wanted to find out if they were temporary or permanent.

"Who's the boyfriend?" Harvey asked.

"I didn't know you had a boyfriend," Elliot said.

Drake was the only one who kept his smile on his face. "I can't wait to meet him if Mother doesn't approve."

Ginny couldn't help the light giggle that came out of her mouth at her youngest brother's statement. None of them wanted to be on Mother's bad side, but all of them certainly bucked against pleasing her all the time.

"None of you carry the same load I do," Ginny said.

"Mother's been telling me since I was six years old that I'd have to marry well."

"Who is it?" Harvey asked again. "He can't be that bad, Ginny."

"It's Cayden Chappell," she said, watching each of them as they absorbed the name. Confusion marred Harvey's face, so he didn't know about Daddy's and Julie Chappell's relationship. Elliot frowned; he didn't either.

Drake shook his head, his smile disappearing. "Why would Mother care if you dated Cayden Chappell?"

"Don't they own the biggest horse breeding farm in Kentucky?"

"It's not the biggest," Ginny said, remembering how Cayden had described it once. "It's just the best." She let her smile linger for another moment.

"Are you ready to order?" the waitress asked, and though none of them had picked up a menu, they put in their orders.

Once she'd walked away again, Ginny leaned against the table. "They're billionaires. All of them. They run a training facility, and they've produced seven Derby champions in the past two decades."

"I don't get it," Harvey said. "He sounds like the *perfect* man to bring home to Mother."

"Yeah," Drake said. "I'm surprised you'd even consider dating him, for that reason alone. It'd make her too happy."

"Remember how she deemed Winston Baybury inadequate?" Elliot asked. "Perhaps this Chappell man is like that."

"Winston was *not* inadequate," Ginny said, her voice tight. "He was a good man, with a good job. We would've been fine."

"Mother doesn't want you to support your husband," Elliot said quietly. "That's all I'm saying."

"Did you hear her say they were all billionaires?" Harvey said. "Cayden doesn't need Ginny's money."

"Let her keep talking," Drake said. "Tell us, Ginny. What did Mother say?"

She glanced at Harvey, her stomach a mess of nerves. "I'll tell you, and then I need you guys to tell me what you think. If there's any solution to this at all. *Any*."

She had ideas in her own mind, and they included living further away from Mother so she wouldn't know when Cayden came over. In short, Ginny wanted to have both Cayden and Sweet Rose. Depending on who she was with, one choice would win out over the other.

Her chest shook with her next breath. "She doesn't like Julie Chappell, because she and Daddy had a relationship once."

She continued with the story, feeling Harvey's impatience and disgust growing. He had the hardest time with their father's behavior, and it often bled into the other two boys as well.

"That's it," she said only a few minutes later. "She's holding a grudge, and that's why I can't see Cayden."

"That's preposterous," Drake said. "You should do what you want."

"Mother is vindictive," Elliot said. "Ginny's right to be concerned and cautious. She really could lose everything."

Ginny felt the weight of her decision down in her soul. "I don't want to lose Sweet Rose."

"You only would," Harvey said slowly. "If *we* allowed it." He gestured to the three of them sitting at the table.

"What do you mean?" she asked.

"Mother won't live forever, Ginny," he said. "Let's say she finds out about you and Cayden. She removes you from the will. Gives Sweet Rose to me."

She picked up instantly where he was going. "It would only stay with you if you didn't then turn it back over to me."

"Precisely." He sat up straight as their food arrived, and Ginny gazed at her farm-fresh salad, with bacon, avocados, craisins, balsamic vinaigrette, and ranch dressing. It was her favorite salad in the whole world, and her mouth watered.

She nudged her club soda out of the way and picked up her fork. "Would you do that, Harvey? Would all of you do that?"

"No one can run Sweet Rose the way you can, Ginny," Elliot said. "I'm content with my role in the family company. I don't want to own it."

"Neither do I," Drake said.

Harvey said nothing, and Ginny turned to look at him. "I think the cruelty and controlling aspect of our family needs to die with Mother," he said quietly. "I think you deserve to be happy, and I've seen Mother drive at least three men out of your life that probably would've made you happy."

Ginny's eyes filled with tears again, but she blinked them back.

"If you want to date Cayden Chappell, and if he makes you happy, then Ginny, I'll support that, and I'll absolutely include you back in Sweet Rose after Mother passes."

"Thank you," she whispered. "Thank all of you."

"It might be a bumpy road until then," Elliot said. "You realize that, right, Ginny?"

She nodded, though she knew Mother was unpredictable and rash, and yes, cruel. She swallowed and kept nodding. "I know," she said. "I sure do like this man, though, and I've already spoken to Drake about living in his country house."

"Smart," Harvey said. "Divorce yourself from as much of Mother's control now, while you can."

"That was my thought," Ginny said, finally forking her way into the salad to get a bite of many things. "What do you think of trying to play both angles for a while?"

"What? Like, date Cayden but don't tell Mother?" Drake asked, his eyes suddenly aglow.

"Yes," Ginny said. "Tell her I'm choosing Sweet Rose, but really, I'm choosing Cayden." She put a bite of the salad in her mouth, getting crunchy bacon and the perfect pop of brightness from the bit of red onion.

"Keep the relationship secret," Harvey mused. "It's not a bad idea."

"Especially if you're living off the block," Elliot said. "I could see it working."

Ginny nodded, her mind whirring as dinner continued. Only Drake said something before the conversation moved on to something else.

You could do that, he'd said. *But only if you're willing to pay the price if she finds out.*

Ginny didn't know what price that would be, but knowing Mother, it would be catastrophic.

5

Cayden turned onto a road that had clearly been privately paved. It wound back through the trees, which finally thinned and opened up to a meadow. A house sat at the end of the lane, with wild grasses surrounding it, a huge wrap-around porch, and the rustic feel of a log cabin though it wasn't made of logs.

The exterior was wood, though, and it shone a bright, earthy orange in the dying light of this Tuesday.

He'd only had to drive for fifteen minutes to get to this "country house," and Cayden wasn't about to complain about that. The house was probably an hour from the lane where her mansion was on the Winters property, and he could see why one would want to escape from there and come here.

He pulled up to the house and parked, not seeing her car or a flicker of life anywhere. The stillness in the air outside almost unnerved him, and Cayden glanced left and right as he went up the steps to the porch.

He knocked and stepped back, hoping she'd answer the door quickly. She didn't, but the barking of her dogs came through the door, and then her voice called, "Come in!"

The door wasn't locked, and Cayden went right inside. He did lock it behind him just before her trio of dogs surged toward him. He grinned at them and bent down to greet them with pats and hellos. They'd all stayed at the homestead until yesterday morning, when Ginny had packed up everything her assistant had brought and moved it out here.

Cayden hadn't seen her since then, and he wasn't sure what to expect when he walked further into the house, her dogs now his shadows. Perhaps an array of food on the counter that she'd picked up in town, with her wearing one of her fancy gowns, heels, and precise makeup.

He found her standing in front of the stove, using a pair of tongs to stir and lift pasta as she coated it in sauce. She wore a pair of loose pants that had an elastic waist and yet somehow still looked elegant as they flowed around her legs.

She turned toward him, a smile on her face, which was as natural as all the wood throughout the house. "You found it."

"I sure did," he said, his voice betraying how cowboy

he was. The scent of garlic and cream hung in the air, along with the saltiness of bacon. "What are you making?"

"Carbonara," she said, going back to the stirring. "You said you liked pasta."

"I do." He took a few more steps, drinking in the black sweater she wore, with the brightly colored apron over that. "You look real nice, Ginny." He put one hand on her hip and looked over her shoulder into the pan. "I didn't know you cooked."

"I enjoy it," she said. "I just normally don't have much time." She looked up at him, her face very close to his when she did.

His heart boomed in his chest, and he stepped back so she wouldn't feel it reverberating through her shoulder blade. "Looks amazing." He turned around, and on the slate countertops, she already had a big bowl of salad and a tray of garlic bread.

His mouth watered, and he rounded the counter as she turned and put the pan of pasta next to everything else. She hadn't said much after her dinner with her brothers the other night, and Cayden was dying to know what was going on.

"Are you going to tell me tonight?" he asked as he took a barstool.

She'd already gotten down plates, and she opened a drawer on her side of the island and pulled out forks. "Yes." She nodded to him. "You want to say grace?"

"Sure." He swept his cowboy hat off his head and ran

his fingers through his hair. His eyes closed, and he said, "Dear Lord, we thank Thee for our bounty. Thank you that Ginny could have the time to do what she likes to do. Thank you that we're able to be here together to talk and eat. Bless her with a clear mind regarding her mother and Sweet Rose. Bless me that all will go well in the joint meeting in the morning and that we'll be able to find a solution to our current obstacles. Bless this food. Amen."

"Amen," Ginny said softly.

Cayden opened his eyes and found her already looking at him. She'd said she wasn't nearly as religious as he was, but she'd prayed with him and Blaine, as well as all the brothers that had come for lunch on Sunday following church. Ginny had not attended, but Cayden usually did, so he'd gone with Blaine and Tam.

"Thank you," she said. "I don't think anyone has ever prayed for me before." Her eyes held a light tonight that made Cayden's whole world brighter. She smiled, her lips perfect and pink and drawing all of his attention.

She didn't wear much makeup tonight, and he wondered if she'd gone to work. Her hair fell over her shoulders, but just barely, and he said, "You cut your hair."

"Yes," she said, reaching up and touching the very ends of it. "It's quite a bit shorter. I'm thinking of dying it."

"Oh?" Cayden stood as she started scooping salad onto her plate. He picked up the only remaining plate and took a couple of pieces of garlic bread with the tongs there. "What color?"

"Blonde," she said.

"That's a huge change," he said.

"I'm ready for a huge change," she said. They finished getting their food, and she led him to a dining room table that could seat eight. With just the two of them, Cayden felt small among this large house.

It was easily three times smaller than the mansion he'd visited before, though, and she probably liked it a lot better.

"Oh, cake," she said, jumping back to her feet and returning to the kitchen. He watched her pull a chocolate cake out of the refrigerator and smile widely as she brought it to the table.

"Wow," he said, admiring it. The chocolate frosting had peaks and valleys, with strawberries and raspberries in little clusters across the top. "Did you make this too?"

"Yes, sir," she said proudly. "I always make my own birthday cake."

He'd just taken a bite of garlic bread, and he inhaled, getting crumbs and butter stuck in the back of his throat.

"I always get my hair cut on my birthday too," she said. "And I always have carbonara." She twisted up a forkful of noodles and put them in her mouth while he struggled to breathe.

He coughed and choked, finally getting the bread where it belonged and the air where it did. He reached for his napkin and wiped his face. "It's your birthday?"

"Yes, sir," she said, that smile still stuck in place.

"Why didn't you tell me?" Foolishness ran through him. He had nothing for her, not even a rose or a card.

"I didn't want you to fuss over me."

"Ginny." Didn't she know that was exactly what he *wanted* to do?

"I got everything I wanted," she said. "The pasta. The salad. The cake." She pointed to each one with her fork as she said them. Her eyes lifted back to his. "And you."

Warmth filled him, and while Cayden had vowed not to kiss her again until he knew more about Virginia Winters, he suddenly wanted to lunge across the corner of the table keeping them apart. He wanted to kiss her until he couldn't see straight. He wanted to find out where her master suite was and go there with her, so she'd have the best birthday possible.

Cayden tried to tame his hormones, managing to get them into submission. "Wow," he said, his voice pitching up a little. "That's a lot to live up to."

"I think you can do it," she said her smile curling up further. She went back to her meal, but Cayden wasn't sure what he'd been doing before she'd said it was her birthday. He held a piece of bread in his hand, so he took another bite.

"Do you normally make your own dinner on your birthday?" he asked.

"Yes," she said. "I celebrated with my family last night."

"Your mother?"

"Yes."

"She doesn't know we're dating, does she?"

"No." Ginny looked at him. "I talked it out with my brothers, and we agreed on several things. One, I'm going to date you. It's what I want, and I'm tired of letting Mother run off the men I like. Two, I'm not telling her I'm dating you. She's going to think I chose Sweet Rose—and her—over you. She gets to feel powerful and vindicated, and no one has to know about us."

"What if I want people to know about us?"

"I don't see why any of them would ever talk to Mother," Ginny said. "It's only the two of us who need to be careful. You can't come see me at work, for example. I put your name in my phone as Bill, for another. If Mother happens to see any texts, I'll simply say you're a supplier or something."

"A supplier." Cayden didn't like the dishonesty that went with a forbidden relationship, even if being in a secret relationship was kind of exciting.

"You are a supplier," she said with a giggle. "A supplier of happiness and charm and amazing kissing."

Cayden laughed, glad Ginny could spin things in such a positive way. "About the kissing," he said, looking at his plate. "I was thinking maybe I—we—should get to know one another first before we do that again. You know, the real you and the real me. Not these fake versions we've been for months."

Surprise covered her face. "Oh."

"No?"

"I mean, it's my birthday. You won't kiss me on my birthday?"

Cayden wanted to. He got up, leaving his dinner right where it was, and slid his hand along her face. "Yes," he whispered. "I'll kiss you on your birthday." He did, everything inside him firing hard.

"Mm," she said against his lips. "Best birthday ever."

He smiled at the way she ducked her head, seemingly shy with him all of a sudden. He took his seat again, laying the napkin over his lap. "Your mother has run off other men?"

"A few," Ginny said. "I guess I'm just done with her deciding my life for me. I'm forty-seven-years-old today. I get to decide who I spend my time with, and who I let kiss me."

Cayden agreed, so he just nodded. He didn't have to understand the complexities of her relationship with her mother. If he didn't have to lie, he was okay. It sounded like Ginny had things worked out on her end too, and while a hint of unease ran through him, he'd simply do what she said. He wouldn't come to her house or her work.

"What about your parties?" he asked.

"I still want you to accompany me," she said. "We'll show Mother how professional we are, and she'll never suspect a thing."

"We'll still pretend for all of those."

"Yes," she said.

"So…let me get this straight. We're going to have a real relationship in secret. But in public, we're going to keep pretending. I'm going to be your escort, as always, to keep the other creeps away and to rescue you from conversations you're done with."

"Just like last fall," she confirmed.

"You'll get to keep Sweet Rose."

"Yes."

"And me."

"Yes."

Cayden watched her, trying to find a downfall here. "It might actually work."

She grinned at him. "It's going to work, Cayden." She reached for the knife that had come on the cake plate. "Do you want a piece of cake?"

"Is that a real question?" he asked, and the two of them laughed. He was thrilled he'd get to keep Ginny in his life too, but something buzzed and pestered him for the rest of the night. It wasn't until he'd kissed her again and sat behind the wheel of his truck, driving away from this cottage in the woods that he realized what he'd been thinking.

"You can't marry her as long as her mother's alive," he said aloud. "You'll be in the shadows until then." He turned onto the highway that would take him back to Bluegrass Ranch.

"Are you willing to live with that?" he asked himself.

He couldn't answer that question, and it haunted him all the way back to the ranch, and into his bedroom with him.

∼

CAYDEN ARRIVED IN THE ADMINISTRATION BUILDING JUST after dawn. He'd been distracted by Ginny Winters for days now—weeks, if he was going to be really honest with himself—and he needed to focus.

He and Lawrence were meeting with both of the marketing firms Cayden had hired for their first-ever race at Bluegrass Ranch. Afterward, they were hosting their usual three-year-old sale, featuring several of the horses in the race.

Cayden was used to putting together sales. He'd done them dozens of times, and he'd worked with Tim Fennyson for the past eight years on events like this. But he'd never done a race before, and he'd met with a couple of former executives for the Kentucky Derby before even deciding to take it on.

"I still can't believe you're doing it," he muttered to himself as he took the few paper agendas from the printer. He went down the hall from his office and into the conference room to lay them out.

Besides Tim and his assistant, Lawrence and Cayden, a representative from the second marketing firm Cayden had hired would be there. He'd asked Lawrence to work with The Gemini Group, as they had vast experience with live, ticketed events, including horse races.

Lawrence claimed to have been in touch with them, and they'd confirmed for the nine a.m. meeting this morning.

Cayden would leave in a few minutes to go get pastries and juice, and he was still undecided about getting milk. He himself was somewhat lactose intolerant, and he never thought about milk. Most normal people liked milk with their doughnut, though, right?

He honestly wasn't sure. He spent a lot of time wining and dining people with a lot of money, and he'd never bring a doughnut to a charity fundraiser or to charm the owner of a stud he wanted to bring to Bluegrass.

He'd entertained men and women from all over the world, and he knew how to dress up while still looking like a cowboy. Today, he already wore a pair of dark, deep black slacks, and a brown, black, and white plaid shirt. He'd put a leather jacket on too, though the weather was getting far too warm for such things.

It would allow him to take it off and sling it over the back of the chair before the meeting started. Something like that gave him time to assess the crowd, read faces, and bask in the energy so he'd know what to say and what not to say.

He wore his cowboy boots, of course, and he'd put his hat on the moment he left the building and keep it there through the duration of the meeting. He'd bypassed the belt buckle this morning though, as that was usually the first thing he did to de-cowboy himself for meetings like this one.

With everything set at the office, he settled his cowboy hat on his head and left the building to get the refreshments. When he returned with far too many cream cheese Danishes and filled doughnuts, he saw Lawrence's truck parked outside the administration building.

Cayden left the juice and yes, the milk, in the back seat and took the pastry boxes inside first.

"There you are," Lawrence said when Cayden entered the conference room. "This all looks great." He looked around at the papers, the flowers in the middle of the table, the screen all lit and ready to go. "I don't see why you need me."

Cayden smiled at Lawrence and put the boxes down on the end of the table. "I need you, because this is too much for me to handle."

"I'm not you," Lawrence said, looking directly into Cayden's eyes. "Promise me you're not going to yell at me when I don't do things the way you would."

Cayden blinked, not expecting Lawrence to demand such a thing. "I won't," he said.

"You probably will," Lawrence said with a sigh. "You save your best self for the press."

"Lawrence," Cayden said. "Am I mean to you?"

"No," he said. "You usually handle all of this so flawlessly. I'll mess it up, and then I'll hear it from Mom, and Spur, and probably you too."

"I don't expect you to know what I know," Cayden said. "If you have a question, ask me. I'm happy to answer it." He swallowed too. "I'm not even sure how this will go. I've never done a race here. We'll all learn as we go."

Lawrence reached up and touched his hat. "All right," he said. "I want to do a good job. I just don't know how."

"You're here," Cayden said. "You're already doing a good job. You've got…who's coming from The Gemini Group?"

"A woman named Mariah Barker," Lawrence said. "She's not particularly nice, I'll say that up front. She's been difficult on the phone."

"She's probably overworked," Cayden said. "That's one of the first things I learned when working with people and not horses. They do things they don't necessarily want to do, because they're tired or stressed or overworked."

"I'll keep that in mind."

"Come help me with the drinks." Cayden retraced his steps out to the truck, where he and Lawrence carried in the juice and milk. He looked around again. "Okay, what else?"

"I talked to Spur, and he said we probably have eleven horses he'd race in this."

"That's only enough for one race," Cayden said, frowning. "We need more than that."

"That's where our marketing execs come in, right?"

The blipping panic in Cayden's bloodstream quieted. "Right," he said. "That's why we've hired them." He didn't have to do everything. Sometimes it only felt like he did.

Knocking on glass met his ear, and Cayden spun back to the hallway. "I thought I kept that unlocked."

"I'll get it," Lawrence said. He ducked out of the room, and Cayden took a deep breath. He should be right here to greet them anyway. He tugged on the hem of his jacket and drew himself to his full height.

Voices spoke down the hall, and Cayden couldn't discern the words as they echoed in the lobby. It was Lawrence and a woman, so probably his rep from the marketing firm. Their voices increased, and Cayden realized that they weren't having a get-to-know-you chat, but an argument.

"Are you kidding me?" he grumbled to himself. He started down the hall, his heart pounding hard in his chest. They needed these people on their side. With a firm as big The Gemini Group, they'd work on the accounts of the people they liked first, and then Bluegrass Ranch would get little attention, or the efforts of the stressed, overworked woman Lawrence had already described.

He strode into the lobby to find Lawrence and a pretty blonde woman facing off. Her fingers were clenched in a fist, and Lawrence looked like he could shoot fire from his eyes. He normally had a pretty sunny disposition. He always had a joke to tell at Sunday dinners, and he was the quickest to laugh at anything anyone else said, even if it wasn't all that funny.

"Good morning," Cayden said, making his voice as pleasant as possible. He went right up to Lawrence and stepped between him and the blonde. "I'm Cayden Chappell. You must be Mariah Barker from The Gemini Group."

He grinned and stuck out his hand, feeling the tension in his brother start to drain away. The blonde woman couldn't see past him, so she had no choice but to look at Cayden. Her anger drained away too, and she finally blinked.

"Yes," she said. "I'm Mariah Barker."

"You found us," Cayden said, keeping his smile in place. "Lawrence has told me so much about you. Let me show you where we'll be." He offered the woman his arm, and she glanced down at it. Then she turned and took it, allowing him to lead her toward the hallway.

He glanced over his shoulder to his brother, a quizzical look on his face. Lawrence just stood there, his chest heaving and a frown marring his eyebrows.

6

Lawrence Chappell didn't know how to walk down the hall and enter the conference room.

He couldn't get his lungs to stop heaving, and he couldn't believe Cayden had charmed the woman so easily.

Everything came so naturally to Cayden, and Lawrence once again had the feeling that he shouldn't be in this building today. His brother should ask someone else to help with this event. The problem was, there was no one else. Trey was splitting his time between Bluegrass and his new ranch, The Triple T.

Spur did enough around the ranch. Blaine worked in the fields and with their pregnant mares until darkness stole the light from the day. He had to make plenty of phone calls already, and he couldn't take on more public relations than he currently did.

Ian, Conrad, and Duke worked with their horses, keeping notes and aligning columns with letters Lawrence didn't understand. That left Cayden and Lawrence, and he finally drew in a breath that didn't shake in his chest.

Not a moment later, the door opened and a man walked in. He took off his sunglasses, his smile wide. Another man followed him, and they both wore white shirts, ties, and slacks. No cowboy boots or hats in sight. More marketing professionals, but not a sassy woman getting right in his face for not telling her how far away Bluegrass Ranch was.

He'd blinked and said, *You got here on time, so you must've seen how far it was.*

He didn't know where she lived, besides. *Shouldn't have added that bit*, he thought. "Good morning," he said, mimicking Cayden. He extended his hand toward the two gentlemen, and they frowned too.

Lawrence's confidence took a dive. Did he have something stuck to his face? He coached himself not to reach up and check.

"Are we not seeing Cayden this morning?" one man asked as he reached to shake Lawrence's hand.

"You are," he said, refusing to let his smile slip even a millimeter. "He's just down the hall. I'm his brother, Lawrence. I'll be working this project with everyone." He shook the other man's hand. "You must be Tim."

"I'm Tim," the first man said. "This is my assistant, Darren."

"Nice to meet you both." Lawrence faced the hall, ready for this meeting to be over already. Maybe he and Cayden could switch firms, and he could deal with Mariah and Lawrence would deal with Tim and Darren.

Even as he thought it, he knew Cayden wouldn't agree to it. He'd been working with Tim at Layered Approach for years, and the two of them knew how the other worked. That was all he needed to do with Mariah—figure out how she worked. Then he could play to her strengths and not get in petty arguments about the distance from her house to Bluegrass Ranch.

He reached the conference room door, where Cayden was laughing with Mariah. He stood to the side so Tim and Darren could enter first, and Cayden practically roared he was so excited to see the two men.

Lawrence slipped into the room last, looking straight at Mariah. She didn't flick her eyes in his direction at all, and his heart pounded with nerves. She was a beautiful woman, and if Lawrence had seen her at church or the grocery store, he'd have been interested.

Today was the first day he'd met her face-to-face, and he could admit she was pretty with that blonde hair that barely kissed her shoulder blades. She had dark eyes, though, with dark eyebrows that made him think her hair color came from a bottle. He didn't care about that, because she wore the blonde well. It had some darker streaks in it, and she wore a navy blue blazer with a white blouse underneath it that had little sparks of color on it. Her skirt hugged her hips and then flared to her knees in waves of pleats, and it was the color of ripe peaches.

She finally glanced at him, and Lawrence felt the weight of Cayden's glance too. Lawrence swallowed his pride and his nerves and stepped over to Mariah. "Can I speak to you for a moment, please?"

"Very well," she said, darting away from him as she left her stacked folders on the table and headed for the door.

He waited for her to leave the room, and then he followed her. He brought the door closed behind him and took a deep breath. "I apologize," he said, employing his most professional voice. It wasn't anywhere near Cayden's, but it would have to do. "I apologize that you had to drive for forty-five minutes to get here. I didn't realize our venue was so far out of your way. Next time, I will come to you with anything we need to discuss."

Mariah's eyes blazed with displeasure for the first half of his speech, but by the end, she looked ashamed. "You don't need to apologize," she said. "I've had a rough morning already, and I just took it out on you. It's my fault. I apologize."

Lawrence suddenly wanted to know more about her rough morning. "Anything I can do to help?"

"Only if you can make my boss less of a chauvinist." She sucked in a breath; her eyes widened; she clapped her hand over her mouth.

Lawrence searched her face, then burst out laughing.

He wasn't sure what he found funny. Her statement or her reaction to what had come out of her mouth.

"I'm so sorry," she said, her voice made mostly of breath. "Please don't repeat that to anyone."

"I won't," he said between his chuckles.

Mariah spun away from him and strode away, breaking into a jog by the end of the hallway.

"Wait," Lawrence called, wondering what had just happened.

The door behind him opened, and Cayden asked, "What are you doing? We need her."

"I was apologizing," Lawrence said, barely glancing at him. Mariah was going to come back any moment now.

When she didn't, Cayden hissed, "Go get her," and stepped back inside as one of the marketing execs asked him something.

Lawrence was fairly sure following Mariah was a bad idea. He felt stuck between a rock and a hard place, but he walked away from the conference room. That would keep Cayden off his back at the very least.

Mariah wasn't in the lobby, and he glanced down the other hallway, which led to their sales offices. They didn't open until ten, and the hallway sat in darkness. He couldn't imagine Mariah had gone that way.

He pushed outside, the sunshine bright this morning. Thankfully, a breeze blew, and Lawrence reached up to press on his hat so it wouldn't get stolen.

She wasn't out here either, but her car sat next to a

fancy, black SUV, as well as his and Cayden's pickup trucks.

"Lord," he prayed quickly. "Where is she?" He didn't get an answer, but his logic told him there was only a couple of places she could be. Down the dark hallway or around the corner out here.

He called, "Mariah?" and walked to the end of the building closest to him. There were no benches or anything here, and she wasn't anywhere to be found.

Lawrence returned to the building and turned down the hall toward the sales offices. Only a few steps later, he heard sniffling, and he slowed his gait. "Mariah," he said softly.

"I just need a minute," she said, her voice high-pitched.

He paused and pressed his back into the wall. There were couches outside the sales offices, and she'd obviously found one. He wished he had something to make her feel better, but he literally didn't know a thing about her—other than she liked to put smiley face emojis at the end of her emails.

After what felt like a long time but was probably only a half a minute, she said, "I need my job."

"I'm not going to say anything," he said.

"I'm normally very professional," she said, her voice cracking again.

"I'm sure you are." He closed his eyes and prayed for help. "Do you want to give me some context?"

"You're my biggest client," she said. "I'm going to do a good job for you."

"I meant about the chauvinistic boss."

Several more seconds went by, and Lawrence suspected Cayden would lose his temper soon enough if Lawrence didn't get Mariah back into that conference room.

"Do you only invite married people to your company parties?" she asked. "Or people with boyfriends or girlfriends?"

"No," Lawrence said, though Bluegrass didn't really have company parties. "That's ridiculous."

"That's my boss." She sighed. "He's having a barbecue tonight, and I was invited...until my boyfriend broke up with me. So you know, I'm just having a great week."

"I'm sorry," Lawrence murmured. A break-up was hard enough.

"My boss talks business at his personal events," she said. "It's how I got this assignment, and you guys are huge. At least Dr. Biggers made it sound like you were. I was thrilled to take you on, and I wouldn't have gotten it had I not been there." She sniffled, and Lawrence couldn't stand her being by herself.

"I'm coming around the corner," he said, and he waited for her to say he shouldn't. She didn't, and Lawrence took a few more steps to get around the corner. The couches he'd been expecting appeared, along with the pretty woman he'd been conversing with via email or phone until today.

"Can I sit?"

"I suppose," she said, her eyes trained on her hands.

"I don't want to freak you out any more," he said. "Cayden's probably going to text me within five minutes, and he'll want to know where we are and when we'll be back."

"I'll be ready," she said, straightening her shoulders.

"I'm sorry. Really."

"I didn't mean to make your bad week worse."

"You didn't." She blew out her breath and looked at Lawrence. She glanced away quickly, a little laugh coming out of her mouth. "My boss did that, and my ex-boyfriend. I just got frustrated this morning when I got the text that said the party tonight was couples-only, and it came in literally five seconds before you opened the door."

Lawrence nodded. "How long have you had this job?"

"A year or so," she said.

"The boyfriend?" He couldn't believe he'd asked that.

He didn't need to know that, and he was surprised when she answered with, "We'd only been dating a few months, but we've known each other a lot longer than that." She looked at him, her eyes sliding down his chest to his knees and then his boots. "You know how couples aren't really couples for a while? Until they have this strange talk about how they are dating exclusively, and now it's suddenly okay to call a man your boyfriend? Or in your case, a woman your girlfriend?"

"I, uh, haven't dated for a while," Lawrence admitted, heat spiking in his face. "I do know what you're referencing, though."

"I'd been with Brady about ten months," she said. "But we weren't officially dating until January. So just a few months."

Lawrence nodded again, glad Mariah wasn't crying anymore and that her voice had returned to normal. They'd spoken on the phone a few times, and she'd never been nasally.

"I could be your boyfriend so you can go to the party," he said, completely shocked as the words came out of his mouth.

She pulled in a breath and swung her eyes to his, hers wide and surprised too.

"I have no idea where that came from," he said, jumping to his feet. Miraculously, his phone rang, and he looked at it. "It's Cayden. We should get to the meeting." He walked away from her before he could say or do anything else that was completely insane.

What are you doing? he asked himself, the voice in his head belonging to his brother. *Who says they'll be someone's boyfriend so they can go to a barbecue at their boss's house?*

He shook his head, glad her footsteps sounded behind him as he retraced his steps to the conference room. He held the door open for her like a perfect Southern gentleman, but he couldn't quite meet her gaze.

"Ah, we're all back," Cayden said, his voice big and

booming and filling the room. "Come in, come in. Let's get this show on the road."

Lawrence took his spot at the table, which happened to be directly across the table from Mariah's. Their eyes met, and another entire conversation happened in that single second of time. Then he glanced away as Cayden said, "I'm going to go through my vision for the event, and I need everyone to identify all the holes. Then we'll work on plugging them."

7

Mariah Barker could listen to the smooth, powerful voice of Cayden Chappell for hours. She could look at his brother for a lot longer than that.

She couldn't believe she'd had a complete mental breakdown this morning. She hadn't wanted to break-up with Brady; he'd ended their relationship on Monday night after a date that Mariah had actually thought went well.

She never saw things coming, and her eyebrows drew down. She told herself to focus, because this was an important client, and she needed every advantage she could get with her boss at The Gemini Group. That text from Dr. Biggers had just been a really rotten cherry on top of a melted sundae.

The barbecue tonight is only for couples, the text had

read. *I'm sorry to hear about you and Brady. I thought you were a handsome couple.*

That was it. *No, you're not invited anymore,* though that message was crystal clear.

Mariah had been working to get invited to Dr. Biggers's parties, barbecues, dinners, and lunches for months. She'd never realized that those getting the invites were in relationships...until that morning.

Shock and anger had swept through her faster than she could blink, and when she'd looked up and seen Lawrence standing there, all she could see was the phony smile of Dr. Biggers.

Embarrassment continued to swirl through her, and it only intensified every time she looked in Lawrence's direction.

I could be your boyfriend so you can go to the party.

He'd back-peddled quickly from there, and Mariah was still trying to figure out what he'd meant by that. He probably was too.

She honestly wanted to go back in time and redo this whole week.

She'd attended two of Dr. Biggers's parties, and she'd gotten new assignments at both of them. She now knew why some of her colleagues seemed to advance quicker than she had. They literally had more opportunities than their weekly Monday morning meetings to get clients. She'd thought they'd brought those accounts to the firm themselves, but she'd been wrong. They simply had spouses or partners and got invited to cider tastings.

The desperation in her voice when she'd said *I need my job* echoed through her whole body. She hadn't been lying; she just wished the person she was going to be working with for the next four months hadn't heard her say it in such a way.

"All right," Cayden said. "That's it. That's what we're thinking for the event. What do you see that I can't see?" He flipped his presentation to a blank screen and positioned his fingers on the keyboard.

"How are you earning profit?" Tim asked.

Cayden typed *profit* on the screen and stepped back from his laptop. "We've got the sales of the horses, obviously. Concessions, which will be new for us. We've never run food and drink through Bluegrass." He paused, his eyebrows going up. "I might have an idea for that. Anyway." He gave himself a shake, and Mariah scrawled a couple of notes on her notebook.

"Ticket sales for people to come watch the races. Merchandise."

She put a check-mark next to merchandise on her paper. "Do you have merchandise?" she asked. "Or is that something you'll have to produce between now and then?"

"We have a few T-shirt designs," he said.

"The Gemini Group has a ton of resource for

merchandising," she said. "Just so you know. I believe I emailed Lawrence about this previously."

"She did," he confirmed, and she cast him a small smile.

When Cayden didn't go on, Mariah opened her mouth again. "You could make money from advertising," she said, glancing at her notes. "Banners along the fences in your arena. Sponsored rows or seats. Ads in your concessions areas. Ads in your parking areas. Paid parking. All of those can bring in additional revenue."

Cayden had moved over to his computer after her first sentence. He finished typing in her ideas and looked up. "This sounds like a lot. Can we get all of that done in four months?"

"Do you have people who'd want to advertise at an event like this?" Tim asked, glancing at Mariah. "No disrespect, Ms. Barker, but money from advertising is only good if there are people who want to advertise to this crowd."

Mariah nodded at him, conceding but not giving an inch. "Very true. I'd imagine the Chappells know quite a few people in the horse racing industry who want to take on an event like this in the first place. They want to sell their horses, of course. But they know the people who'd buy their horses already. So what else are you looking to accomplish here? Increased awareness? Other local business partnerships? You could bring in a food truck and partner with them. They bring their customers to you;

you bring yours to them. It's about increasing awareness." She glanced down at her paper.

"You could partner with a local distillery or brewery," she said. "For drinks. Their brand brings in their fans, and that crowd might be new to horse racing. Your horse racing crowd might not have heard of Barreled and Brewed. It's a win-win."

"Partnerships are smart," Tim agreed. "It can become more than a single horse race. That can be the culminating event, as you said you only have eleven horses right now."

"We can bring in money through entrance fees," Lawrence said. "From other owners who want to be involved in the race and sale."

"That makes it more of a racing event," Tim said. "Different ages, genders, lengths."

Mariah took several more notes as the discussion continued, and the event just got larger and larger. She put a star next to the one question she needed answered. *How big do you really want this to be?*

With a deadline and a budget, not everything could be accomplished.

"This is great," Cayden said several times throughout the discussion. At the end, he said, "Thanks so much, you guys. Good work today." He shook hands all around, and Lawrence did too. They walked Tim, Darren and her out to the lobby and all the way outside.

More smiles. More handshakes. More promises to

follow-up on all the items they'd all taken on. She had to get quotes for banners, as well as put together merchandise opportunities. She needed to make a list of possible companies that might want to advertise at an event like this, and Lawrence said he'd help with that.

She'd definitely get to talk to him again, and Mariah shouldn't be so excited about that. She told herself that she enjoyed speaking to all of her clients, and that she loved planning events, and that was why she left Bluegrass Ranch with a smile a mile wide and her heart thumping irregularly in her chest.

As she thought about Lawrence, though, she knew he was a large reason why too.

I could be your boyfriend so you can go to the party.

She thought about that sentence the entire way back to the office, and when she arrived, she found it very quiet. "Hey," she said to Jane, the woman who sat only a couple of cubicles away from Mariah. "Where is everyone?"

"Biggers took a few people to the food truck rally," she said, rolling her eyes. "Look around. Do you see any of his favorites?" She went back to her computer, and Mariah glanced around.

All of Dr. Biggers's favorites were indeed gone. All those he invited to his parties too. "Two meals in one day," she mused, wondering who she could possibly call about his behavior. Surely it was unethical, but Mariah didn't even know who to complain to. Her frustration with her job kept rising with every passing day, though, and she needed to do something about it.

Her phone rang, and Mariah lifted it from the cradle. "Mariah Barker," she said, glad her emotions from that morning had disappeared.

"Hello, Mariah," a man said, and she recognized the voice. "It's Lawrence Chappell. I'd love to talk more about the merchandising without Tim and Darren around. Are you free for dinner sometime this week?"

By the end of his question, a smile had filled her whole face. She leaned back in her chair and gave time a couple of seconds to fill the line. Then she said. "I'm sure I can find an evening for dinner."

He chuckled, and she could just see the handsome, dark-haired cowboy ducking his head as he did. "Great," he said. "Should we say Friday?"

"Friday is fine," she said, knowing full-well that couples went out on Friday nights. She wasn't going to make him define the relationship right now though, because their relationship had always just been a business one. She hadn't even thought of him as anything but her biggest client and most important assignment right now. She hadn't met him face-to-face until today either, and that had changed things.

His kindness had too, and as she hung up after confirming a pick-up time of six-thirty and that she'd text him her address, she wondered if she could take Lawrence up on his offer to be her boyfriend for Dr. Biggers's parties.

"Just ask him on Friday," she said, making a note of it and then getting back to work, the image of his worried eyes and kind smile as he'd come around the corner filling her head for the rest of the day.

8

*G*inny stepped over to her mother when she turned, her unspoken request all that was needed. She zipped up the dress, noticing how bony her mother had gotten. Perhaps she'd always been this skeletal.

"There," she said.

Mother turned, and she was flawless in her pale pink gown. She reached for something on her bureau. "Ears?" She put on a pair of tasteful white rabbit ears with silver for the inner ear linings, which matched the metallic sparkles in her dress. "Or no ears?"

"It is an Easter gala," Ginny said with a smile. She wore a robin's egg blue dress, sans sparkles but with plenty of train. It was easy to pretend with Mother; Ginny had been doing similar stints with her counterparts for years.

She'd confessed that she'd ended things with Cayden, and that since she was doing so much work with the Founders Association that spring and summer, she'd decided to live in Drake's country house, which was decidedly closer to the Association's office.

Mother hadn't questioned it at all. She rarely asked how things were going with Ginny, and it had been easier than Ginny had even anticipated to have her cake and eat it too.

Kiss it too, she thought, her smile turning genuine on her lips.

Cayden hadn't allowed much kissing, though, and Ginny's grin went back to plastic. The last time had been on her birthday, almost a month ago now. They'd had plenty of conversations since then, though, and she could admit that getting to know him was almost as fun as the explosive feelings that moved through her whenever he got near.

Her phone buzzed, and she checked it. "This is Bill," she said. "Excuse me, Mother." She swiped on the call from "Bill" as she strode away from her mom. "Hey," she said, her voice low but filled with anticipation.

"I thought you'd have left by now," Cayden said. "Sorry. Did I cause you to run out?"

He had, but Ginny said, "Not at all. We're just leaving," in a much more normal voice.

"I'm here," he said. "I thought maybe I should go in alone? Or did you want me to wait for you?"

"Up to you," she said. "If you go in alone, Mother certainly can't think we're seeing each other."

"Right," he said, but he was distracted. Ginny could hear it in his voice. "What is it?"

"We've met for your social events in the past month," he said. "She hasn't had a problem with me being your arm candy."

Ginny kept one hand on the bannister as she went down the steps. She'd have to climb them again to assist Mother, but she needed a few minutes alone. She knew what Cayden was going to say next.

"Maybe she wouldn't have a problem—"

"She will, Cayden," Ginny said, glancing over her shoulder at the bottom of the steps. "Aren't we okay?"

"I don't know," he said with a sigh. "I don't want to pretend."

"I can get someone else to stand at my side," she said.

"No," he said in a flat tone.

Frustration filled her; he felt it too, she knew. She simply didn't know how to erase it. This was the situation they'd both agreed to. "I'm sorry," she said, because she didn't know what else to say.

They'd discussed the difficulty of the situation, and every time, he said it was worth it. That she was worth it.

"It's okay," he said. "I'm gonna go in. I see Lolly."

"Okay," she said, and the call ended. Ginny stood near the exit and drew in a deep breath. "It's fine." Her whispered reassurance to herself didn't get very far, but it had to be enough for now.

She turned and gathered her skirt into big handfuls before she went back upstairs. "Ready, Mother? We're going to be late."

"You're never late when you're the guest of honor," Mother said, reaching up to adjust her earring.

Ginny didn't argue with her, though neither of them were the guests of honor at tonight's party. It was simply a ham and potatoes dinner at the Winchester's, but they owned one of the largest plantations in Kentucky, and they'd serve their salted, cured meat on family heirloom china, sterling silver forks and knives to complete the settings.

Everyone would be in gowns and suits, and everyone would fit in the dining room. Ginny and Mother had been invited for the past two years, and this would be their third appearance.

This year, Colton Winchester had called Ginny and said they'd only be serving Sweet Rose whiskey and bourbon, and she'd gushed at him for a solid ten minutes. He also had a son who'd just turned forty, and Ginny suspected she'd be somehow strategically placed next to Emerson Winchester for dinner.

"I hope there's someone there I can latch onto," Ginny said. "To avoid Emerson." She met Mother's eye, who frowned.

"I agree," she said. "He hasn't quite lived up to his potential, has he?"

"I heard his last girlfriend was only twenty-two," Ginny said, and that was the honest truth.

"There will be someone there," Mother said with confidence. "Let's go." She reached for Ginny, and together, they went down the wide hall, and then Ginny went first down the steps, her skirts gathered into her fists and Mother's hand on her shoulder.

Step by painful step, they made it to the first floor, and Ginny said, "Mother, you need to consider moving to the main level."

"There is nowhere for me here."

"Mother, it's a four-thousand-square-foot level. There has to be something here."

"If you find me a bedroom, a bathroom, a kitchen, and a sitting area on this level that does not include that front bedroom, I'll consider it."

Ginny could rise to this challenge, and she said so as she opened the back door and helped her mother to her SUV. "I'll get someone to look into it," she said. The kitchen in this house was massive and meant for a professional to man it. Mother couldn't use it, and there was no other place to cook.

A library and ballroom sat on the main level as well, as did a drawing room and a music room. "The music room would work," she said. "There's a bathroom right next door, and we can modify it the way we did the room upstairs with what you require to make your tea and toast."

"I don't want all those men in the house," she said.

"Mother," Ginny said. "Don't be unreasonable. If you want the house modified, it'll take people to come modify it."

"*I* don't want it modified," Mother said haughtily. "You do."

"For your safety," Ginny said, driving slowly as she left the property. Mother didn't like fast driving, and Ginny was doing everything she could to stay on her mom's good side these days. When she did that, Mother didn't look too closely as what she did in other areas of her life.

Several minutes later, they arrived at the Winchester's mansion on the east side of town. It didn't look like there was a party here at all, though the entire front face of the house was lit up with tasteful lights.

Ginny followed the arrow and turned down a lane just past the house. A valet met her, opening her door and helping her from the SUV while another helped Mother. Someone met them on the sidewalk and escorted the two of them into the house through a back door, where light and music spilled into the darkening night.

One step through the door, and Colton Winchester spotted her instantly. "There she is," he said, his loud voice filling the whole house.

Heat filled Ginny's face, and she told herself not to look anywhere but at Colton's smiling face. He was serving their liquor exclusively, and she had to please him. She had limits, but playing to his ego was well within them.

"Colton," she said, making sure Mother was steady on her feet before she stepped away from her. She laughed as she got engulfed by the bear of the man wearing a cowboy hat. He lifted her right up off her feet and Ginny let out a giggle as his laugh covered hers.

He set her down, and Ginny kept her hands on his shoulders. "We're not late, are we?"

"You're never late," Colton said, smiling down at her. "Look at you, Wendy." He grinned at Mother and stepped over to her. She offered him her hand, and Colton lifted it to his lips like a perfect Southern gentleman. "You are beautiful."

"Thank you, Mister Winchester." Mother didn't have a giggling bone in her body, and Ginny found it a miracle if she even smiled. She also wondered why she tolerated Colton and his cowboy hat but not Cayden and his.

"My daughter will show you to your places," Colton said, turning back to Ginny. "You're coming with me, Missy. I have someone I want you to meet."

"Is that right?" Ginny asked, finally allowing herself to sweep the room. She couldn't find Emerson or Cayden. She told herself it couldn't be Emerson, because she'd met him several times.

"That's right," he said. "There's a gentleman here who's putting together a race at his ranch, and it's the perfect opportunity for the two of you to combine your audiences."

Ginny knew who Colton was going to "introduce" her to before Cayden came into view. He stood with a couple of other men, a drink in his hand he hadn't touched. She knew, because the amber liquid was much higher than the others in the group, and even when he lifted it to his lips, none passed into his mouth.

His eyes met hers, and he lowered his glass.

"Here she is," Colton said. "Virginia Winters." He indicated Cayden. "Cayden Chappell. He's putting together a summer ending event at Bluegrass Ranch. Have you been there?"

"Once or twice," Ginny said, her smile cordial and professional. "It is beautiful land."

"These boys know what they're doing, and they're pushing into the future with their own race this year."

"Is that right?" Ginny asked, though she'd heard all about the challenges and successes Cayden had experienced over the past few weeks as his initial planning stages of the race had been put into motion.

"They're looking for advertisers," Colton said. "Sweet Rose might be interested in that. They're also looking for sponsors for their concessions, which might fit your brand too. Or perhaps you'd simply be interested in attending the race. You've been to the Derby before, I believe."

"Once or twice," Ginny said again, because she had.

"You have?" Cayden asked, and Ginny nodded. "I'd love to see the hat you wore."

"Virginia has beautiful clothes," Colton said, and Ginny beamed up at him.

"Stop it, Colton. You're embarrassing me." She removed her hand from his arm and extended her hand for Cayden to take. "Good to see you again, Cayden."

"You know each other?"

"Yes," Ginny said as Cayden took her hand and lifted it to his lips. Her skin sizzled with his touch, and Ginny wished that mouth would claim hers again. "He's attended several of the same social functions as me in the past several months."

She didn't need to keep such things secret. If she did, and Colton found out, he'd feel stupid, and she didn't need that.

"I think he came to my New Year's Eve party," she said.

"I did," Cayden said. "It was fantastic." He put down his glass of whiskey and tucked Ginny's hand into his arm. "I'd love to talk more about the Derby. Maybe you have some insight for how the race should go at Bluegrass." His eyes fired like dark diamonds, and Ginny's blood ran hotter and hotter with every moment he looked at her.

"Dinner is in ten minutes," Colton said, grinning at the two of them.

"Thank you," Cayden said, looking at Colton. "This has been an amazing night already."

"Is your son here?" Ginny asked as Colton started to leave, and he turned back to her.

"He's in Belgium currently," Colton said, his face darkening.

"I see," Ginny said. "Tell him I said hello." She added a bright smile to the statement and turned back to Cayden. "You're not here with anyone?"

"No, ma'am." He grinned at her. "You?"

"Just you now," she said, well aware of the others around them. "Tell me, Cayden, what kind of race is this you're planning? Certainly not as high-stakes as the Derby."

"Ho, no," he said with a chuckle. "Have you seen the gardens here, Ginny? They're lovely right now."

"Once or twice," she said as he led her toward the door in the corner that led out onto the patio. She happily went with him, the train of her dress tailing behind her. She hoped Colton would say something to Mother about this "great opportunity," while simultaneously her heart jumped over itself at the thought of him saying anything to her.

Mother would say that yes, of course Ginny knew Cayden, because they'd been building a relationship last fall and winter.

Outside, away from listening ears and prying eyes, Cayden bent his head toward Ginny's and whispered, "You steal my breath," in a voice full of only air. "You should wear blue every single day."

"Thank you," she murmured, pressing into the kiss he touched to her jaw. She wanted to ask him again if they were okay, but she didn't want to open any wounds he'd managed to close in the past half-hour.

"Horseback riding lesson at my place tomorrow?" he asked, his lips catching on her ear.

"I'm still planning on it," she said. "Three o'clock?"

"Mm."

"I had Mel clear my afternoon."

"Perfect," he said. "Blaine said he's cooking for Tam, and we're welcome to join them for dinner at the homestead. How do you feel about that?"

"That sounds great," she said. "I always enjoy Blaine's food."

Cayden finally straightened, and Ginny felt the absence of him against her neck and cheek. "You never did ask me to sponsor your race," she said.

"No," he said. "I didn't want you to feel like you had to."

"I'm surprised you think I'd do something I don't want to do."

He chuckled as they reached the railing and gazed over the gardens in front of them. The last light of the sun cast everything in an orange glow, and Ginny said, "This is a stunning garden." She looked up at Cayden. "I'd love to do something for your race."

"Yeah? Because you want to? Or because Colton Winchester will think he made the deal happen?"

Cayden was extremely smart, and Ginny saw no reason to lie to him. "Both," she said with a grin. "Let's discuss it whenever you can come to my office."

His eyebrows went straight up. "Your office?"

"Yes, sir," she said. "I do business deals from my office, and no one will think it odd if you come there to get this deal done."

"I see."

Ginny looked up at him, the sexy curve of his mouth making her so happy.

"When should I come get the deal inked?"

"Let's see," she said. "I'll have Mel check my schedule and set something up with you."

"Perfect," Cayden said.

9

Cayden walked down the aisles of the family stable, the scent of horseflesh and dirt calming him in a way he couldn't explain. He loved being outside with the horses, and he didn't get to do it nearly often enough.

His boots scuffed against the ground, and the jeans he'd pulled on in his office felt like soft cotton for how dirty they were. A smile touched his face as he approached Raven's stall. "Hey, girl," he said softly.

He felt more like himself with the horses than he did in suits and shiny shoes—not that he wore those. Even last night at the Winchester party, he'd worn cowboy boots. They were shiny though, and they'd never visited the outdoors here at Bluegrass Ranch.

The blue roan lifted her head over the gate and sought Cayden's palm. "I need to come see you every day, don't I, girl?" he said to her, bending his head down to get closer to hers. "Sorry I haven't. I will, okay?" He stroked both hands down the sides of her neck and watched her eyes close halfway.

"You're going to take Ginny on your back today," he said. "She's got eyes about the same color as your coat, and all this long, dark hair she thought about dying blonde but never did. She's gorgeous, and kind, and I kinda like her." He smiled at the horse, who'd keep his secrets until the day she died.

Not that how he felt about Ginny was a secret. *Only from her mother*, he thought.

Cayden had moments where everything between him and Ginny was plated with gold and nothing could go wrong. Other times, he spiraled into self-doubt, and he'd call or text her and try to get the reassurances he needed that they were okay.

She always gave them too, patiently, and Cayden wished his insecurities weren't so strong.

"Who should I ride today?" he asked Raven. "I think I'm gonna go with Honeyduke."

Cayden always rode Honeyduke, and he loved the palomino more than anything. He'd bought her several years ago, and she'd produced three golden colts in that time, remained his best friend, and knew all of Cayden's secrets, inside and out.

He looked down the aisle, but Honey's stall wasn't open. "Be right back," Cayden said, digging in his pocket as he went. He pulled out a single serving of honey roasted peanuts and ripped open the bag.

Several horses lifted their heads over their gates at the rustling of the plastic package, and Cayden grinned at them. "Not for you guys," he said, knowing Spur wouldn't be happy about Cayden feeding the horses peanuts. Especially his, and Cayden went right past All-Out's stall without hardly a glance at the horse.

He arrived at Honey's stall and unlatched the top half of the door. She met him there, and he did feed her a few of the candied peanuts. "Hey, my friend." His soul finally soothed all the way, and he couldn't let so much time pass between now and his next visit.

He did get out on Honey every Sunday afternoon, but he hadn't yesterday because of the Easter dinner. His thoughts wandered to Ginny, and he'd already told Honey all about her.

"You're going to meet her today," he said. "Be nice, okay? You'll have to tell me what you think once she's gone."

He'd never been engaged, and he'd never asked a woman to marry him. He'd only been dating Ginny for a month now, and he was considering whispering secrets to Honey about his feelings.

"I'm not going to tell you how I feel about her," he said. "I've babbled on long enough about her." He backed up and opened the bottom half of the stall, reaching in to drape a lead around the horse's head. "Come on, girl."

He led her outside and saddled her, throwing her reins around the post there so he could go get Raven. He retrieved that horse too, and while he'd left this office early, he was sure three o'clock had come and gone.

With Raven saddled and ready for Ginny, he finally pulled his phone out of his back pocket to check it. His heart skipped a beat when he thought of her canceling their horseback riding this afternoon, and then another when he saw he had texts from her.

I'm coming, she'd said. *I'm just late.*

Sorry, Cay, she'd said in her second text. *Maybe twenty minutes out.*

That last message had come in about five minute ago, and Cayden quickly sent a text back to let her know where to come and that he was ready whenever she arrived.

Several minutes later, he heard the crunching of gravel under tires, and he walked around the side of the stable and lifted his hand when he saw Ginny's SUV. He couldn't see her through the windshield because of the sun's glare. After she'd parked and turned off her car, she got out, and Cayden could only stare at her.

He'd seen her in soft, stretchy pants and flip flops in her own house, scrambling eggs for dinner while he made coffee. He'd seen her in ball gowns and tiaras. He'd seen her in long, flowing pants paired with silk blouses and an expensive, billowy robe.

He'd never seen her wear jeans and boots, and his

mouth turned dry. His breath left his body. His heart pounded.

He'd never been in love before, and he needed to talk to Blaine and Spur to find out what such a thing felt like. Ginny had always ignited a spark in his blood, and they'd shared some fiery, amazing kisses.

He wanted more than physical passion, and he'd taken his time this past month to get to know her as much as he could. She had a lot of walls up, and a couple of times he'd had to remind her they weren't at one of her fancy parties. They could talk freely and learn about each other.

Ginny obviously hadn't done that with very many people, and she'd been opening up to him more and more with each passing day.

"Look at you," she said, walking toward him. Her eyes dropped to his feet and rebounded back to his eyes. "I like this cowboy version of you."

"Look at you," he said, his voice only slightly hoarse. "I've never seen you wear jeans."

"I just bought these today," she said with a smile. "They're okay?" She looked down at her legs and back to Cayden with hope in her eyes.

"They're great," he said. "New boots too, I see."

"What gave them away?"

"The price tag hanging off the side there." He nodded to the left one, grinning.

"Oh my gosh," Ginny said, stooping to remove it. "How embarrassing." She straightened and looked at him.

Cayden laughed as he crossed the distance to wrap her in a hug. "You didn't have to go shopping to come horseback riding."

"I didn't have anything to wear."

"I've seen your closet," he said. "You have plenty to wear."

"Not for horseback riding."

"Even for this." He stepped back and secured his hand in hers. "You're going to be on Raven." He nodded to the two opposite-colored horses. "Which one do you think she is?"

"Too obvious," she said.

"She's a blue roan," he said. "Can you see the blue-black shimmering in her coat?"

"Totally," Ginny said. "She's as beautiful as you said she'd be."

"The other one is Honeyduke. She's mine, and she's a palomino." He led them over to the horses and stroked Raven's neck. "Have you ridden a horse before?"

"Yes, when I was twelve," she said. "Remember I told you about that birthday party I went to?"

"That's the only time?" he asked. "That was a pony ride around the block."

"Yes." She reached out and touched Raven's neck where he had too. "She's so wonderful."

"I find them so therapeutic," he said. "I come out and tell them all my secrets."

"Lucky horses," she said, plenty of teasing in her voice.

"You already know all my secrets," Cayden said.

"That is not true," she said.

"What do you want me to tell you that I haven't?"

"So many things," she said, looking up at him. "Who was the last woman you went out with? What's your favorite food? Do you like dressing up like we were last night or wearing these dirty jeans?"

"The last woman I went out with is Terri Wilson. My favorite food is deep dish pepperoni pizza with tons of extra cheese. I'd choose jeans any day of the week, any time of day. I feel...centered when I'm with the horses. I don't mind the office, but entire weeks can slip by without proper spiritual care if I don't get out to the stable."

"Proper spiritual care," she repeated.

"Mm." He unlooped the reins for Raven. "What do you do for that?"

"I'm not sure," she said.

"Who's the last man you went out with?"

"Russell Troy," she said.

"Was it serious?"

"Not particularly," she said. "I've had a few serious boyfriends over the years, though."

Cayden kept his head low. "Ever been in love?"

"Yes," she said, her voice barely audible. "You?"

"No, ma'am," he whispered. "Not yet." He flashed her a smile and rounded Raven's head. "Stay in front of the horse, Ginny. These are super calm animals, but they don't like it when you're behind them. Makes 'em nervous."

"Stay in front," she repeated. "Got it."

"Come on over here," he said. "I'll help you up."

"I don't know if I can get on a horse," she said. "The most exercise I get is yoga."

"You just put your left foot in there, and boost yourself up."

"It's the boosting I can't do," she said wryly. She did lift her left leg, but there was no way she was even getting it to the stirrup.

Cayden handed her Raven's reins. "Hold these. I'll be right back."

"I can't hold these," she said, plenty of panic in her voice as he jogged back into the stables. "Cayden."

"Just stand there, Ginny," he called, grabbing the step they used with kids. He hurried back to her and found her standing there, gripping the reins with both fists. He laughed as he took them from her. "Ginny, you're in charge of the horse. She goes where you tell her."

"I've never done this," she said, her eyes sparking with that navy lightning he liked so much.

He shook his head and set the step down. "Climb up on that, baby."

She cocked her eyebrows at him and folded her arms.

"I forgot." He held up both hands in surrender, pulling a bit on Raven as he held her reins. "You don't like baby. Climb up on that, sweetheart."

She smiled, nodded, and stepped up on the block. "This is way better," she said. She put her left foot in the stirrup easily then, and Cayden held Raven still while Ginny pushed with her right foot and swung that leg over the horse's back.

"I can't believe I just did that," she said. "There is no way I'm getting off this thing." She gripped the saddle horn like it would save her, and Cayden found himself chuckling again.

"Yes, you will." He handed her the reins. "You're in charge of the horse." Raven would just follow Cayden, so he moved the step out of the way, got on Honey, and looked at Ginny.

"You just hold the reins here," he said, demonstrating how he held them loosely in front of him. "You don't really use them unless you want her to turn quickly. We won't be doing any of that, so you basically just let her walk."

"Let her walk," she repeated, and it sure was nice to see some fear and apprehension on her face. She was always so confident, and she knew exactly what to say and do in every situation he'd seen her in.

"Yes," Cayden said. Then he nudged Honey into that walk, expecting Raven to come right along easily. She did, and he smiled over at Ginny. "See?"

"I'm riding a horse." She looked like an eight-year-old on her birthday.

"Yes, you are, sweetheart." He took a long, deep breath

of the afternoon air, and while it had started getting hot in Dreamsville the past few days, he still loved the scent here.

He couldn't believe he'd told her he hadn't been in love...yet. She'd asked, though, and he wanted to be truthful with her.

Truthful.

"Do you think this is really going to work?" he asked, not wanting to open a can of worms but needing to get this out in the open.

"I think so," she said. "I think it's going well so far, don't you?"

"I do," he said. "I'm just...I guess I'm wondering if you're thinking long-term or not." He glanced over to her. "To me, this doesn't end unless your mother accepts me or dies. Like, honestly, Ginny."

She said nothing, and Cayden wished he hadn't brought it up. *No,* he told himself. *Better to bring it up now instead of after you fall in love with her.*

"Or we break up," he added. When she still didn't say anything, Cayden told himself to stop talking. She'd heard him; she had to decide what to do with the conversation next.

10

Ginny wished she could split herself down the middle. She'd send half of herself to the office in the skirt suits and heels, the plastic smile and the perfectly painted lips. The other half of her would wear jeans, ride these beautiful horses with this beautiful man, and soak in the afternoon sunshine every single day.

She had no idea what to say to Cayden. It felt like beating a dead horse, but she knew he deserved answers too.

Annoyance ran through her at the situation. She enjoyed spending time with him, and she'd liked all of the things she'd learned about him. He didn't miss much though, and he could see through Ginny's carefully crafted façades that no one else could. She actually liked that, except for when she just wanted to be left alone about a topic.

This was a losing conversation, in her opinion, and she'd been hoping he'd simply drop it. Cayden didn't drop much, though. She wasn't overly religious, but she tipped her head back and drew in a long breath of the heated air.

"The sun is nice today," Cayden murmured.

Ginny found the strength she needed in his quiet and powerful voice. "I don't want to break up," she said in an equally quiet and powerful voice. "My goal, Cayden, is to bring my mother along gradually to the idea of us. That is not going to happen overnight, or even in a month."

He looked at her, and she marveled that he could ride a horse without looking. She could barely stay in the saddle as it was, and her fingers tightened on the reins as she attempted to meet his eye.

"That's not going to work," she said, giving a light laugh. "I have to watch where I'm going or I'm going to fall off." The movement of the horse beneath her wasn't entirely unwelcome; it was just new, and she was still trying to calibrate how she sat so she felt balanced.

The weight and brilliance of his smile touched her peripheral vision. "What do you think is going to happen?"

"I don't know," she said. "That's the point." She smiled too, and it felt real and comfortable on her face.

He chuckled, but the sound didn't last long. "It feels like I get two different Ginnys," he said. "I'm not sure how you split yourself like that."

"I've been doing it for decades," she said. "That's how."

The smile slipped away, and while something had interrupted them in the past, or Ginny had reassured him until he stopped asking, she wanted to hash this out. "I realize I'm splitting myself, but I can honestly say I haven't lied to anyone. Mother has not asked me if I'm still seeing you. If she does, I suppose I'll have to decide at that point if I'm going to tell her the truth or not."

There were versions of the truth, Ginny knew that. She could easily say that of course she was seeing Cayden. They were working together on his forthcoming race. She was sponsoring it, and she had to meet with him to sign contracts and approve banner designs.

That would be the truth, though probably not a direct answer to what she knew Mother really wanted to know.

Was that a lie?

Ginny wasn't sure, and she took another long breath. "Could I...could I come to church with you next week?"

His surprise wasn't hard to feel, and Ginny managed to glance at him quickly. "Sure," he said easily. "What brought that on?"

"I want to be honest," she said. "With you, and with Mother. It's something I've always strived for in my work."

"I want us to be honest too," he said. "Sneaking around doesn't seem that honest."

"We're not sneaking around," she said. "Do you detail every date you go on with your mother?"

"I don't talk to my mother about dating at all," Cayden said, his voice turning a shade darker.

"There you go," Ginny said. "I sense a story there I'd like to hear very much."

"It's somewhat boring," he said.

"I think I'll be the judge of that," she said with another smile. "If I'm about to nod off, I'll surely fall off this beast, so I'll let you know to stop."

He chuckled again, and she sure did like the low, rumbling quality of it. When he finished, he cleared his throat. "When I wanted to go to college, my parents weren't very supportive of it. Well, Daddy was."

Ginny knew the reason why before he even had to say it.

"Mom didn't understand why I needed to leave the ranch for four years, spend a bunch of money, and then come back to run the public relations. I do most of the customer service here as well."

"What's your degree in?" she asked.

"I have a business degree, with a couple of things added on. One in public relations, and one in hospitality management."

"Sounds like the perfect training for what you do." Ginny took in the breadth of the sky as they went past the last building and the vast blueness spread before her. A breeze kicked up that was no longer stifled by the barns and row houses, and the last of Ginny's tension fled.

This was what relaxation was made of. Sunshine, blue sky, and the scent of leather. No wonder Olli's colognes for men had gotten off to such a great start. Ginny reminded herself to call her best friend that night after she left Bluegrass, because Olli wanted an update on Ginny's relationship with Cayden—and how *The Stars Align* perfume had gone.

Cayden hadn't even seemed to notice the new scent, and Olli might have to go back to the perfumery to spruce it up a little bit.

Perhaps Ginny simply didn't bring the missing ingredient to the scent. She wasn't sure, and she pushed the insecurity away as Cayden continued his story.

"I told my mom that I wanted the credentials to back up my role here. That I *needed* them."

Ginny heard something desperate in his voice, and she dared to look over at him again. His beautiful, pale horse plodded along, seemingly undisturbed by the big cowboy on her back. Cayden rode with his head down, his cowboy hat shading his face. He wore a burnt orange shirt with tiny black lines to indicate the plaid, with shirtsleeves that rolled back to reveal a much thicker plaid in brown, orange, and white.

With the dirty jeans, real cowboy boots, and that dark brown hat, Ginny sure did like looking at him.

"Why did you need them?" she asked.

"To matter," he said, looking up. He focused on the horizon for a moment, the miles of green grasses and white fences before them indicating the pastures. He turned his attention to her and gave a small smile. "I told my mother I needed the degree, because I wasn't significant around here."

"That is simply not true, Cay."

"True or not, it was how I felt as an eighteen-year-old, with a perfect older brother who would run the ranch. Trey right behind me showed a ton of talent in the organizational systems of the ranch and he was great with horses too." He looked away, his eyes still harboring something dark and dangerous.

"College, to me, would prove my worth. Anyone can do what I do around here, but at the same time, they can't, because I have the training and the degrees."

Ginny could've pointed out that he could've earned the training through experience, no college degree necessary. But she didn't.

"My mom didn't understand. She came from a family of two—just her and her sister. She has no idea what it's like to be one of eight boys. Loud, opinionated, capable men now," he said. "I had to have a way to matter."

"I'm sure you do matter to them all," Ginny said gently. "To this ranch as well."

"I honestly don't know," he said. "I love and respect my brothers, and I get along with all of them. It's my mother I've never really gone to again with any problems in my life. With anything, really, and that includes the women I've dated."

"Ah, I see," Ginny said. "You don't trust her to take you seriously."

"Something like that," he said.

Ginny's heart tore for him, and she wished she could reach out and touch his arm or hand. "I'm sorry," she said. "I know a little bit about not having a close, personal relationship with your parents."

"Thank you," he said. After that, the whispering of the wind dominated the conversation, and Ginny let her thoughts wander where they may.

"Look at all those flowers," Ginny said several minutes later, her soul as quiet and peaceful as it had ever been. "They must be Olli's."

"This is her land here, yes," Cayden confirmed. "Should we head back?"

"Sure."

He started to turn around, but Ginny had no idea how to do that. As he peeled away from her, she increased the grip on her reins. "Wait. How do I turn this thing?"

"C'mon, Raven," Cayden said, and the horse started to turn on her own.

Ginny's heartbeat danced in her chest, especially when the horse increased her speed to catch Cayden and his palomino. "Whoa," she said, not thinking it through all the way.

The horse came to a stop, and Ginny almost flew forward. "Um." She squirmed in the saddle like that would tell the horse to keep walking. "Go?" she guessed.

It took Cayden a few more steps before he realized she

wasn't at his side. He twisted in his saddle, and how he did that, Ginny would never know.

"Help," she said, her voice getting somewhat stuck in her throat. "Do I spur this thing, or what?"

He started to laugh, swung his animal around, and came back to her as easily as if he was born on horseback. His grin was infectious, and she returned it. "I'm bad at this."

"You're fine." He came right up next to her, his gaze serious and his smile faltering. "Thank you for listening to me this afternoon."

"Of course," she said, holding his eyes. "I like talking to you, Cayden. Are we...are we okay? What else do you need from me to feel okay about us?"

"Nothing," he said, ducking his head. "I'm trying, Ginny. Trying not to get too far into my head, and trying not to go too fast with you."

"I don't have a speed limit," she said.

"I do." He looked up, his eyes wider and full of vulnerability now. "No sense in falling in love tomorrow if it's going to take a year for your mother to come to a place of acceptance, right?"

Ginny's eyes widened too. *Love?* screamed through her head. He'd said he'd never been in love, but she knew why men and women dated.

He started to laugh, and all of the fear stomping through her dissipated. "You look like I just hit you with a frying pan." He reached over and touched her thigh.

"Come on, sweetheart. Let's get back and put these horses away. Blaine won't like it if we're late."

He swung around again and came to her side. "You just say, 'Let's go, Raven. Get us back to the barn,' and she'll do it."

Ginny looked into the dark depths of his eyes again, utterly mesmerized by him. "Thank you for taking me riding," she said. "It's been really amazing. I can see why it cleanses your soul."

He nodded, his smile genuine and so handsome. "Church is at ten-fifteen on Sundays. I can come pick you up about thirty minutes before that if you're serious about coming. I usually ride on Sunday afternoons too, and you're welcome to come with me."

"Done," she said, grinning a genuine grin too. "To all of that."

"All right," he said, nudging his horse without saying a thing. Honey started plodding along again, but Ginny's horse just stood there.

She tried copying his movement and touching the heels of her boots to the horse's body, but Raven didn't even move.

"Come on, Raven," she said, trying to remember the exact wording he'd used. "Get us back to the barn."

The horse stayed stubbornly still.

"Let's go, Raven," Cayden called. "I've got candy at the barn."

The horse immediately started moving, catching up to Honey and Cayden before matching her pace to theirs.

After they'd returned to the stable, as Ginny brushed Raven's beautiful blue-black coat, she giggled and dared to run one hand down her neck. "You like him as much as I do, don't you?"

The horse didn't answer, but Ginny knew what she would've said.

∽

"THERE'S A CHEESE BALL HERE," BLAINE SAID WHEN CAYDEN and Ginny arrived in the kitchen at the homestead.

"Someone knows exactly how to sweeten me up," she said, smiling at Cayden's brother.

Blaine grinned back at her, a slightly lighter version of his brother. He was softer too, in ways Ginny couldn't adequately articulate. He didn't seem to hold everything so tight, his cards pressed against his chest in pure terror.

"Cayden told me you like the green onion cheese ball with those chicken-flavored crackers." He turned back to the stove, picked up a wooden spoon, and kept stirring.

"That I do," Ginny said, glancing up at Cayden. "You remembered that? I told you that back in the fall."

He just looked at her, his mask almost in place but not quite. She squeezed his hand to let him know they didn't need to wear masks in his own home, and he seemed to relax a little bit.

"Where's Tam?" he asked as he led her closer to the counter and the crackers.

She released his hand as she picked up a paper plate for her crackers and dip.

"She's out front," Blaine said. "A customer called, and she's in her truck talking to him."

Ginny understood that; she'd had hundreds of conversations in her car too, the other person's voice coming over the speakers so she could drive and do business hands-free and literally all the time. She piled crackers on her plate and then took a good-sized chunk of the cheese ball before retreating to the table.

She'd been in this house before, and she only saw people eat at the table for big meals. Otherwise, they sat at the bar. Cayden came with her, but he didn't get any crackers.

"How was the ride?" Blaine asked.

"Great," Cayden said. "I wish it could be April in Kentucky all year long."

"It's been great weather," Blaine agreed. "But April all year long? That's insane."

"That's because you're swamped." Cayden looked at her, and when she raised her eyebrows, clearly asking him why Blaine was swamped when he wasn't, Cayden said, "The foals are all born in the spring. Then he moves right into covering, and that takes months too."

"The reproductive cycle of a horse ranch," Blaine joked as the back door opened.

Tam's voice came down the hall, and when she entered the kitchen, she said, "I really have to go. I'll call you later," with a disgruntled look on her face. She hung up and moved over to Blaine first. He leaned down to listen to whatever she said, and then he kissed her quickly.

She turned to Cayden and Ginny, a completely new light in her eyes. "Heya, Ginny."

"Good evening, Tam." Ginny didn't mean to sound so formal; it was simply how she was, but she glanced at Cayden to see if she'd come off as pretentious. It wasn't the first time she'd met Tamara Lennox, as Ginny had stayed at the homestead twice now. "Who were you talking to just now?"

"Oh, this guy." Tam sighed as she sat down at the table too. "I want some of those crackers."

Ginny pushed her plate toward Tam, a clear indication they could share. Tam reached for a cracker and sliced off a healthy chunk of cheese with the edge of it. "Blaine and I are doing a redesign and build of my front porch, and he's the construction manager."

"I need a construction manager," Ginny said, several lightbulbs going off inside her head. "You sounded frustrated with him, though. I need someone good."

"What for?" Cayden asked. "We know lots of people in construction."

"My mother's house," Ginny said, looking at him. "She

lives on the second floor right now, and she can't go up or down the steps without help."

"That doesn't seem safe," Tam said. "What if she needs to get out?"

"She has an assistant," Ginny said. "Though there are times she's alone in the house." She didn't like going up and down the steps with her mother's weight leaning into her, but she hadn't actually thought it unsafe for Mother to be in the mansion alone.

She did now. "I want to move her to the main level, but she wants a suite with a bedroom, kitchen area—it doesn't have to be a full kitchen—a bathroom, and a living room so she can watch her shows."

"There's nothing like that in that huge mansion?" Cayden asked.

"There is," Ginny hedged, glancing at Tam and then Blaine as he arrived at the table and set up a contraption with a flame underneath it, then put a steaming pot right over that. The wonderful smell of cheese and salt met her nose, and Ginny's mouth watered.

"Be right back," Cayden said, and he bustled back around the peninsula and into the kitchen.

"What is this?" she asked.

"Fondue," Cayden said. "Blaine loves to impress with fondue." He spoke the last part in a near-whisper, and when Ginny met his eyes, he carried laughter in his expression. "Right, Tam?"

"The man loves to impress with everything he makes,"

she said, her mouth barely moving. "Not that I'm complaining. He's a genius in the kitchen." She plucked up another cracker and dunked it in the cheese sauce this time. She blew on it while it steamed, saying in a much louder voice, "Baby, this smells amazing."

"The pork broth is coming," he called. "Don't fill up on bread."

All Ginny wanted was bread, and she dipped a cracker in the cheese fondue too. "The only living area on the main floor belonged to my father," Ginny said. "Mother won't go in there."

"Why's that?" Tam asked. "You don't have to say if you don't want to." She cut a glance at Cayden, who still hadn't put anything in his mouth. Ginny felt like a pig, but the call of the sharp, salty cheese was too much for her.

She ate her cracker, her taste buds yelling at her to get some more as quickly as possible. "Daddy cheated on Mother a lot," Ginny said, just laying everything out. It wasn't like it was a Winters family secret anyway, even if Mother and Harvey pretended like it was.

Apprehension swam through her when she looked at Cayden. He'd been downright solid on his denial that her father and his mother had engaged in anything illicit. He'd said he'd speak to his mother about it, but if he had, he hadn't told Ginny about it.

"Oh, wow," Tam said. "I wouldn't go in that room either."

"Everything else on the main level is meant for entertaining," Ginny said. "The kitchen is huge, but industrial. It hasn't been used in years, and Mother wouldn't know how to do much more than boil water to make tea anyway."

She sought out Cayden's hand to ground herself. "There's a library, though Mother prefers to knit and crochet to reading. A huge ballroom where my parents used to host massive parties before we built the event center at the distillery storefront. A conservatory, if you can believe that." She shook her head, her smile anything but happy.

She'd gotten one of the worst tongue-lashings of her life in that conservatory, and she hadn't been inside it since.

"My father was not a nice man," she said, deciding to sum it up and move on. Blaine set up another burner, this one with a much higher and brighter flame, and put another pot down. His eyes met hers, questions there.

She imagined a lot of people had the same types of questions as him, Tam, and Cayden.

"He used to entertain in the drawing room, which he actually called a smoking room back in the day. Only men were allowed in there." She swallowed. "There's a music room as well, with two pianos—one of them grand—as we all had to learn to play as children."

"You play the piano?" Cayden asked. "I didn't know that."

"I can," Ginny said. "We needed to be able to entertain." She flashed him a smile that felt so warped. "It's been a while since I've sat at a piano, I'll admit." She looked around at the three of them. "I think I've identified that as the room Mother could convert—it's large, and we can easily section it into two spaces. The room she's in now really just has a small kitchenette along the back wall, and a bedroom big enough for a king-sized bed. The music room could hold that."

"It would still require construction, though, right?" Blaine asked, going back into the kitchen. "Our guy is good, Tam. Everything is always delayed in construction."

"I want that porch done before the wedding," Tam said. "That's not a crime."

"Things always come up," Cayden agreed. "We can give you some names."

Blaine returned with two platters, saying, "Help me, Cay."

Cayden jumped to his feet and took one of the platters, which held a variety of raw meats and vegetables. Ginny had never seen anything like this as far as fondue went, as her experiences were limited to desserts.

He and Blaine set down the trays, and Ginny soaked in the beauty of this meal. She'd expected steak and baked potatoes, as the Chappells hadn't ever had anything much more elaborate than that, even when Blaine cooked.

This was something else though, and Ginny felt like she'd stepped into a five-star restaurant and would have an amazing dining experience that evening.

"Al right," Blaine said with a sigh. "I've got the chocolate slowly heating, but we can start with the first two courses." He indicated the cheese fondue. "This is a Wisconsin sharp cheddar, with parmesan and aged mozzarella. It's great for the apples and pears, smoked hams, salami, and sausages, and the pickles, pretzels, cauliflower, and roasted potatoes."

He pointed to the other tray. "This is all raw meat and veggies. You skewer these and put them in the pork broth to cook. Most of it is cut to an appropriate size so each item will take about five minutes, depending on how full the pot is." He reached over to adjust the thermostat on the burner under the pork broth, which was boiling away.

"There's steak, chicken, and pork. Potatoes, broccoli, mushrooms, and squash. I'll bring out the dessert spread once we've eaten as much as we want here." He pulled out a chair, sat down, and took off his cowboy hat before looking at Cayden.

Everyone looked at Cayden, and he flinched when he realized it. "Okay. I'll say a prayer, and then we'll eat."

"Don't feel like you have to do the cheese course first," Blaine added. "Eat what you want whenever." He smiled at Ginny and reached for Tam's hand.

Ginny smiled back and took Cayden's hand in one of hers, and then stretched to meet Tam's across the table from her. With the four of them joined, Cayden bowed his head and started his prayer.

Ginny barely heard it, because the powerful feelings moving through her drowned out his voice.

When everyone else said, "Amen," she opened her eyes and withdrew her hands from the others. As dinner began, and chatter broke out among them, Ginny knew one very important thing: She belonged here.

She wanted to be here, in this homestead, for a good long while, and she just needed to figure out a way to make that happen that would allow her to keep Sweet Rose and the decades of her life she'd already invested in the family company.

Please bless my mother, was all she could come up with as she reached for a skewering stick and poked it through a roasted potato.

11

Cayden knotted his tie at his throat, his nerves out of control already and he hadn't even left to pick up Ginny for church yet.

He hadn't taken a woman to church in a very long time. Longer than Terri Wilson, even. He'd only dated her for a few months, and she hadn't been that interested in attending church with him. In the end, she hadn't been that interested in doing anything with Cayden, and they'd broken up over a text.

He looked at himself in the mirror, and said, "Calm down." He knew the source of his anxiety, and it was a petite, blonde powerhouse who'd run a family of eight boys, a beyond-busy husband, and a six-hundred-acre horse ranch.

His mother.

As he looked into his own eyes, he realized how complicated parental relationships could be. Sympathy for Ginny filled him, and he regretted all the times he'd asked for her reassurance that their relationship would survive being in the shadows.

"It works in proportion to how much you put into it," he said, a repeat of something Blaine had said to him last night after Ginny and Tam had left. He and Blaine had stayed up far too late—so late that Cayden had enjoyed a second round of dessert fondue by the time the conversation wrapped—last night, discussing their girlfriends.

Cayden had been the focus of most of the conversation, which he normally hated. Blaine was the best brother to talk to about matters of the heart, though, and he'd told Cayden that he and Ginny were "the perfect couple."

He could see easily how much they liked one another, and Cayden had liked that Blaine could see Ginny's affection for him. Sometimes, he couldn't see it.

Cayden turned away from the mirror and picked up his phone. He could text his mother, and she'd answer in moments, as she never went very far without her device. He called, though, because he knew that brightened her whole day.

"Cayden, my darling," she said, and he smiled.

"Hello, Mother," he said.

"What's wrong?" she asked immediately, the cheerfulness in her voice extinguishing.

"Nothing," he said easily. "I have a few minutes before church, and I thought I might stop by for coffee." He left his bedroom as he said it, his words smooth and even as they came out of his mouth. There was a reason he ran the public events on the ranch. He didn't stutter. He always knew what to say and how to say it. He could cover surprise in the blink of an eye and smooth over any problem.

"That would be great," she said.

"You have time?"

"Yes, I'm ready too."

"See you in a few." Cayden didn't stop in the kitchen where Blaine sat with Lawrence and Conrad. They were poring over something in one of Conrad's notebooks, and none of them looked up at him as he left the homestead.

It was a quick six-minute drive down the lane to the T-junction and then down the road and around the curve of the ranch to his parents' house.

Spur's horse was tied out front, but his oldest brother came out of the front door as Cayden got out of his truck. "Morning," he called, and Spur wore a smile as he came toward him.

"Morning yourself," Spur said. He grabbed onto Cayden and hugged him. "It's good to see others coming to see Mom and Daddy."

Cayden hugged his brother back, knowing full-well that his toxic feelings toward Spur had nothing to do with the man himself. He'd never done anything wrong. It was simply trying to live up to him that sometimes sent Cayden into a tailspin. He'd always been able to get himself out, and he'd never said anything to Spur.

"You said to," he said. "I just haven't quite known how." He still didn't, but as the two brothers separated, Cayden looked toward the front of the house to find Mom leaning into the doorjamb.

"Just say whatever comes to mind," Spur said. "She really is a lot better these days. She listens."

Cayden nodded and swallowed. "I didn't run you off, did I?"

"Nope." Spur grinned at him, and he seemed abnormally happy this morning. Cayden narrowed his eyes at him, but Spur only laughed. He clapped Cayden on the shoulder and said, "I'm not telling yet. See you at church," and walked away.

He swung onto his horse and got it moving into a trot as he headed back to the property adjacent to Bluegrass, where he now lived with his wife, Olli.

"Mornin', baby," Mom drawled in her Kentucky accent, and Cayden turned toward her.

"Mornin', Momma," he said, and he set his feet moving in that direction. He'd always gotten along with his parents, even through his teenage years. Daddy expected everyone to work around the ranch, and Cayden hadn't cared about sports or football. He had participated in FFA, and since that hadn't taken him from the ranch very often, he'd never had an issue the way some of the other boys had.

He went up the steps, where his mom greeted him with a hug. "You haven't been here in a while," she said. "Come see my new coffee maker."

"Okay," he said, wondering if her comment was meant to be a jab or not. She smiled, her eyes bright and happy, so he concluded she hadn't meant anything by saying he hadn't been there in a while.

Sometimes the truth was pointed anyway.

Inside, he listened as she detailed how she could program the coffee maker to come on when she wanted, and she and Daddy had been waking up to fresh, hot coffee for a couple of weeks now.

"That's great," he said, pouring himself a cup.

"You didn't come to listen to me gush about appliances," she said, taking her cup to the counter. Cayden joined her, where he spooned in a lot of sugar and stirred everything around.

"Momma," he said. "I guess I just want you to know a few things."

She didn't even speak then. Her eyes stayed wide and clear as he searched for the right thing to say. She sipped her coffee, the silence between them deafening.

"You made me feel really stupid for wanting to go to college," he said, unable to maintain eye contact with her. "You dismissed my feelings, and because of that, I stopped coming to you for advice."

A huge burden lifted with just those few words, and he nodded. "I guess that's the only thing I needed to say. I want to come to you and talk about things, but I'm worried I'll just get written off again."

"I'm so sorry," Mom said, her voice barely more than air. "I didn't realize I'd done that."

He looked up and right into those light brown eyes he could see in Blaine's face when he faced his brother. "Do you realize it now?"

"Yes," she said. "I didn't mean to do that. I suppose I was trying to tell you that you were already good enough, but I can see how it just drove you away." She swiped at her eyes. "I apologize." She pressed her palm over her pulse. "Sincerely."

"Thank you," he murmured, dropping his gaze back to the dark liquid in his mug. "I'm seeing Virginia Winters." He cleared his throat and ignored the gasp that came from his mom's throat. "Her mother doesn't approve of us, because she does not like you."

He raised his head again, focusing out the window on the other side of the bar. He wasn't sure how to ask his mom if she'd ever had an affair with Harvey Winters.

Digging down into a deep well of bravery, he swallowed only to find his throat bone dry. "She thinks you may have cheated with her husband."

"I did not," Mom said instantly. "They were not married when Harvey and I dated."

Cayden nodded, relieved at the indignation and

strength in his mother's voice. "He didn't...I don't know, Mom. You tell me." He barely dared to glance at her, and when he did, he found that familiar fire blazing in her eyes.

"Harvey and I dated a little in high school," she said. "It wasn't anything serious. We dated after he returned from his brief service in the military. It got serious, but then I found out he was also dating Wendy Winters. I broke up with him and told him to never call me again." She scoffed and set her mug down a little too hard. "Harvey was the kind of man who did whatever he wanted. He called. He kept coming over. The night before he and Wendy were to be married, he took me on a long drive and said he still wanted me in his life. He could have mistresses. Wendy wouldn't know."

Cayden said nothing as his mind whirred.

"I said no, that wasn't the kind of relationship I wanted or believed in. I kissed him good-bye. They got married. He only came back once, and that was about five years later. I'd just brought Trey home from the hospital, and Daddy was in Georgia at a horse auction. There was Harvey, standing on the doorstep." A certain level of bitterness came with her words, and Cayden didn't dare look at her now.

"He wanted to come in. He and Wendy had just gotten into a fight, and he had nowhere to stay. Well, I knew what that meant, and I turned him away."

"Just like that?" Cayden asked, finally looking at her.

"Just like that," she said, hitting all the consonants heavily. "I love your daddy. I had three boys under the age of five. I didn't need another lover. I didn't want him, Cayden. I didn't."

"I believe you," he said, lifting his mug to his lips. The coffee was sweet and hot, and he liked the way it coated his throat. "Do you object to my relationship with Ginny?"

"Of course not," Mom said. "It has nothing to do with me. If you like her, that's perfectly fine with me."

Cayden nodded, glad this weight was out of his mind. "I like her."

Mom linked her arm through Cayden's. "How much do you like her?"

"More than I should," Cayden said. "Our relationship is in the shadows, Mom. Her mother does not approve." He glanced at her. "She is not as forgiving as you, I suppose."

"Oh, baby, that's not it at all." She reached up and ran her hand down the side of his face. "She simply has so much more to forgive than I do." She gave him a kind, motherly smile and leaned her head against his bicep. "You're such a good boy, Cay. You always have been. As a toddler, you helped me the most. You've always been the one to get along with everyone and find solutions all ten of us can live with. That was why I didn't think you needed the college degree. Not because I didn't think you could do it."

"I know," he said. "College was more about me earning my place here—and for you not to dismiss how I feel because it's not how *you* feel."

She nodded and drew in a deep breath. "I am still working on that."

"I guess we all are," he said.

They sat together for several minutes, the silence between them comforting and calm now.

"All right," he said with a groan. "I have to go pick up Ginny. She's comin' to church with me today."

"Is that right?" Mom asked, keen interest in her eyes as she watched him. "I didn't think the Winters believed in religion."

Cayden went around the counter and rinsed out his empty coffee mug. "I'm not sure about all Winters," he said. "She asked if she could come with me, and I said yes." He smiled at his mother. "Don't go gettin' ideas about how you can get me to introduce the two of you. I'll do it when I'm ready."

"Yes, sir," she said, giving him a mock salute along with her smile. "Go have fun."

He grinned at her and went back to where she still sat at the counter. "I love you, Momma." He bent down and hugged her, glad she still had the fierceness in her grip that she'd always possessed.

"I love you, too, son," she whispered, plenty of emotion in her voice.

Cayden's heartstrings strummed, and he straightened. They nodded to each other, and he turned to leave. Things between them weren't perfect—how could decades of a relationship be mended with one twenty-minute conversation and a cup of coffee?—but so much had been stitched back together.

Fifteen minutes later, he stood on Ginny's front porch, his cowboy hat in his hand. She opened the door and curled her fingers around it as her mouth inched up into a grin. "Morning, cowboy. You look lost."

"Do I?" he asked, enjoying this game immensely. "You look amazing." He let his eyes linger as they slid down her body. She wore a black, sleeveless dress with white butterflies splashed across it, a wide sash around her waist, and bright red heels on her feet.

"Thank you." She glanced at the ground as her trio of dogs came to greet him.

He crouched down to give them all a hello scrub, and when he straightened, Ginny had her purse and was stepping out onto the porch.

"I talked to my mother this morning," he said, causing her eyes to fly to his.

"Is that right?" Her voice stayed calm with the question, though she definitely looked interested.

"I'll have to tell you about it later," he said. "I don't want to be late for church, and I still have one thing to do."

Her eyebrows went up. "You do? What's that?"

He slid the hand not holding his cowboy hat along that sash at her waist, drawing her into his personal space. "I think it's time for another kiss, Miss Winters," he whispered, half playing and half scared. "What do you think?"

"I think I've been wishing you'd kiss me every day for a month now," she whispered, stepping into that space and putting her hands flat against his chest. "You're feeling like you know me better now?"

"Yes," he said. "A lot better."

"You still like what you see?"

"It's about more than liking what I see," he said, frowning. "That's the point of getting to know you. I know we have great chemistry. I want to feel like I know the woman I'm kissing, not that I just think she's gorgeous."

"I know," she murmured. Her fingers curled up behind his head, weaving through his hair. "I've enjoyed getting to know you better too, Cay. The real you."

"Yes," he said, ducking his head but pausing with a couple of inches between his mouth and hers. His eyes drifted closed, and his pulse picked up. "The real you, and the real me. No masks. No pretending."

"No pretending," she murmured, and Cayden closed the distance between them and kissed her.

A wave of heat rolled over his shoulders, especially when she lifted up onto her toes trying to get closer to him. He dropped his hat and ran his fingers through her hair, every cell in his body firing exactly right with this woman in his arms.

The chemistry was definitely explosive between them, but Cayden slowed the kiss in the next moment, glad he'd slowed everything between them so he could have a truly meaningful kiss with the woman he was starting to fall for.

12

Ginny had been kissed passionately before. She'd been kissed by men who proclaimed to love her. She'd kissed men she'd said she loved.

None of those men or those kisses even held a candle to Cayden Chappell. There was simply something else about him that existed on a higher level. He kissed her with his hormones, then his head, and finally his heart.

When he pulled away, he immediately touched his mouth to her neck and said, "We'll be late if we don't go in the next sixty seconds."

"Okay," she said, her voice barely audible above the pounding heartbeat in her ears. So she wouldn't be part of the problem—Cayden really didn't like being late—she stepped out of his arms and bent to pick up his cowboy hat. It was a tough thing to do in those heels, but Ginny had decades of experience wearing such shoes, and she accomplished the task without too much difficulty.

She handed him his hat and asked, "Do you want to come back here for lunch today? I can whip us up something decent."

"I'd love that," he said.

"Your brothers won't miss you?"

Something odd crossed his face, and then he shook his head. "It'll be fine."

"Okay." She laced her arm through his as he passed, and she leaned on him to get down the steps without falling. "I want to hear all about your visit with your mom this morning."

"I can do that," he said. "I also have a list of contractors for you. I can bring that over."

"Perfect," she said, smiling at him as he opened her door and helped her into the truck. Nerves clawed at her during the fifteen-minute ride to the chapel, and Ginny had only felt like this on a handful of other occasions.

Once when her mother had transferred all the legal ownership and responsibility of Sweet Rose Whiskey onto her. Once when Phillip Carlson had proposed. A few times when she'd encountered her father in one of his drunken rages.

The feelings came from fear, and while Ginny had learned to tame them over the years, she also knew they couldn't be boxed up and thrown away.

Fear had to be faced and dealt with.

"I'm scared," she blurted out when Cayden pulled into the parking lot at the little white chapel. The steeple reached high into the sky, piercing the blueness of it with a gold-tipped top.

"Of what?" Cayden asked, and the question was so sincere that Ginny's trust for him grew.

"I don't go to church," she said. "Everyone's going to be looking at me. I'm going to have to talk to people I don't know. I don't know the songs, or how to pray, and—" She cut off, hearing the panic as it lodged in her own ears.

"Do you feel like you don't belong here?" he asked, reaching over and taking both of her hands in his. They immediately stopped winding around one another, and she looked at him. If he was nervous, it certainly didn't show.

"Yes," she said. "I know I don't belong here."

He looked out the windshield at the church. "Everyone belongs here. Everyone belongs to the Lord." He said it without a waver or a stutter, and Ginny had a hard time disbelieving him. "Everyone comes to the Lord on their own terms," he added. "We're all new once."

He met her eye again, and he smiled. "New things are so scary."

Hope rose within her. Maybe he could just take her home right now. She'd start on a bread dough that would be ready to bake by the time he attended church, drove home to change, and made it back to the country house.

"Sweetheart." He lifted one hand to his lips and kissed

her wrist. "You talk to a ton of people you don't know. Everyone is always looking at you. You can read, so you'll look in the hymnal and sing the songs. You don't have to pray. You just bow your head and nod along."

She nodded now, some of her panic ebbing away. "Okay."

"I'm gonna be right beside you. If there's something you don't know, just ask me. I'll tell you."

"Okay." He was right; she wasn't alone. He was with her.

He studied her for another few moments. "If you really don't want to go in, I'll take you home."

She found herself shaking her head. "No, I can do it." She looked at the church too, and it was obvious someone took very good care of it. To do that, that person had to love the building very much, and as Cayden released her hands and got out of the truck, she realized they didn't love the building.

They loved what it stood for. They loved the Lord.

Cayden opened her door, and Ginny faced him. "With you at my side, Cay, I can do this." She'd never said that to a man before. She'd always had to rely on her own strength and her own convictions. Mother had taught her to do exactly that. *Never put your trust in a man, Ginny*, she heard in her mind. *They only let you down.*

As she linked her arm through Cayden's once more and they faced the church together, Ginny knew her mother was wrong.

Daddy had let Mother down, because he wasn't trustworthy. He hadn't married her because he loved her. He'd married her for the bounty she brought with the Winters name.

In that moment, she realized how utterly smart Cayden had been this past month or so, insisting that they eradicate the barriers between them, take off their masks, and be real with one another.

He'd wanted to build that trust that every strong relationship needed. He wanted to fall in love with *her*, not the idea of her. He wanted the real Ginny Winters, flaws and all, and Ginny wasn't sure anyone—male or female—had ever allowed her to be the messy, chaotic, emotional woman that existed inside her.

"Thank you," she whispered after he'd led her up the steps, through the door, and to a row near the back of the chapel. She wasn't sure if he heard her or not, but the gratitude wasn't for his escort services. It was for him being him, and for the Lord blessing her to realize that she could be herself when she was with Cayden.

If she got the song lyrics wrong, or didn't understand what the preacher said, it wouldn't matter. She'd already learned more about herself, Cayden, and the Lord that morning than she'd ever anticipated.

"Thank you," she whispered again, and this time Cayden pressed his lips to her temple and tucked her into his side.

"Yes, right over here," Ginny said, leading Ben Roth into the house. "If you need to widen these hallways, that's fine." She continued to talk over her shoulder, wishing she'd hired a cleaning service to come scrub the mansion from top to bottom before the construction crew showed up.

"I'm not really sure what you'll find," she said. "No one's lived on the main level in about oh, four years." She gave a laugh that was filled with nerves. She finally reached the end of the hall and went past the doorway there. "It's right through there."

Ben touched the brim of his ball cap as he ducked into the music room. He'd been here before, of course, and Ginny didn't even need to meet him at the back door and show him where the construction zone was.

He'd taken measurements and pictures three weeks ago, and he'd sent over three remodel renditions for her to choose from. Ginny had sat down with Mother one evening, her favorite soup and salad on the small table between them, and they'd gone over the designs.

"I was able to get the furniture out, like we discussed," Ginny said, following Ben into the room. Cayden and four of his brothers had come to do that, actually, but Ben didn't need the specifics. "It's empty and ready for you."

"That it is," he drawled, looking around. "Such great height in here." He smiled at the walls like he could hear them whispering things to him that no one else could.

"I'm excited to be able to work on this." His gaze migrated to hers. "Thanks for the opportunity, Miss Winters."

"Of course," she said, her voice full of propriety. "Cayden said you were the best." She smiled at him. She'd interviewed four contractors, and she'd liked Ben the best, besides.

"I'll thank him too," he said as his phone went off. "That'll be my guys. We'll be doing demo today, and every day this week. I'll keep you abreast of everything going on."

"I'd appreciate that." She checked the clock on her phone and turned back toward the door. "I do have a meeting in an hour I can't be late for." She flashed him a smile over her shoulder. "My mother is upstairs, but she can't get down the steps by herself. Her assistant is Sydney, and she'll be here in an hour."

"Right, I have her number too," Ben said from behind her.

"Yes," Ginny agreed. "I've told her not to let Mother come downstairs, but my mother does whatever she wants. Sometimes Sydney has to do something just to appease her, but she'll usually call me first." Worry gnawed at her as she exited the mansion through the narrow doorway at the rear of the house. "Mother can—"

"Ma'am," Ben said. "I deal with...particular customers all the time. I can handle your mother."

Ginny turned and looked at him, trying to find a way

to make him understand. "I don't know if you've ever met anyone like her," she said.

"If I get in over my head, I've got my bets foreman with me today." He nodded to a man named Alex Samuels, who Ginny had met before. She'd known his family for a while too, as his father was one of Sweet Rose's annual investors in their children's parade over the Fourth of July.

He owned a huge car restoration shop in Dreamsville, and he often donated a number of bicycles to children in need as part of the parade. Alex had started as a mechanic and quickly moved on to construction.

Anything to be working with my hands, he'd told Ginny a year or so ago.

"Hello, Alex," Ginny said pleasantly, stepping into him and kissing both of his cheeks.

"Morning," he said. "Don't worry about us." He exchanged a glance with Ben.

"You know I will," she said with a smile. "Tell Ben here that he can't underestimate my mother." Her stomach quaked, and she considered rescheduling her meeting for the tenth time that week.

"No one underestimates anyone out in this part of town," Alex said, grinning at her. "Now, go on. I know you have a meeting, and we don't need you here."

"I know when I'm not wanted." Ginny smiled and ducked back into the house, where she opened the closet behind the door and took out her purse. She paused to let Alex go by with an armful of tools and various supplies, her eyes widening at the amount of equipment being brought in.

"Just go," she murmured to herself, because she wasn't going to wield a saw or a hammer, knock down any walls, or fill in any doorways. In the driver's seat, she took a moment to grip the wheel and close her eyes. "Help Mother to have a good day today and bless Ben and Alex to get a lot done today."

The faster the demolition got done, the better. Mother had mentioned to Ginny at least twenty times how she couldn't abide "hammering all day long."

"It's fine," she told herself as she drove off the property. She and Cayden had brainstormed a back-up plan, and that back-up plan had a back-up. She could put Mother in any number of nearby hotels, and if worst came to worst, Ginny was prepared to move Mother into her house.

She glanced left as she drove by the street where her house was, but she couldn't see it from the corner. It sat back far enough from the street that she almost had to be in front of it to see it. That, plus the mature trees that towered on the whole family block, kept the Winters family residences fairly private.

She continued on to her office, carrying in her protein shake and her purse, a measure of tiredness already moving through her and she'd just arrived at work.

The scent of cinnamon and honey met her nose, and she smiled at Mel as she approached. "Morning, Mel."

"Good morning, Ginny." Her auburn-haired

assistant looked up at her, her dark green eyes bright and wide. "You've got your nine o'clock in your office."

"Already?" Ginny picked up the stack of messages on the edge of Mel's desk. A bit of mail sat there too, and while Mel went through most of it, she always sorted out the items Ginny needed to see.

"He's a little early," she said.

"Of course he is," Ginny said, glancing toward her closed office door. "How was your date with Michael?" She wasn't going to run into her office just because someone was waiting for her. In fact, she didn't like it when her appointments were early, and had she been here at her normal time, Mel would've held Martin Gold out here.

"So amazing," Mel smiled and leaned forward. "I'm not sure he's ever had a hush puppy before." They laughed together, and Ginny liked these softer moments with Mel. She didn't have very many friends, but she'd count Mel as one of them.

"Where is he from again?"

"Nevada."

"Yes, I don't imagine they'd eat a lot of hush puppies in Nevada."

"He claimed to like it, but I think he drank at least three glasses of water and three or four glasses of Diet Coke during the meal."

"Maybe he just has severe dry mouth," Ginny said,

which caused Mel to laugh again. "You're seeing him again, though, right?"

"Yes, tomorrow," Mel said. "Now go on. You only have a few minutes."

Ginny frowned as she straightened. "Only a few minutes?"

"Go now," Mel hissed, looking past her and getting to her feet. "I'll buy you a few minutes, but not if you're out here chit-chatting with me." She rounded the desk, and Ginny turned to see Martin Gold facing the wall near the door, his phone pressed to his ear.

"Wait a second," she said. If Martin Gold was down there, who was waiting for her in her office?

Her curiosity piqued, Ginny hurried to the closed door and opened it, almost peeking in cautiously. Her office seemed empty, but there was definitely a presence here. A scent too, and Ginny's nose got her pheromones firing.

"Cay?" she asked, and he rose from the wingback in front of her desk. Joy burst through her at this surprise. "What are you doing here?"

"I brought breakfast," he said, holding up a bag. "I know you have four meetings today, and you're stressed about your mother." He shrugged and took a couple of steps toward her. "I hope this helps."

She met him and took the bag from him. "This is a cinnamon scone from Doughboy, isn't it?"

"What gave it away? The giant logo on the bag?" He grinned at her, one hand sliding down her arm.

"I could smell the cinnamon out in the hall." She grinned at him. "Thank you so much."

"There's honey-lemon tea on your desk," he said. "Did everything go okay with Ben and Alex this morning?"

"They were right on time," she said. "I'll admit I'm worried about it." He knew all of that already, because Ginny had been venting to him every time Mother brought up her reluctance to the construction.

"I know." He touched his mouth to her cheek. "It's going to be okay."

She nodded and tipped her head back to receive a proper kiss from him. She didn't let it last long, because she did have another appointment in only another sixty seconds, and she'd need all her wits about her to deal with Martin's demands.

"I have your final banner design," Cayden said. "It's on your desk too. Final cost and donation amount. There's a copy of the invoice, and I've already given one to Miss Oscarson out front."

"Thank you," she said, her voice taking on a crisp quality too. "Anything else I need to do for the event?"

"Nothing on our end," he said. "I do need your approval in writing, but you can have Mel email it over."

"How are things going for you and Lawrence?"

His expression darkened for a moment. "We've had some ups and downs in the past twenty-four hours alone. Things are still coming along, though."

"What happened?"

"Our biggest horse was pulled," he said. "A real draw for other owners to sign up their horses, and for the deep-pocket buyers to come to the race." He sighed and turned to set her scone on the desk. "Thankfully, Lawrence fielded a call this morning from Mariah, and she's found a fairly large owner to enter his horse."

"I'm glad," she said. "If I had a horse that anyone cared about, I'd enter it in your race."

Cayden smiled at her, the moment tender and soft between them. "Thank you, sweetheart." He started for the door. "I won't keep you. No sense in starting your day out behind." He paused with his hand on the doorknob. "I'm in Louisville for a couple of days, but we're still on for dinner on Friday and Blaine's wedding on Saturday?"

"Yes, of course," Ginny said. "Good luck in Louisville. You'll call me tonight?"

He smiled, nodded, and left the office.

Ginny took a moment to sip her tea and take a single bite of her scone. While she chewed, she searched for a breath mint in her desk drawer and thanked the Lord for a sweet, kind, thoughtful man like Cayden to take care of her.

She jerked her head up, the mint in her hand. "That's what I want, isn't it?" She'd been trying to figure out why she'd want to get married this late in life, especially because she couldn't have children. Now she knew—she wanted someone to take care of her.

With a smile warming her soul, she quickly popped

the mint into her mouth and went to open the door for Mel to send back Martin Gold.

~

A FEW DAYS LATER, GINNY'S STOMACH ROARED AND SHOOK at the same time. She hadn't eaten since breakfast, and that had only been a few swallows of her strawberry protein shake. She'd survived a very busy week, and Cayden should be arriving to take her to dinner at any moment.

She smoothed her hand down the front of her dress and over her stomach. It wasn't flat, and Ginny couldn't remember the last time it had been. She didn't care, because some days required potato chips or pretzel crisps to survive. Really bad days had her opening a specific drawer in the credenza in her office and taking out a bag of Reese's Pieces.

She hadn't told Cayden about her secret candy stash, just like she hadn't told him about her inability to have children. They'd been seeing each other on a near-daily basis for just over two months now. She'd shared many things with him, but not this.

They hadn't started talking about long-term things like marriage and family, but a voice had been nagging Ginny since Tuesday, when Cayden had shown up at her office with her favorite scone and tea.

He knew so many little things about her, and she

wanted him to know the big things too. All the intimate things that could really bond them.

"It could also drive us apart," she whispered to Sarge, who lifted his puggy head and looked at her through squinted eyes. Minnie stood up and stretched, a yawn squeaking out of her mouth. Ginny smiled at the little dog and picked her up.

"We've had a good afternoon together, doggies," she said. She'd left the office at one-thirty and done the rest of her work from home that day. That had allowed her to take the dogs for a walk and shower, catch up on emails, and schedule her June appointments.

Her phone chimed, and Ginny looked at the bright screen on her bed. She didn't catch the name, and she quickly put Minnie back on the bed with Sarge and Uncle Joe in favor of her device.

Olli had said, *Don't overthink this, Ginny. I love you, and you're beautiful, strong, and smart.*

Ginny's emotions caught in her chest. She'd met Olli at the perfumery to get a new scent to try that night, and she'd finally confessed to her about the hysterectomy that was seven months old now.

She'd asked Olli how she could possibly tell Cayden, and she'd asked her best friend if she and Spur were going to have children. Olli was in her mid-forties, and she and Spur had been married for ten months, and there hadn't been any announcements of the two of them having a baby.

"We want kids," Olli said. "We're working on it." She'd given Ginny a sad smile, hugged her tight, and told her to just be herself. "Bold, articulate, and kind. If children are a deal-breaker, wouldn't you rather know now?"

Yes, Ginny had said. She did want to know now if her ability to have children was a deal-breaker for Cayden.

She quickly sent back a couple of hearts and promised Olli she'd update her tomorrow. As she sent that text, another came in.

Ben had texted a picture, and she stared at the chaotic state of the music room. Everything looked coated in a white dust, and while Ginny hadn't gone back to the mansion this week, she'd never thought it would be this bad.

Trash littered the floor, along with various power cords. Big, black garbage cans overflowed with what looked like chunks of sheetrock, some large and some small. Splatters of something that looked like mud marred the trashcans, the floor, and the walls.

"It's like a murder scene," she said, horror plain in her voice. The text read, *Only one more day, and then we're going to be onto the rebuild!*

He seemed so happy about the progress, but Ginny seriously doubted they'd even taken one step forward. It sure looked like they'd taken ten steps backward.

She took a deep breath and closed her eyes. She'd been to plenty of construction sites in the past, and they all looked like someone had opened their hand and dropped a hardware store.

She couldn't bring herself to send a celebratory text, though. Instead, she typed out, *Thank you for all your hard work this week,* and sent that.

Her doorbell sounded, and Ginny's nerves vibrated. She tucked her phone in the pocket of her dress and headed down the hall to the living room. Through that, she entered the lobby and pulled open the door.

Cayden stood there, and he was pure perfection after a few days of not being able to see him in person. Their eyes met, and he said nothing before he swept her into his arms and held her close.

"You're back," she said, holding onto his strong shoulders and wondering what good deed she'd done to get this cowboy in her life.

"Mm," he said. "You smell amazing."

"I saw Olli this afternoon," she said. "She gave me a new scent."

"What's this one called?"

"*Glass Slipper*," she said. "Or *Midnight Magic*. She's still working on the name."

"I like *Glass Slipper*," Cayden said. "Smells really clean and really clear."

"She calls that blue," she said. "She usually only puts those kinds of things in her men's scents, but she used it as the base for this one, claiming Cinderella's dress for the ball that night was, indeed, blue."

A smile landed on his face, and Ginny felt herself falling for him. "What else is in there? Smells a bit like pink lemonade." He leaned closer and breathed her in again.

"She did say lemonade. Not sure if it's pink or not. But she called it blue-lemonade-seashore."

"I *really* like this one," he said, capturing her waist with one hand against her back and holding her close.

Ginny enjoyed the warmth from his body and the pressure from his hand. He smelled like aspens and clouds and musk, and if Ginny had to guess, she'd say he was wearing Olli's *Saddled and Spurred*.

She'd burned her *Get Your Man* candles every time Cayden came over, but she'd need to get this new scent in a candle as soon as possible.

"What would you name it?" she asked, and she wrapped him in her arms.

"Let's see." He started to sway, his other hand coming up to stroke her hair down her back. "*My Perfect Princess*."

Ginny smiled slowly, the moment absolutely perfect between them. Could she really ruin it tonight by telling him she couldn't make him a father?

They breathed in and out together, neither of them in any hurry to go anywhere. Finally, Cayden said, "I'm starving, sweetheart. Should we go?"

"Yes." Her stomach swooped as she stepped away from his warmth and his spirit. "They're almost done with the demo," she said. "Mother only texted that one day, so I'm counting this as a win."

"That's great," he said, holding the door for her. "How long on the rebuild?"

"Three or four weeks," she said. "There's a bit of plumbing that has to be done, and then everything after that isn't too bad." She let him open her door and steady her as she got in the truck. He'd kept it running so the air conditioner was still blowing. The sun went down later and later each evening, and the closer summer got, the hotter the days became.

She watched him round the truck, and Ginny wondered how to start this conversation. She'd had plenty of serious discussions in her life, and this one shouldn't be any different. Ginny felt like it was though. She felt like she'd climbed twenty flights of stairs and couldn't get a decent breath.

The next time she opened her mouth, she was going to fling herself off the tall building she'd just climbed to the top of.

"You okay?" Cayden asked, and Ginny blinked, realizing he'd already turned around, gone down the lane, and set the truck on the highway.

She cleared her throat. "Yes." She shook her head, though. "No."

"Yes and no," he repeated.

Ginny swallowed and bent to reach into her purse to

get out the bottle of water she never left home without. "I have to tell you something."

He glanced at her with one hand draped over the top of the wheel while the other rested on the console between them. "All right."

She slicked her hands down her thighs, glad she'd worn this thick denim dress. It had a wide belt the color of children's bubble gum that made her barrel-shaped torso look somewhat like an hourglass instead. She'd put on a bright white pair of running shoes to complete the fun, flirty look, and she wished she felt the same way inside.

"I've never told anyone this before."

He reached out and turned down the radio.

Ginny didn't have the right words. She sighed and looked out the window on her side of the truck. "Do you want children, Cayden?"

He took a few moments to answer with, "I think so, yes."

Of course he did. He had no reason not to want children, and he came from a family of eight boys.

"Do you want children, Virginia?" he asked.

She nodded, her throat clogged with emotion. "Yes," she said right through it, causing her voice to pitch up. "I do want children, Cay, but I can't have them." She swung her head toward him, feeling like her upper half was encased in quicksand.

Cayden continued to drive, but he looked only at her. "I'm sorry," he said, his voice catching on all the syllables.

He opened his mouth to say something else, but he quickly closed it again.

He shifted in his seat and looked out the windshield.

Horror shot through Ginny when a tear splashed her cheek. Her hand flew up to her face to wipe it away, and she turned away from Cayden. If she could just take a breath in—*nice and slow*, she told herself—he wouldn't know she'd started to cry over this.

The next thing she knew, a sob had wrenched its way out of her throat, the sound loud and completely out of place in the cab of the truck. She covered her face with both of her hands, her mind buzzing at her to *control this*.

Ginny didn't lose control. She didn't.

The truck slowed and stopped, and she had no idea how long it took for Cayden to get out of the truck and come to her door. He was just there, and when he said, "My sweetheart, it's okay to cry."

She lowered her hands, both eyes filled with tears now. She met his gaze for only a moment, because she wasn't strong enough to hold it for longer than that. Tears tracked down her face, and she flung her arms around him, pressing her cheek to his so he couldn't see her.

His strong arms encircled her, and where Ginny was weak and flawed, Cayden was strong and perfect, and she needed him more than ever as she fell apart for the first time in many years.

13

Cayden didn't know what to say to Ginny. His own emotions battled inside him, and he wondered how long he could stand on the side of the road while she cried.

As long as it takes, he thought, keeping her tight and flush against him.

He didn't know how to reassure her, but eventually, he said, "Let me take you home." She wouldn't want to go out now anyway.

"You're hungry," she said, her breath hitching in her chest immediately afterward.

"I'll call for something." He released her, and she slipped away from him. He dropped his eyes so she wouldn't feel overwhelmed. A woman like Ginny required privacy to put herself back together, and she'd be horribly embarrassed that she'd broken down like this.

Cayden rounded the hood again and got behind the wheel. He swung the truck around and headed back to her country house while Ginny continued to sniffle on the other side of the truck.

He helped her down back at the house and took her right back inside. She kept her hand in his as she went through the living room and down the hall that led to her bedroom. She spun back to him, reaching up with both hands and cradling his face.

"You are a beautiful, wonderful man," she whispered. "Will you wait while I change, and then can we just sit together?"

"Of course," he whispered. "I'll call for pizza while you change."

She nodded and slipped into the bedroom. He didn't call; he used the pizza delivery app to get the pies, salads, and desserts he wanted.

Ginny took a long time in the bedroom, and when she came out, she wore a sexy, black sweatshirt that hung off one shoulder, revealing a lot of skin there he'd never seen before. She wore a pair of wide-leg pants, also in black, and she'd scrubbed her face clean.

Cayden stared at her, as he'd never seen her without makeup. She didn't paint herself up like a clown, but Ginny knew how to wear the exact right colors on her face, in the precise amount to enhance her natural beauty.

He wanted to take her into his arms and whisper that

he loved her. In so many ways, he did. In others, he knew he wasn't quite there yet.

He gathered her close and said, "Ginny, I don't know what to say or do right now. I don't know what's happened or not happened. I just want you to know that there are other ways for a couple to have children, and if that's a point we find ourselves at, I'm confident that we'll make the right choices for us."

He liked speaking in plurals like *we* and *us*, and he hoped he hadn't jumped too far ahead for her. He hadn't asked her about her mother in several weeks now, and she hadn't brought her up either. He'd made a little bit of peace with himself regarding the whole thing, and he could make peace with this too.

Easing back, he looked down into her face. "You're gorgeous," he whispered. "I like you so very much. So much that sometimes I think I'm in love with you."

"I can't have children," she said again, those navy eyes so full of anguish. "That's not a deal-breaker for you?"

"Not at all," he promised. "Okay? Not at all."

She closed her eyes and nodded. He watched her draw in a big breath and put all of her strongholds back into the proper positions. When she looked up at him again, the fierceness had re-entered her gaze. "Thank you, Cay."

He smiled and reached up and wiped her face for her. "For the record, Ginny, I love this fierce version of you. I love this woman with no makeup on too. I love the woman who was vulnerable enough with me to cry in front of me.

I love the honesty of your heart." He took a breath and smiled. "I love the woman who knows how to wear her professional clothes and the perfect makeup and run a massive family company almost single-handedly."

Running his fingers over the soft, bare skin on her shoulder and neck, Cayden added, "I *really* love this sweatshirt," as the final thing he was going to say.

She laughed, the sound so much better than that sob he'd heard in his truck. He joined her, hoping he hadn't said "I love" too many times.

One time was probably too many, he thought, but he didn't want to regret anything about tonight.

"Come show me the best seat in the house," he said, lacing his fingers through hers. "Will the dogs come sit with us?"

"You and those dogs," she teased.

"I like them," he said. "There's something comforting about dogs."

Out in the living room, Ginny led him to the end of the couch that was a chaise, and she pointed to it. "This is the best seat in the house."

"I can see that." He sat down and stuck his legs straight out in front of him, grinning up at her. "I'll take my boots off."

"I'll get us something to drink." She padded into the kitchen while Cayden removed his boots and let them drop to the floor. When Ginny returned, she handed him a bottle of diet cola and climbed onto the chaise with him.

She cuddled right into his side, and he lifted his arm around her shoulders. "Now this *is* the best seat in the house," he murmured.

She sighed and pressed her cheek to his chest. Cayden closed his eyes and basked in the warmth and safety of the two of them, in this moment, together.

It certainly felt like love to him, but he kept those thoughts and words to himself, and when Ginny asked him about the forthcoming Bluegrass Ranch race, he shared his real life and real feelings with her, something he'd always wanted to do with a woman.

14

*B*laine Chappell stood in front of the huge picture window in the master bedroom at the homestead. The wind made the tree limbs outside lash around, and he frowned. The weather in Kentucky at the end of May should be beautiful. Warm, sure, but not insufferably hot like August or September. It did rain sometimes, but a cold snap had been hovering over the state for a day or two now, annoying him and causing his mother to fret.

His heart boomed in his chest, as it had been doing every so often for the past two weeks. *Probably more like a month*, he thought as he turned from the window.

"The wind hasn't died down," he said to Spur, who turned from what he was doing at the dresser.

"It's going to be fine," Spur said. "The tents are solid in

the ground, and I sent Jules and Peter to set up the wind block."

"Tam's not going to be happy." Heck, Blaine wasn't happy.

It was his wedding day, and he didn't want to battle the elements when he was already fighting the urge to get behind the wheel of his truck and go a lot farther than Tennessee this time.

Spur abandoned the cufflinks he'd bought for all eight of the brothers and approached Blaine. "You want to do this, right?"

"Yes," Blaine said, having a hard time looking at his older brother.

"You love her, right?"

"Yes." His voice scratched in his dry throat. "Spur, it's never been about me."

"She loves you," Spur said. "You need to start believing that, Blaine. It's never going to work if you don't."

Blaine set his jaw and nodded. He hated this softness inside him, but he hadn't been able to root it out or turn it into something hard. He could lift weights and run miles and his body turned into steel.

His heart steadfastly refused to toughen up, and so Spur wouldn't see the emotion on his face, he grabbed him and held him tight.

"Okay," Spur said with a chuckle. "Everyone's going to be here in a minute. You better get out of those jeans and into your tux."

"Right." Blaine stepped back and stripped down to his boxers. His mother had laid his tux on the bed, and Blaine started getting dressed, taking precious seconds to get every piece in the exact right place, savoring each moment as he thought about the blonde who'd walk down the aisle with her father in only an hour's time.

He did love Tamara Lennox, even if she drove him to insanity from time to time. She was talented and talkative, and Blaine loved making her laugh and holding her as the sun went down. For so long, he wasn't sure he'd ever learn how to trust himself again. He wasn't sure he'd ever be able to trust another woman. He had no idea how to love someone and believe it was real and not just something he told himself.

Tam had been patient with him, and they'd talked through everything. Literally, everything, from who would cook in the evenings—Blaine—to who'd primarily take care of any children they had—Tam.

He would be in charge of their money, and Tam was going to keep her business incorporated in her name only. She was going to take the Chappell last name, but she wasn't going to carry it into her business license.

She hadn't signed a prenuptial agreement, despite Ian's urgings that she do so. Blaine had talked to Trey for a few hours one afternoon while he helped his brother put in the corn at the ranch down the road where he now lived with his wife, Beth.

"Beth didn't sign one," Trey said. "Not before...when

things weren't entirely real, and not now either." He'd shrugged as if protecting himself was not a big deal. "I trust her."

Blaine trusted Tam too, and they'd gone back and forth on the topic for what felt like months. In the end, he'd looked her straight in the eye and said, "I trust you. I don't want or need you to sign a prenup."

She'd dropped it after that.

The door opened just as Blaine looped the bowtie around his neck. He let it dangle there as Cayden, Lawrence, and Trey entered the room. The three of them were engaged in a conversation that had Lawrence rolling his eyes while Cayden laughed in that smooth, rolling voice of his.

Trey grinned at them both and looked to Blaine first. "Wow, look at you, brother."

Blaine smiled back, the gesture genuine and sitting perfectly on his face for the first time in weeks. Trey gripped him in a tight hug, and Blaine returned it. So much was changing in their family, after what felt like a few years where nothing had.

Families were definitely dynamic, and while he wasn't the first brother getting married, Blaine felt like he was stepping way out of his comfort zone. Gratitude filled him that he had older brothers to look to as good examples.

Spur's bravery inspired Blaine to be strong too. Trey's fearlessness helped Blaine take steps into the darkness when he wasn't sure what path he was even on. Cayden's spirit reminded Blaine to challenge himself physically, mentally, and spiritually.

He waited his turn to hug Blaine, and when Trey stepped back, Cayden took his spot. "I'm so happy for you," he said, and he sounded like he was.

"It'll be you soon," Blaine said. He'd seen Ginny Winters with Cayden, and it was clear to him that they belonged together.

"We'll see," Cayden said, his voice giving nothing away. When he stepped back, though, he wore a smile, and Blaine hadn't heard that things with Ginny weren't absolutely perfect. Quite the opposite, in fact.

"Congratulations, Blaine," Lawrence said, and Blaine hugged him extra tight for extra long.

Though Ian was fifteen months older than Lawrence and technically, he and Blaine made up the middle block of brothers between the three older men and the three younger ones, Blaine had always felt that kinship with Lawrence.

Number one, he was more open than Ian. He didn't slam doors when one thing went wrong, and he stayed for hard discussions.

"You're just happy you can move in here," he joked as he stepped back, his emotion surging up his throat.

Lawrence chuckled and shook his head. "I am happy about that; I can't lie."

With Spur gone next door to Olli's now, and Trey living at The Triple T with Beth, and Blaine moving into

Tam's grandmother's house, only Cayden remained at the homestead. Lawrence and Duke were moving out of the house they shared with Ian and Conrad and into the homestead to even out the living conditions.

He looked around at the good men in the room with him. They all wore the same midnight black suit, each tailored just for them. Because of the long engagement, they'd had plenty of time for tailoring, and only Ian had refused to go into the shop with everyone else. He'd assured Blaine he'd be presentable for the wedding, and Blaine couldn't do much more than accept his brother at his word.

He was coming to the wedding, and Blaine had chosen to be glad about that. He knew how hard some things were, and that not everything could be explained.

The door opened again, and the rest of the brothers arrived. Conrad and Ian spoke to one another, and Blaine wasn't sure if the two of them ever stopped talking. Duke, the youngest, seemed to have more maturity than they did, and he grinned at Blaine as he beelined toward him.

He whistled as he scanned Blaine down to his shiny shoes. "Tam is so lucky," he said, laughing.

Blaine laughed with him and hugged him, then clapped Conrad on the back and finally faced Ian. His brother's jaw jumped, and a tornado blew through his expression.

"Congratulations," Ian said stiffly, and Blaine's heart broke for him all over again. Something must've shown on his face, because Ian looked away, anger in the set of his jaw now. "Don't, Blaine."

"I'm not," he said, but his voice definitely choked with emotion. He wanted to say Ian would find someone to love—who would actually love him in return, not just love the size of his bank account.

He grabbed onto Ian, because he didn't think anyone hugged him enough. After a couple of seconds, Ian yielded and returned the embrace. He didn't say anything either, like, *Don't come crying to me when she breaks your heart*, and he could have.

So much was said with silence anyway, and Blaine knew exactly where he'd go if Tam broke his heart. Misery did love company, and Ian had been miserable for so, so long.

"All right," Spur said above the chatter. "Get over here and get your cufflinks." He frowned at the closed door. "Daddy should be here by now. Maybe I need to call Mom."

"He was just pulling in when we got here," Duke said, crowding around the bureau with everyone else.

Blaine just stood back and watched them, this loud mess of brothers he'd been dealing with his whole life. He loved them; he always had. Sometimes, though, they were simply a lot to handle. At occasions like this, though, he was grateful for his big, loud family and the man they'd helped him become.

Daddy entered the room, and he too wore the suit.

He'd paired his with a brand-new cowboy hat in a matching shade of darkness and a pair of deep, dark brown cowboy boots. He wore a smile the size of Texas, and Blaine hurried over to him.

"Daddy." He breathed in the scent of his father's cologne, recognizing it as one of Olli's. She had half a dozen scents for men now, and she'd been working with one of the Chappell brothers for each one she developed.

Blaine himself wore *Horsing Around*, the scent she'd developed just for him. It was sold all over the country now, and he did like the notes of licorice buried down deep under the pine and straw, which were the dominant scents.

"What's yours called?" he asked his father as he stepped back. He blinked back the few tears that had gathered in his eyes.

"My what?"

"Your cologne." He gestured to Daddy's throat. "That's got Olli written all over it."

"Oh, it's called *Perfectly Patriarchal*." He grinned again, and Blaine hoped he would take his dad's optimism and joy into the future with him. For years—decades—no one had worked harder than Daddy around Bluegrass Ranch. Now that he was retired, he hadn't lost his drive to do good things, but he sure had a lot more free time to enjoy his life.

Blaine wanted to enjoy his life day-by-day, and he had

the sudden vision of him and Tam sitting on their new porch in the evenings, doing just that.

His fears settled, and he went with Daddy over to the dresser to get his cufflinks.

"All right," Spur drawled. "That's everyone." He looked at Blaine. "Did you want to say something?"

Blaine wanted to say so much to each of them individually. He felt like he had a good relationship with each brother, and as he looked around at them, their eyes meeting and catching, his love for his family swelled again.

"Spur, thank you for leading us and being the best oldest brother there is." He smiled at Spur, who just blinked back at him. He probably had no clue how much his example meant to Blaine.

"Cayden, thank you for showing us how to hold our tempers and be proper Southern gentlemen."

Cayden grinned and touched the brim of his black cowboy hat. It looked so foreign on him, as Cayden usually wore a white hat.

"Trey, thank you for your undaunted spirit. Nothing ever scares you or stops you, and I want to be like that too."

Trey simply smiled at him and pressed his fist to his chest, right above his heart.

"Lawrence, you're my favorite of all the brothers." He grinned around at the others, hoping they knew there weren't really favorites. "You have a pure heart, and don't ever let anyone tell you that's a bad thing."

Lawrence looked at him with wide eyes and nodded.

"Ian, I know you're hurting, and I wish with everything inside me that I could take it for you. I would, you know. I'd carry it for as long as you needed me to, for as far as I needed to." He swallowed, unsure what else to say to the man who studied the floor instead of looking at Blaine. "I think we all would, and I guess I just want you to know you don't have to be alone. We're all here for you, anytime."

He switched his gaze to Conrad. "Conrad, I wish I had your talent with horses. It's crazy how smart you are, and you deserve a life of goodness that's as amazing as you are."

"Wow, thanks, Blaine." Conrad actually looked surprised, and Blaine knew he didn't tell his brothers how much he admired and appreciated them often enough.

"Duke." Blaine's voice cut out at the end of the name. "I couldn't do my job without you, and I think the Lord sent you just to take care of me." He slung his arm around his youngest brother's shoulders. "I love you, and I'm glad we get to work together every single day."

"Me too, Blaine," Duke said softly, a glow on his face.

"I love you all," Blaine said, looking at the last man in the room. The one who'd taught them all. "Daddy, what else is there to say?" His chest shook, and he pulled in a breath to try to steady it. "You've given us all this good life, this beautiful ranch, and some sort of tenacity we don't understand." He put both hands over his heart. "I love you, and I owe everything I have and everything I am to you. Thank you for showing me what it means to be a Chappell, and I hope I can live up to the name."

Daddy wiped his eyes and said, "I wish your mother was here."

Blaine had already spent an hour with Mom that morning, and she knew how he felt about her. "All right," he said. "Huddle up."

They all stepped in a couple of times, creating a tight circle, each of them lifting their arms around the men next to them. Blaine bowed his head, leaning toward the center of the huddle.

"Lord," he said. "We thank Thee for this day—my wedding day." Joy filled him, and he smiled. "Bless us all to be safe and experience some measure of happiness today. We're grateful for each other, and for our family all over Kentucky."

The perfect picture of Tam entered his mind, and he said, "Bless Tam to be calm and filled with light. Bless Momma to be pliable, and bless us all to forgive her for whatever is still plaguing us."

His mind blanked, and he figured that meant he'd said enough. "Amen."

Instead of a rousing "Amen," the brothers usually gave, they each said it in a much more subdued tone. They stayed in their huddle for a couple of moments, and then Blaine straightened, breaking the moment and the group.

"Let's go," Spur said, his voice rough, starting to turn toward the door. "Wait." He looked around at the brothers, lingering on Blaine. "I have some news, but I don't want to steal anything from your wedding day."

"Good news?" Blaine asked.

Spur nodded, and Blaine waved at him to go ahead and say it.

"Olli's pregnant," he said slowly, a smile creeping onto his whole face.

A moment of silence passed, and then congratulations started going around. He accepted hugs and kept smiling and laughing.

"Okay, okay," Spur finally said. "We're going to be late, and I think we all know what that does to our mother." They started streaming toward the door, and Blaine just watched them go.

It was Cayden and Lawrence who paused at the door and turned back to him. "You comin' or what?" Cayden asked. He and Lawrence both held out one arm, beckoning for Blaine to come with them.

"Yeah," he said, grinning. "I'm coming."

15

*L*awrence stood in line, the fifth brother instead of the sixth. Blaine stood next to the altar, which was an elongated saddle attached to a rough-hewn log with all the natural bark still on it. Tam had made it herself, and it was a gorgeous dark leather carved with flowers, little birds, and her and Blaine's names.

A large C sat in the middle on top of it, and while Lawrence couldn't see it from here, he'd already admired the custom altar, marveling at the way Tam's mind worked. The fact that she could pull her thoughts out through her fingers and into leather astounded him, and he found himself praying for a woman like her to walk into his life.

"Welcome," Mom said, and Lawrence shook his lonely thoughts out of his head. He'd been busier than ever around the ranch in the past couple of months, and he didn't have time for dating anyway. Blaine and Spur were some of the busiest Chappell brothers, and they'd still managed to find time to fall in love and start families.

Lawrence's thoughts moved to Mariah Barker and the idiotic thing he'd said to her months ago. *I could be your boyfriend so you can go to the party.*

He'd never brought it up again. She hadn't either. They'd kept their relationship strictly professional, and every time he spoke to her, she was perfectly composed and knowledgeable about everything going on in preparation for the big race.

Tam didn't have many girlfriends, so she only had her sisters for bridesmaids, along with three cowgirls that she'd gotten close to over the years as she made saddles for them. Combined, there were only five women, and seven brothers.

Olli had her arm hooked through Spur's, and they stood at the front of the line, of course. Trey had his wife Beth on his arm, and that left a bridesmaid for everyone else.

He watched as Tam's sister Cara approached Cayden, and the perfectly pleasant smile on his brother's face. Cayden should have Ginny Winters on his arm, but he'd said nothing to Blaine or Tam—or anyone else—about the situation.

Ginny had come to the wedding; Lawrence had seen her standing with Olli twenty minutes ago.

"You must be Lawrence," a woman said, and he turned toward her. She wore a pale pink dress, and he had the distinct impression that she rarely wore anything but rough cotton blouses and jeans.

"Yes," he said, smiling at her. "Pauline?"

"Yes, sir." She linked her arm through his, and Lawrence shook off his disappointment that there had been absolutely no spark. She was a pretty woman, he supposed. Her tight, curly hair wasn't his favorite, and she was a bit shorter than he'd like. She'd be perfect for someone, as Lawrence believed there was someone for everyone.

He wanted to meet his someone.

The music started, and he drew in a breath. "Ready?" he murmured to Pauline.

"Sure thing," she drawled, and she didn't seem to have any nerves whatsoever.

The line moved in front of him, and when it was his turn to step, he did. One foot in front of the other, then both feet together again. They'd practiced the spacing for forty minutes last night, and Lawrence was determined not to be the one who messed it up.

Only Ian remained in front of him, and Lawrence started looking out over the crowd. They'd all gotten to their feet and were watching every couple as they stepped down the aisle. Lawrence began to sweat, despite the shade under the tent and the breeze that kept everything cool.

He really didn't like being in the spotlight like this, and he hoped that when it was his turn to get married, he could convince his girlfriend to elope.

Ian moved, and Lawrence took his spot. He had several seconds to survey the crowd before he moved, and as he did, he saw a woman who definitely made his blood run hotter in his veins.

Mariah Barker.

His eyes hooked onto hers, and he lifted his eyebrows when she looked back at him. What in the world was she doing here?

She stood in front of an older gentleman—her father, obviously—and Lawrence started connecting dots in his head. Her daddy must be friends with Tam's—

"Go," Conrad hissed from behind him. "You're late, Larry. *Go.*"

Lawrence blinked; his heartbeat accelerated; he took one giant step forward, dragging his partner with him. She couldn't take that big of a stride in her dress, and she stumbled. Horror moved through Lawrence as he tried to steady her and himself at the same time.

He was still behind, too, and he whispered, "Sorry. Another big step."

Pauline's grip on his arm intensified as he got them caught up in two steps, and the harsh glare on the side of his face didn't ease his discomfort.

He should just look straight forward and get down the aisle and out of the limelight. Instead, he locked his gaze back onto Mariah, who wore a beautiful smile now, miming a few beats of applause as he passed her.

Warmth and pride filled his chest, and he hoped to all of heaven that she found him as attractive as he found her. She wore a pretty green and purple flowered dress, perfect for a springtime wedding in Kentucky.

He wanted to dance with her and eat dinner beside her. He wanted to hold her hand and steal her away from the wedding once darkness fell. His fantasies got out of control, and he told himself to focus—at least until he delivered Pauline where she needed to go and he took his place behind the altar between Ian and Conrad.

Once there, he had a good view of Mariah again, and he couldn't help lifting his hand to the brim of his hat and grinning at her.

She ducked her head and tucked her loose hair behind her ear.

Tam appeared at the end of the aisle, and even Lawrence's breath caught in his throat. He switched his gaze to Blaine, who'd moved to stand right in front of the saddle altar. He waited perfectly still, and Lawrence could only imagine the smile on his face.

Tam wore one on her face, and she stepped the same way down the aisle, her father at her side. When they reached Blaine, she kissed her father's cheek and leapt into Blaine's arms, which caused the crowd to laugh.

Blaine kissed her, and the pastor said, "We usually save the kissing for the end."

"Right," Blaine said, and the two of them positioned themselves in front of the altar, facing each other, their hands joined and hanging in front of them. "Right."

He grinned at Tam, and Lawrence could see enough of her face to taste her joy too.

Lawrence let a sigh move through his whole body. He hadn't dated a lot, but he was ready to change that. His gaze moved back to the crowd as they sat, and he lost sight of Mariah, as he couldn't see her past all the cowboy hats in the crowd.

"We gather here today for one of the most wonderful reasons in the world," Pastor Clements said. "Weddings are always beautiful, but especially when I see two young people in front of me who obviously love each other more than the sky loves the moon."

Lawrence grinned again, because he loved that imagery. He wanted a love affair as fierce as the sky loving the moon, and he determined to ask Mariah to dinner as soon as he possibly could.

16

Mariah loved weddings. The spirit of happiness and joy and love was unlike anything else, and there was something special about this particular event. She'd worked dozens of events, and none—even the anniversary parties and business grand openings—held the same magic as this wedding.

She suspected it had something to do with the hoard of men crowding around the most gorgeous altar she'd ever laid eyes on. They all had one hand in the air, gripping a cowboy hat as they surrounded Blaine Chappell, who'd just married Tamara Lennox.

The cheering, applause, and whooping died down, and people started moving out into the aisle to go give their congratulations too.

Mariah hung back, because she didn't really know Tam or Blaine all that well. She knew Cayden and

Lawrence Chappell just fine, but she'd come to the wedding with her father, who'd been friends with the Lennox's for about eight years now.

"You go ahead," she said to him, and Daddy inched his way up to Shirley and Kenneth Lennox.

Mariah got out of the way, something she was extraordinarily gifted at doing. She knew how to be in charge of an event and then fade into the background once it began. She'd watched many of her plans execute themselves at that point, and she couldn't remember the last time something she'd been in charge of hadn't gone off without a hitch.

This wedding had a very good planner behind it, because everything had been seamless so far.

After several minutes, Julie Chappell stepped up to the mic and said, "We're moving over to the wedding pavilion for dinner, dancing, and drinks. If you'll start making your way over there, you'll find a name tag on the front table. Take that and place it at a spot of your choosing. You should find the meal you selected on the underside of the tag. Please do let Hillary here know if y'all have any questions."

She beamed out at the group of people, some of whom were actually listening, and a tall brunette with perfectly curled hair lowered her hand as she realized no one was looking at her anyway. If there was a problem, Hillary would handle it, but people would likely go to Julie first.

Mariah scanned the dispersing crowd, looking for two people: Daddy and Lawrence Chappell.

When his eyes had met hers, that electric tether that had bound them together months ago had roared back to life. She hadn't forgotten his kindness, but her embarrassment and professionalism had prevented her from ever bringing up what he'd said to her at their first face-to-face meeting.

I could be your boyfriend so you can go to the party.

She'd missed three more shindigs that Dr. Biggers had thrown, and there was a summer kick-off bash coming up in three weeks. He'd once again bypassed her for a new assignment for June, citing her busyness with the race here at Bluegrass ranch.

Mariah was busy getting everything finalized, contracts signed in a timely manner, and dealing with what felt like constant changes. *Not so busy you can't take on another client, especially in the early phases of planning,* she thought.

She hadn't gotten the clients, though. Suzy Mays had, and she had two big-name clients having events in July and August already. Suzy was also recently married, blonde, and about twenty pounds lighter than Mariah.

Familiar bitterness coated her throat, along with the complete and utter helplessness. She wasn't sure what she could do about her situation, short of quitting. Everyone outside of the Favorites talked in low tones about what happened at The Gemini Group. No one actually did anything.

Mariah wanted to find the grenade that would blow the whole thing up, pull the pin, and toss it in Dr. Biggers' office. She simply didn't know what that was yet.

Her dad gestured to her that he was going to head over to the tent by exiting near the front instead of coming back down the aisle. She lifted her hand in acknowledgement, wondering if she could make up a work emergency and get out of there. She did like weddings, but she didn't really know anyone here she wanted to spend the next three hours with.

Her couch, Diet Coke, and bottle of coconut-flavored syrup sounded so much more enticing than the promised prime rib, and Mariah couldn't believe she'd rather drink soda than eat red meat.

"Hey."

She blinked her attention away from the altar, where Blaine and Tam had just linked hands and started their pilgrimage to the wedding pavilion, and toward the man who'd spoken.

Her natural reaction was to suck in a breath at the handsome man in front of her. Her heartbeat twittered in her chest, and she actually pressed one palm against it to get it to calm.

"Lawrence," she said.

"I didn't mean to startle you." He put his hand on her

elbow as if they'd touched so intimately many times in the past.

They hadn't, but Mariah found her mind sparking in all kinds of new directions tonight. She'd only met with him in her office once since the meeting here in the administration building, and she suddenly needed to find a way to get him behind closed doors again.

Her thoughts surprised her, and she covered them with a smile. She dropped her arm, which caused him to pull his hand back, and said, "I'm fine."

"You looked like you were looking for an escape," he said, his smile so symmetrical, revealing perfectly straight, white teeth. He had a nicely trimmed beard, which was different than the last time she'd seen him. She wanted to reach out and run her hand along the length of his cheek to see if his whiskers were soft.

"Maybe I was," she said, adding a little bit of coyness to her tone. "I don't really know anyone here."

He stepped to her side instead of standing in front of her and cocked his arm for her to take. "Now you do."

Again, Mariah let her natural instincts take over, and she laced her hand through his arm. "You look great in that suit."

"Thank you," he said. "I like your dress as well."

She looked down at herself as if she'd forgotten what she'd put on for this ranch wedding. A splashy, bright floral dress—her favorite item of clothing. She had them in blue and white, pinks, reds, and yellows, and this one in purple and green. "I like patterns," she said. "Dr. Biggers doesn't, so I don't get to wear my fun dresses very often."

"It's gorgeous," he said, and when Mariah looked at him, she found him gazing right back at her. The crowd and noise fell away. All that existed for a moment was him. Only him.

He cleared his throat and took a step, breaking her out of the bubble she'd fallen into. "I can't be late. My mother is not one to be trifled with at family weddings."

Mariah giggled quietly and walked with him. "I bet she isn't."

"I wasn't expecting to see you," he said. "Your family must know Tam's?"

"That's right," she confirmed. "My father worked for hers for a while, and they've been friends since."

Lawrence nodded as he led her out from underneath the wedding tent. The sun was just starting to arc west, and it would still be a couple of hours until dusk. She suddenly didn't want to leave, especially alone.

Or before you make sure Lawrence knows to call you for anything other than what he needs for the race.

Mariah had no idea how to do that, but pressing her hip into his seemed like a good idea as they squeezed by another couple standing in line to get their name tags. "I need my tag," she said as Lawrence seemed to be bypassing the front table to the wedding pavilion completely.

"Not when you're with me," he said, his voice slow and

low but filled with confidence. He paused next to the table, not in front of it, and said, "Olli."

"Right there, Lawrence," she said, pointing without looking. "Family tags."

"I need Mariah Barker's," he said, and Olli looked up. Mariah knew her; everyone knew Olivia Hudson since she'd gotten her perfumes, colognes, and candles in every Renlund Association store across the country.

"I have three of your perfumes," she said, smiling at the harried brunette. "I love them."

Olli grinned back at her, suddenly unconcerned about the crowd she still needed to serve. "Which one are you wearing tonight?" She leaned closer as if she could smell it.

Mariah stepped closer and let her sniff her collar. "What do you think?"

"*Petals and Passion*," Olli said, smiling. Her gaze switched to Lawrence, her eyes missing nothing, including how close Mariah stood to him and her hand through his elbow. "Two things really quick." She started searching for a tag on the table. "One, spray that perfume in your hair, girl. Make him *lean in* to smell it." She looked up. "Have you seen my videos?"

"I have to admit I haven't," Mariah said.

"Three minutes will change your life." Olli handed her the tag. "Second, for a man like Lawrence, you want *Leather, Lace, and Laughter*." She grinned at the two of them, pressing her hip into the table. "Trust me on that."

"*Leather, Lace, and Laughter,*" Mariah said. "I thought that one smelled a little...outdoorsy."

"Exactly," Olli said, her eyes glinting now.

"We're not..." Mariah let the denial of a relationship with Lawrence die on her lips when Olli raised her eyebrows. Mariah shifted her feet and dropped her eyes, a smile inevitably crossing her face.

Olli focused on Lawrence. "Cayden was looking for you. I might keep my hands to myself when I see him." With that, she looked at the next guest at the table and asked for their name.

Lawrence grabbed his name tag and walked away, taking Mariah with him. He went to one of the front tables and put his name tag down. "Do you need to sit by your father?"

"No," she said. "I'm thirty-seven years old. I can sit by myself." She smiled at him, and he returned the gesture as he shook his head.

"What were you going to say back there?" he asked.

"When?"

"We're not...what?"

She searched his face, trying to find what he'd like for her to have said. "I don't know, exactly," Mariah admitted.

The noise in the pavilion increased, but Lawrence didn't look away from her. "I think—"

"Larry," a man yelled, and the next thing Mariah knew, Lawrence had been plowed into by one of his brothers.

She stumbled too as she got out of the way, and she smiled at his exuberance.

"Sorry," he said, laughing. "Are you guys full at this table?" He barely glanced at Mariah, his eyes flitting away quickly.

She was used to being overlooked, especially by tall, handsome cowboys with a lot of money.

"I think just Cayden and Ginny, and Spur and Olli are here." He glared at his brother. "Don't tell me you've found some giggling girl, Conrad."

"I have to have someone," his brother said, his smile slipping. "Hilde wouldn't come."

"That's because she broke up with you months ago." Lawrence pulled his arm around from Conrad. "Have you met Mariah Barker?" He indicated her. "She's working with me and Cayden on the race."

She stuck out her hand, not liking that introduction at all. Her heart wouldn't be pounding so hard if she was about to eat dinner with a client. "Good evening," she said. "So nice to meet another Chappell."

Conrad grinned at her and shook her hand. "Nice to meet you too, ma'am." He stepped past her and put his name tag on the table. "I'm going to sit with you guys. Ian is driving me crazy."

"Duke's going to get stuck with him."

"Yes, but Duke has a woman with him, so he can suck it up." Conrad wore a dark look and surveyed the line of people entering the pavilion. "Now, I just need to find someone to sit by..." He took a deep breath and walked away.

Mariah twisted to watch him go, sure he wasn't going to bring a complete stranger to the table with his brothers and their wives and girlfriends.

You're neither of those, her mind whispered.

Then Lawrence's hand landed lightly on her waist. "Would you go to dinner with me sometime?" he whispered, his lips right at her ear. "You don't have to answer right now. It's crazy, and my oldest brother is heading this way." He stepped back and hugged Spur Chappell when he arrived. He introduced her the same way he had for Conrad, and when Cayden came over with Virginia Winters, Mariah started to freak out a little bit.

"I love Sweet Rose," she gushed at Ginny. "The harvest holidays you guys do are amazing. My nieces love going there." She trilled out a laugh. "I think I took them six times last fall."

"Thank you," Ginny said, a pleasant smile on her face as she sat down. She glanced at Lawrence and back to Mariah. "Did you come with him?"

"No," she said with a grin as she took her seat too. "No, my father is good friends of Tam's parents. I'm working with Cayden and Lawrence on their marketing and publicity for the Summer Smash."

Ginny's face lit up. "I knew your name sounded familiar. You're the one who contracted my banner."

"That's right." Mariah loved talking to other successful

women, and when Ginny asked her if she was seeing anyone, she saw Lawrence perk up right next to her. "No," she said. "Not for a while now."

Ginny nodded as her attention got diverted by Cayden. She leaned in close to him, listening as he said something right against her ear. Mariah shivered, remembering the heat from Lawrence's breath on her skin.

She reached out and touched the decorative spread in the middle of the table. "It's like a little cowhide," she said, utterly charmed by the brown and white spotted hide on the table. From it rose a tower of rough-cut logs with all the bark on them, like the post that had supported the saddle. Clear glass lanterns, crystal horse figurines, bottles with baby's breath, ripe, red apples, and candles rested on the different levels. Woven in among the rustic wood and charming décor was an assortment of flowers. White, red, orange, and rose gold roses, along with greenery and sprayed of what looked like the tops of wheat.

Mariah loved everything about it, and she once again thought there was something very special about this family and this ranch. She wanted to bottle the magic here and pour it into her life whenever it became too dull.

She also needed to figure out how to bottle it so she could give everyone a sip over the next couple of months to fill the stands for the Summer Smash.

Just as the first waiters started serving dinner, Mariah pulled out her phone, the question Lawrence had posed infecting her mind. She needed to answer him so she could enjoy the rest of the wedding.

Her thumbs flew across the screen as a smile curved her lips.

I'd like to go to dinner with you, she said. *But I have a strict policy not to date clients. What do you think about what you said a couple of months ago? My boss is having a summer kick-off party I'd love to be at...*

She wasn't sure if his phone was on silent or vibrate. She didn't hear it go off, and with everyone else at the table now—including a dark-haired woman with a smile as nervous as a sinner in church who'd sat next to Conrad—she and Lawrence didn't have a chance to continue the conversation.

She would, though. She wasn't going to let this drop the way she had last time.

∼

"He's going to be here any second," she said, dashing through the living room and back down the hall. "You're sure you haven't seen them?"

"No," Alicia called after her. "The last time was sometime last week."

Irritation built in Mariah's chest, because that just wasn't true. Alicia had borrowed Mariah's little red sandals on Thursday night for her date with Malcom, and Mariah darted into her sister's bedroom.

Clothes littered the floor, as did shoes. Mariah came to a stop, wondering how she and Alicia were related. Where her sister was a slob, Mariah liked everything lined up and neat. She hung her blouses and dresses in the closet in a rainbow configuration, for crying out loud.

"Red," she muttered, telling herself that her younger sister would be moving out in a week. Seven more days. She could survive. "Red."

Most of Alicia's shoes were down at the end of the bed, and Mariah dropped to her knees to look under the bed, her heartbeat racing. Her jumpsuit was a little too tight around the hips to be down on all fours, but she needed those shoes.

She'd just yelped in triumph and closed her fingers around one sandal when the doorbell rang. "I'm coming!" she yelled, but Alicia would let Lawrence in.

A wave of dizziness hit Mariah as she lifted a pair of Alicia's skinny jeans and found the other shoe. She couldn't believe she was going out with Lawrence.

"You're not," she said, flopping onto her sister's unmade bed and slipping on the first shoe. "This is a pretend date for a business party."

He'd said yes to the idea of being her stand-in boyfriend for the parties this summer. She wouldn't date him until the Summer Smash had ended, and they'd texted hundreds of times working out the details.

If they weren't dating, there would be no kissing.

If they weren't dating, they were both free to date other people.

If they weren't dating, he didn't have to pay for everything.

They hadn't been out yet, and the work between them hadn't suffered a bit since the wedding, about three weeks ago now.

Every night, they texted a little bit, though as Mariah slid on her second shoe, she knew some nights were more like texting marathons. He'd reasoned that they'd need to know a little bit about each other to come off as a believable couple in front of her boss.

Mariah honestly didn't think Dr. Biggers would even notice she was there. She'd had Lawrence call The Gemini Group a few times and ask for her, each time telling the receptionist that he was her boyfriend.

Karl, who had a direct line to Dr. Biggers, had told the boss, and Mariah had an invite in her box for this summer kick-off pool party at the doctor's mansion north of Dreamsville.

With the shoes finally strapped in place, Mariah jumped to her feet and nearly fell right on her face again as she tripped over an article of clothing on the floor. "Stupid skirt," she muttered as she kicked it out of the way.

She wiped her hand through her hair, feeling clammy and sweaty. She couldn't go out in to the living room and greet Lawrence like this. Panic built in her chest. What had she been thinking?

Alicia appeared in the hallway, her shorts far too short for a woman her age. "There you are. Are you coming?" She approached, her eyes scanning Mariah from head to toe. A smile touched her face. "You look so pretty. He's going to go nuts."

Mariah resisted the urge to ask how he looked. This was a fake date. A façade. She couldn't think it was real until the Smash ended. Then she and Lawrence could become a real couple—if he was still interested at that point.

To be honest, Mariah didn't have much hope that he would be. Most of the men she dated seemed intrigued by her at first, but the charm and allure wore off after only a few weeks.

She took a deep breath and smoothed her hands down the front of her jumpsuit. "I look okay?"

"Okay?" Alicia said, embracing her. "You look like a million bucks, Mya."

"I'm going to burn my shoulders." She looked at her bare shoulders, save for the thin strap of the jumpsuit. She'd loved this piece the moment she'd laid eyes on it, and she thanked the heavens above they'd had her size. The black material was lightweight and breathable, with bright red, yellow, and purple flowers scattered across it. Because they were small, the pattern wasn't splashy, and she liked that.

It was classy.

The red sandals completed the look, and Mariah combed her fingers through her hair, which was properly spritzed according to Olli's instructions with *Leather, Lace, and Laughter*.

"All right," she said. "Here goes nothing."

17

Cayden couldn't believe he only had three more weeks until the Summer Smash. He had everything laid out in front of him in the cool, quiet administration building, and he adjusted a piece of paper that indicated an entire section of the stands.

They were all grayed out, because by some miracle, they'd sold every single seat in their arena. With Tim's help, Cayden had made drastic improvements to their facilities, with a few simple construction projects that had wrapped last week.

He reached out and touched the row of paper that represented their corporate suites. These could be rented by anyone, and he'd offered them to all the owners entering their horses in the sales event for free. The others they'd rented for a flat fee of one thousand dollars for the day, with a maximum of eight guests per suite.

They were located on the second level of the stands, spanning the width of arena, except for one large area right in the center.

That was the Bonfire Room, and it held a maximum of fifty people, with tables and chairs for dining inside, and seats to watch the race on the balcony.

The moment the pictures of the Bonfire Room had come back, Lawrence had forwarded them to Mariah Barker, and she'd put them on the website, along with the availability. As there was only one room, with a large occupancy, they'd listed the rental fee at ten thousand dollars.

Mariah had called fifteen minutes after the room went up and said it had been booked.

Cayden let his eyes drift along the second level, his thoughts tangling around Mariah and Lawrence. Now that his brother lived in the homestead with him, Cayden knew more details of Lawrence's life, and he knew he'd accompanied Mariah to at least three events that summer.

"Three in less than a month," Cayden muttered, wondering if Lawrence was dating her. After the first party, where Lawrence had sighed like a man in love when he'd returned home, Cayden had asked him if he was seeing Mariah romantically.

Lawrence had burst out laughing and said, "Who talks like that, Cay? Seeing her romantically?" After another round of laughter, Lawrence got up and took a bottle of his favorite fruit punch out of the fridge and had disappeared upstairs.

Because he'd had Ginny on the couch with him, Cayden hadn't realized until after that Lawrence hadn't exactly answered the question.

They'd gone to a water park with The Gemini Group, and Lawrence had returned after a full Sunday away from the ranch the color of boiled lobster. Cayden and Duke, who'd started sleeping in Blaine's old bedroom for some reason Cayden hadn't discovered yet, had tended to him for days and weeks afterward, spreading cooling aloe vera over his back and shoulders while the heat radiated off of him.

Lawrence had complained the whole time about how many people worked at The Gemini Group, and how the boss there barely knew all the employees. He did say he was impressed they had big company parties like that, and Cayden had a bug in his head now about holding a huge Bluegrass-Ranch-wide party for anyone on their payroll.

They hadn't done that in the past, to his knowledge. Daddy used to give out bonuses during the holidays, and Spur had stuck to that tradition. Cayden didn't want to admit he'd started another folder on his computer for a holiday party, where the bonuses would be handed out in person. Not until the Smash was over.

He looked up a tier to the third level. The kitchen for the café, restaurant, and bar at the arena was on this level, and the chef would also cater to anyone who rented any of the suites.

"Their food orders have to be in by Friday," he said, tapping his phone to wake it. Friday was tomorrow, and he quickly picked up his phone to text Lawrence about who still needed to turn those in.

We have seven outstanding, Lawrence answered a few seconds later. *I'm meeting with Mariah this afternoon to go over all the last-minute loose ends.*

Cayden sent a thumbs-up and put his phone down, though something zipped through him at the words *I'm meeting with Mariah this afternoon.*

He and Mariah had made up and patched over whatever they'd fought about that day they'd all met together for the first time.

He picked up his phone again and typed, *Come see me in my office when you get back to the ranch.*

Will do, Lawrence said, and Cayden sat down and tapped to call Ginny.

"Hello," she said crisply. "I have about forty-five seconds before my brothers are arriving."

"I won't keep you," he said. "It's just something silly anyway."

"Tonight?" she asked, clearly distracted.

"I thought you guys had another family emergency meeting at Old Ember's tonight."

"Later," she said. "About ten?"

"All right," he said, and she agreed and hung up.

Cayden sighed and looked out his window as he thought about Ginny. Things with her had been going amazingly well, despite his busy schedule combined with hers.

Sometime at the beginning of June, she'd texted him dozens of pictures of her mother's new living conditions, and Cayden had enjoyed that. She seemed happier now that her mother wasn't living on the second floor of the mansion, but he'd also had to hide in Ginny's supply closet once when her mother showed up unannounced at her office.

She was certainly more mobile now, and Ginny had been dealing with pop-ins for weeks. Cayden had stopped going to her office, which was probably just as well, as it was a long drive there and back, and he had plenty keeping him busy here.

He stood up again to gaze down at the plans. The arena could hold nine thousand people in the stands and on the grass, and those fifteen-dollar tickets had sold out in forty-eight hours. The Bluegrass Suites on the third level—six of them, three on each side—had been booked by The Gemini Group for their employees. They'd paid tens of thousands for all six rooms, and Cayden wasn't complaining about that.

He'd reserved the Chappell Coatroom on the fourth and top level for his family, and he'd turned in his menu a week ago. Three more suites took up the top floor, and then their premier space sat on the rooftop, with open-air, nearly three-hundred-sixty-degree views of the track and grounds.

That space had been divided in half, and each sold for twenty-five thousand dollars. They'd taken a bit longer to sell, and Tim had handled those high-rollers. Cayden had written personal emails to owners, breeders, the other horse farms around Dreamsville and Lexington, celebrities, and anyone else he'd encountered throughout the years in his job at the public relations director at Bluegrass Ranch.

In the end, the Darvill Family had bought one, and they were bringing their entire family. They ran a ranch south of Lexington, where three of their Derby winners and studs were buried. They'd definitely turned more to the tourism aspect of Horse Country, and the one time Cayden had checked to see if he could get a van tour to see the graves of the great horses, they'd been booked for eight months.

The other rooftop space had gone to celebrity chef Lisa Long, as she owned several racehorses that her trainers worked right there at Bluegrass Ranch. She wanted to bring her employees from her start-up restaurant in New York City, and they were planning a company retreat for the few days before the Smash.

He admired the arena on the individual pieces of paper, then gathered them all up and slipped them back into the right slot in his expandable file folder. He pulled out the papers in the next slot back, which were all the entry forms for the horses. The racing would begin at one-thirty, and he, Tim, and Darren had sorted the horses into age brackets, gender races, and length heats.

All in all, there would be eleven races, one about every half an hour, with a culminating event at the end of previous high-stakes winners. No one from the Belmont, Preakness, or Derby had been allowed to enter, but if a horse had won over two million dollars in their career, they could enter the high-stakes race.

He'd been surprised they'd gotten as many entries as they had.

All the horses racing in the Smash could be bought, and all of those sales were being handled through their Sales Office or the app that Cayden had commissioned back in January. He was dang proud of that app too, and it worked just like an auction.

Every horse would enter the auction the moment their race ended, and it would last until the starting bell rang for the next race. Whoever was the top bidder at that time had just bought himself or herself a horse.

Bids could be done through the app, which updated in real time, or through any window in the arena. Their signage would update in real time too, and Cayden's stomach buzzed with anticipation to see how this would go.

He, Tim, Darren, Lawrence, and Mariah had been testing the app for two months now, and everything seemed to work. Last time, he and Lawrence had stood in the arena with all their displays on, and as the app updated, so did they.

They'd found a few bugs they'd passed on to the developer, who was a younger guy in his late twenties who'd made six figures to drop everything and create the app Cayden described to him.

All purchases had to be paid for in the Sales Office, and Cayden had his full veterinary staff coming in for the Smash, the same way he did for their other sales. This part of the Smash didn't concern him, as he'd run dozens and dozens of horse sales over the years.

"What else?" he asked, sliding the entry forms back into the folder. It had cost five hundred dollars per horse to be entered, and all of that money had gone to the programs, so people could see which horse was running in which race, what kind of horse they were, age, winnings, times, the full nine yards.

The proof for the program would be in on Monday, and Cayden and Lawrence had an appointment with the print shop already.

Once the menu selections came back, Cayden would need to meet with Chef Bryson to go over the food order. He fingered those papers in the folder, but he didn't take them out. The food would cost thousands, and Cayden closed the file folder and turned to his computer.

The Summer Smash needed to turn a tidy profit if they were going to keep doing it. The hours he and Lawrence had invested in it alone required that. He opened the master financial spreadsheet, which he looked at every single day.

Several other people had access to it, and as they updated their expenses and included revenue, the numbers changed.

He only needed to know one—the profit. It sat down at the bottom of over one hundred lines, several columns over, highlighted in red, with the text white.

Right now, with their entry fees, seats sold, sponsorships, banner costs, construction costs, app building cost, and several other items, their profit sat just above five hundred thousand dollars.

He frowned, because he wasn't sure that was enough. "For six months of work?" he grumbled. "We still have three weeks to go."

The food costs hadn't been put in, but neither had the percentage of each sale Bluegrass would collect when someone purchased a horse. There were parking fees too, and likely thousands in concessions, as well as bar, restaurant, and café income.

"Knock, knock," Lawrence said as he entered Cayden's office.

"Hey." Cayden minimized the spreadsheet and leaned back in his chair as his brother sat down. "How'd it go with Mariah?"

"Good. We got four more menus." He passed over one piece of paper. "She's emailing the others to me and you. We have calls and emails out for the last three, and she said she'd run them down tomorrow no matter what." He grinned, and Cayden smiled back.

"Thanks for working on this with me," he said. "You've been amazing."

"Thanks," Lawrence said, his smile growing and his dark eyes shining like moonlight off dark water. "It's actually been fun." He glanced around the office. "The air conditioning can't be beat."

They chuckled, with Cayden sobering first. "You sure it's the air conditioning you like? Or Mariah Barker?" He watched Lawrence closely, because this particular brother had always been terrible at hiding how he felt.

"All of it," he said airily, which gave everything away.

"I'm concerned about you dating her," he said. "Doesn't she have some policy through her company?"

"No," Lawrence said, his eyes flat now. "Her boss loves it when people date—and besides, we're not dating."

"You go out with her." He raised his eyebrows.

Lawrence folded his arms, and while he usually wore more cowboy casual clothes, today, he had on a dark blue shirt with white pinpricks all over it. It was still cotton, but not flannel, and he'd probably looked like he fit right in at The Gemini Group.

"No," he said. "I don't."

"No? Didn't the two of you go to a movie screening on Monday night?"

"That was for her work," he said. "It wasn't a date."

"I see." Cayden didn't really see, but he thought he

knew where Lawrence was driving. It felt a lot like the truck he and Ginny had been in last Christmas. "So she has events she needs to attend, and you...accompany her."

He lifted one ankle to his opposite knee, his chin going right up. Cayden had hit close to the bullseye but not right on it. He leaned his elbows on his desk. "I don't care either way. I'm just trying to figure out what's going on."

"Why does it matter what's going on?" Lawrence asked. "I didn't sit and hound you last year when you went out with Miss Winters every other day."

Cayden smiled, because it wasn't every other day. He didn't argue; this was one of those times where he didn't have to be right. He also didn't want to drive Lawrence further away, nor did he want to make him feel like he was doing anything wrong if he wasn't.

"I didn't mean to hound," he said, leaning back and picking up his phone. "Ginny's gone with her family tonight. Do you want to go get wings and frozen custard at the Lionshead with me?" He looked up, though he'd tapped on their app already.

They sold a limited number of tickets for Thursday night wings, all-you-can-sip beer, and the best chocolate custard in Kentucky. They put on sports from around the world, and while Cayden wasn't a huge sports fan, he'd become addicted to their wings the very first time he'd gone with Duke.

"Or we can get pizza and stay home." That option

sounded like heaven to Cayden, and he wondered when he'd gotten so old.

Lawrence shrugged, and that only annoyed Cayden. He knew precisely how to hide that, though, and he tapped on the big red button at the top of his screen. "I'm getting two tickets at the Lionshead."

"The Gemini Group doesn't have a policy against clients dating their associates," he said, and Cayden looked up from his phone, his fingers frozen in mid-air. "It's Mariah who has a personal no-dating-clients policy." Lawrence cleared his throat and dropped his foot back to the floor. "She needed a boyfriend to get invited to the parties her company throws, because her boss is a complete chauvinist and he only invites married couples or people with partners to his events. He hands out the best assignments there, and I said I'd be her—boyfriend—for the summer."

He really ground out the word *boyfriend*, and Cayden just kept watching him. He had more to say, and knowing Lawrence, he'd say it just fine.

"When the Smash ends, we're going to give the real dating thing a try."

"You've talked about this with her?"

"To death," Lawrence said. "We talk about *everything* to death."

Cayden burst out laughing, glad when his brother at least cracked a smile. "When did you ask her out?"

"Blaine's wedding."

"What did she say?"

"The whole policy thing, and I already knew about the unfair parties. She told me about them way back in March when she first came out here and we argued."

"You like her?"

Lawrence pressed his lips together and nodded. That was a big, old *heck yes*, not a tiny nod, and Cayden grinned.

"All right then. Just a few more weeks, and then the two of you can see where things will go." He got back to work on his app, and a few seconds later, he had his two tickets. "Got 'em. We can go any time after four."

"Cayden?"

"Hmm?" He glanced up, abandoning his phone though Ginny had just texted when he saw the look on Lawrence's face.

"What if she doesn't want to take things from fake to real?"

"Has she said that?"

"No, but." He exhaled and looked out Cayden's window too. "I know my track record with women, and it's not good."

"Do you think she doesn't really like you? What indication has she given of that?"

"I think she likes me right now, because I can help her get into the parties she wants to go to."

"Well, that won't change once she's no longer working for us."

"Right." His voice faded, and Cayden knew exactly what he was thinking.

He didn't want to be used. He wanted a real relationship with Mariah, not a fake one so she could get through the door at a work event.

He didn't know how to say it would be okay or that it would work out. Not everything was okay, and not everything worked out.

He stood up. "Come on. Let's go get Duke, saddle up, and ride for an hour before we stuff ourselves with wings." He rounded his desk and grabbed onto Lawrence's arm. "Okay?"

Lawrence finally chuckled a little as he got to his feet. "Fine, but I'm not going to stuff myself. It's just you who can't control himself with the wings."

"Hey, we all have flaws," Cayden said with a grin. He led the way out of his office, glad he was getting outside that day. He had a ten p.m. date with his girlfriend that didn't sound like it would be good news, three weeks to the biggest event he'd ever tried to pull off at Bluegrass Ranch, and perhaps years before he could make Ginny Winters his wife.

He definitely needed to get outside today.

"You better get a ticket for Duke to the Lionshead," Lawrence said behind him. "He's the only person I've ever seen eat more wings than you."

18

Ginny stared at the folder Harvey had put in front of her. "Is this what I think it is?" She tore her eyes from the seemingly simple and innocent manila.

"Yes," he said.

"What is it?" Drake asked, reaching for the folder. He picked it up while Ginny folded her hands in her lap.

She should be panicking, but all she could feel was... calm. She should grab her purse and storm from Old Ember's, her destination Mother's mansion.

She should practice her explanation on the drive over.

She sat very still and looked Harvey in the eye, as he sat across from her tonight. He wore a look of resignation and sympathy. "I'm going to stick to our agreement."

Ginny nodded, her gratitude rising up to choke her. She'd been attending church with Cayden each week, and every time was easier than the last. She fit there now, and she couldn't imagine not being able to go and bask in the warm sunlight pouring through the stained glass windows, listen to the pastor's rolling Southern voice, and feel like her life had more purpose than making money.

Didn't they have enough money?

Nothing will ever be enough for Mother, Ginny thought, and that was probably the truest thing that had ever moved through her mind.

"She's changed the will," Drake said. His voice carried equal parts awe and shock. "Ginny. What are you going to do?"

"What am I going to do?" She gently took the folder from Drake and handed it back to Harvey. "Nothing. I'm not going to do anything. My boyfriend is coming over tonight, and I'm going to talk to him. His brother's vow renewal is on Saturday, and I'm going to attend."

She couldn't believe how calmly she spoke, so her brothers' shocked looks weren't hard to understand. "I'm in love with him," she said quietly. "I'm going to choose him over Sweet Rose."

Her throat scratched then, and her chest constricted painfully.

"Ginny," Elliot said, and that was all.

She heard the unspoken words. *Good for you. You deserve to have someone you love.*

"She's not going to choose for me again," Ginny said, his voice deadly now. "I've let her run my life for so long, and I just—" She exhaled, a sense of mania moving through her. "I just don't care.

"I want you to be happy," Harvey said. "If he makes you happy, that's good enough for me."

She nodded at him, tears stinging her eyes.

"Mother won't live forever," Drake said.

"Could be another decade though," Ginny said, the thought of being without Sweet Rose for that long horrifying to her. She painted a smile on her face anyway. "Good thing Cayden's a billionaire too."

That somehow broke the tension, and the four of them laughed together.

Ginny's chin started to wobble, and while she'd cried more in the past four months since she'd gotten back together with Cayden than she ever had, she didn't try to tame the tears. "I love you guys," she said. "I'm sorry about the salary blocking last year. We should've gathered to this table and done this. Talked it all out."

"We all have plenty to apologize for," Elliot said, glancing at Harvey. "It's not necessary. We're family, and we forgive each other."

Ginny nodded with the others and when the waitress arrived, she ordered the goat cheese beet salad and a plate of fried calamari. "I have something else to tell y'all," she said, her emotions already rearing their ugly heads. "It's personal."

Drake flipped his phone over and looked at her, and Harvey and Elliot hadn't stopped looking at her.

"I guess it's more of a request," she said, her tears already flying down her face. "I can't have kids of my own, and I'm hoping you'll let me take yours to do everything in Lexington and Dreamsville in the near future." She wiped her face clean. "The far future too. All the futures."

A few seconds of silence descended on the table, and then Harvey said, "I will pay you fifty grand to take Sullivan for a weekend. I'm not even kidding. He's driving us *nuts*."

Ginny burst out laughing, though her tears still spilled from her eyes. Drake lifted his arm much the same way Cayden had and drew her into his chest. "I'm so sorry, Ginny," he said, and the other two nodded and murmured their assent.

Elliot was right; they were family, and they did forgive each other. More than that, though, they loved one another. That was the kind of family she wanted too, and when she closed her eyes, that family was with Cayden.

Now she just needed a plan to deal with Mother.

∽

"How did she find out?" Cayden asked later that night.

"I don't know," Ginny said, her eyes closed as she laid on her couch, her head and shoulders in Cayden's lap. "Harvey didn't say. All he knows is the lawyer sent him a copy of the new will; that Mother requested the changes on Monday."

His fingers slid through her hair again. Then again. "What do you want to do?"

"This," she whispered.

Cayden's unrest carried like a scent on the air. He'd give her a few minutes, but then he'd want to know what she was really going to do.

"I spoke to Gloria today," she said. "She said we can pick up the cakes either tomorrow night about eight, or Saturday morning at seven-thirty. They're going to freeze them either way, and even if we pick them up in the morning, they'll thaw by the time brunch and the renewal is over."

"You're still going to come?"

"Of course," Ginny said, sighing. She sat up, glad when Minnie and Uncle Joe came padding over and curled into her side. They were warm and comforting, and she did love her little dogs.

"Mother isn't going to decide what I do anymore," she said. "It's taken far too long for me to get to this place at all." She turned to look at Cayden, intending to tell him she loved him. She'd said the words before to another man. She knew how they felt in her mouth, and she knew how they sounded in her voice.

Their eyes met, and Ginny offered him a smile. "I love you, Cayden."

Before she'd even finished saying those four words, he

started shaking his head. "No," he said, standing up. He paced away from her, and that so wasn't the reaction she'd been expecting.

"What?" she asked.

"I'm not going to come between you and Sweet Rose," he said. "I'm so stupid." His cowboy boots clunked against the floor as he strode into the kitchen. "*We're* stupid. This isn't some little game. This is a hundred-billion-dollar business that *you* run. That you've ran for *two decades*."

He came back into the living room and knelt right in front of her. "No. You're not giving that up."

"It's out of my hands," she said. "I made my choice. I always knew Mother would follow through."

"This is insane," he said. "Are you even listening to yourself?" His eyes harbored a wild edge Ginny didn't like. "I'm not worth giving anything up."

Her heart started to pound, mostly because it sounded like he was going to break up with her. "Cayden, my brothers will give it back to me once Mother dies."

"In what? Five years? Ten? Fifteen? She's only seventy-seven, Ginny. She could live for *twenty* more years. Then what? You'll run a whiskey distillery, event center, and a dozen annual events when *you're* almost seventy?"

He shook his head and straightened again. "No. No, no, no." He paced away from her again, and Ginny got to her feet too.

"What are you saying?" she asked.

He stopped, his back to her. She watched those powerful, sexy shoulders lift as he drew in a breath. Pause as he held it. Lower and deflate as he released the air in his lungs. He turned back to her, his face a carefully arranged mask she could not see through.

"It's not only your choice," he said, his voice strong and steady. "I'm going to do what your mother asked me to."

"Cayden," she said, true fear pinching her lungs. "Don't do that."

"You're not losing everything because of me. It's idiotic. It's not smart business." He shook his head, the emotion sliding away as easily as if he'd shaken it off. "I don't think we should see each other anymore."

"No," she said, just as he had. "No, that's not going to work for me."

He simply looked at her, and Ginny found herself grasping for straws. "I have to come to the vow renewal. I'm in charge of all the cakes."

"I can ask my mother—"

"No," she said again, louder this time. "No. I'm going to do it. Beth ordered from Whiskey Cakes because it's my brother's company. I'm going to pick up those mini bundt cakes tomorrow night, and I'm going to make sure they're beautiful for that vow renewal on Saturday."

Cayden looked away, and Ginny wanted to rage at him. How could he give up on them, especially after what she'd said to him only five minutes ago?

How?

"If you'd like to break up with me, can you please have the decency to wait until Saturday, after the vow renewal?"

"I don't *want* to break up with you."

"Then don't."

"Some things are bigger than a relationship," he said.

"No, they're not," she said. "You used the wrong word, Cay. It's not a relationship. It's love. Nothing is bigger than love. Sweet Rose is not more important than love."

He dropped his chin to his chest, his cowboy hat coming between them. He stayed quiet for so long, Ginny was sure he'd changed his mind. He finally shook his head and said, "I can't do it, Ginny. I'm sorry."

He started for the front door, and shock had rooted Ginny's feet to the floor and rendered her voice silent.

"I'm sorry," he said again, and that got her to thaw.

"Please," she said, hurrying after him. "Don't do this. If you walk out that door, I will lose everything I want. Absolutely everything."

Couldn't he see that? Couldn't he see that he was who she wanted? If he couldn't she didn't know how to make it more plain.

She'd said *I love you*. She'd just told him he was everything she wanted.

He held her gaze for a few seconds, then twisted the doorknob. "I'll come help you with the cakes tomorrow night. You said eight?"

She nodded, her fingers curled into fists. Her fingernails pressed into her palms, and that pain kept her sobs at bay.

"See you then," he said, and in the next blink, he was gone. The door clicked closed.

Ginny collapsed onto the couch and curled into herself, hugging a pillow as her anguish and agony rolled through her and spilled out of her mouth and eyes.

The worst part was she didn't know if he'd broken up with her or not.

～

"More citrus blossoms," Olli said, putting another basket inside the empty one. "Spur's bringing the lavender and pansies."

"Thank you," Ginny said without looking up. She'd been working for about thirty minutes, and she'd beautified about two-thirds of the miniature bundt cakes.

"Can I help?" Olli asked, and Ginny knew that tone.

"Of course," she said anyway. She couldn't deny her best friend, and she found she didn't even want to. She'd always made people work really hard to be her friend, and no one had tried harder than Olli. Once Ginny had let her inside the inner circle, they'd been closer than ever.

"I don't know what's going on," Olli said. "I can simply feel your misery."

Ginny just nodded, carefully placing a pretty white citrus blossom on a chocolate cake.

"Do you want to tell me?"

"Can I come over tonight and do it?" She lifted her head and met Olli's eyes. They swam with concern, and Ginny grabbed her in a hug before she could burst into tears.

"Yes," Olli said. "Of course you can come over tonight." She held Ginny tightly and refused to let go. "I'll kick Spur out, and we'll make whatever kind of cookies you want. I'll burn all my good juju candles, and everything will be fine."

Ginny nodded against her best friend's shoulder. "I want the triple chocolate chunk."

"I'll send Spur to get the ingredients after the renewal."

Ginny calmed, finally realizing what she could feel against her stomach. She yanked herself away from Olli, her mind racing as her eyes widened. "Olli." She sucked in a breath as she looked at her midsection. It was definitely swollen, and Ginny had felt the hard bump of it. "You're pregnant."

Olli's whole face lit up. She nodded, her eyes turning glassy. "I wanted to tell you Ginny. I did. We haven't told anyone but my parents and Spur's. Well, he told his brothers at the wedding a month or so ago. It's just...I'm high-risk because of my age, and I wanted to make sure I wouldn't lose the baby."

Ginny exhaled, the sound soft and full of awe. "Can I?"

She reached out toward Olli, hesitating before she touched her.

"Yes. Of course."

Ginny put her hand against Olli's baby bump, so many things in her life aligning. At the same time, the harsh reminder of what she'd never have sliced through her like a hot, sharp knife. Her smile wobbled, and she wasn't sure if it had come from joy or pain.

"I'm sorry," Olli said. "I also didn't want to tell you, because I thought it might upset you."

Ginny shook her head, her tears falling softly. "I'm not upset." She pulled her hand back and looked Olli in the eyes. "You're my best friend. I love you, and I want you to be happy. I'm thrilled for you and Spur." She gathered her into a hug again. "Just thrilled."

"Thank you, Ginny," Olli whispered. "What happened with Cayden?"

Ginny pressed her eyes closed, wondering how she had the strength to even be where she was. Surrounded by Chappells, another happily-ever-after that wasn't hers right in front of her face.

"He wants to break up with me," she said, stepping back and returning her gaze to the bundt cakes. She'd promised Beth they'd be perfect, and they were going to be. Ginny didn't deliver anything but perfection.

"What? Why?" Olli asked.

"Mother found out I've been seeing him," she said.

"She took me out of the will, and I'm not sure what her plan is, but when she confronts me, I'll lose Sweet Rose."

"No." Olli pulled in a breath and covered her mouth with her hand.

"Pansies," Spur said, putting the bowl on the table. "Lavender."

"Thank you," Ginny said, her voice as proper and poised as always.

"What's goin' on here?" he asked.

"Nothing," Ginny said at the same time Olli said, "Your brother is going to break up with her."

"What? Why?"

Ginny smiled, wondering if they noticed their separate reactions had been identical.

"Because he is a stupid, stupid man." Olli paced way from the table. "Where is he? I need to talk to him."

"Don't, Olli," Ginny said, keeping her head down as she picked up a delicate purple flower and added it to a carrot cake. "Help me finish these so you can get off your feet."

"I don't get why Cayden would break up with you," Spur said. "He's in love with you."

Ginny laughed, the sound high-pitched and somewhat cruel. "I can assure you, Mister Chappell, that he is not." She did throw Spur a glare then, and she poured all of her disdain and annoyance into it.

"I'm Mister Chappell now?"

"You're not helping," Olli said.

"Why am I not helping?" he asked. "Wouldn't she like to know he loves her?"

Olli shook her head as she put a leaf of lavender next to the citrus blossom Ginny had already put on the cake.

"I love how rustic the lavender is," Ginny said, and she wasn't sure if it was a beautiful moment to find joy in something so small, or pathetic that she'd chosen to focus on a sprig of lavender when her entire life was crumbling around her.

"He does love you, Ginny," Spur said.

Ginny stopped working and looked at Spur. Those Chappells had strong genes, and she could see so much of Cayden in him. "He has a terrible way of communicating it then," she said coolly. "I told him right to his face that I loved him, and do you know what he said to me?"

Spur swallowed and glanced at Olli, who likewise stared at Ginny with wide eyes. "What?"

"No," Ginny said, barking out the word. "That's what he said, Mister Chappell. *No.*" She bent over the cakes again. "So you'll pardon me if I don't believe you. Also, yes, right now, you need to be Mister Chappell to me. Otherwise, I actually think my head will explode and my heart will crack right in half." Her voice broke on the last word, as if proving her point.

She placed a pink flower on a vanilla bean cake. "Please," she added in a whisper. "I just want to get these cakes perfect for Beth." She added another pansy, this one in yellow, and Olli put on a blue one, completing the little vanilla cake to perfection.

"Go on, Spur," she said a moment later. "I'll stay with her."

"I'm real sorry, Ginny," Spur said. "Honestly, I am."

She could only nod, pick up another citrus blossom, and place it just-so on a chocolate bundt.

Twenty minutes later, she and Olli had all the cakes decorated with edible flowers. They spiraled on a circular table, climbing up a circular staircase Tam had carved out of wood to the very top tier, where Ginny carefully placed a vanilla cake completely drenched in flowers, a little cowgirl bride and cowboy groom poking out of the blooms.

She sighed and stood back, the wedding "cake" the most wonderful thing she'd ever created. "I love it."

"It's gorgeous," Olli agreed, slinging her arm around Ginny's waist.

"Oh, my goodness," Beth said as she entered the room. "Look at that." She took a few hesitant steps toward it. "It's like the whole table is the wedding cake." She turned and looked at Olli and Ginny, her bright, brown eyes filling with tears. She engulfed them both in a hug, and Ginny closed her eyes and held Beth, a smile on her face.

She wanted to be Beth's friend too. She wanted to belong to these women.

You don't, though, she thought, and she let Beth go as she stepped back. "Get over there by it," Beth said as she pulled out her phone. "I want a picture with the masterpiece and the artists themselves."

Ginny giggled and stood with Olli next to the table-cake. Beth snapped pictures, her face full of joy. "Okay," she said. "I'll text these to you guys. I better go get dressed."

"Yes," Ginny said. "You can't renew your vows in jeans and a tank top."

Beth grinned at her, thanked her again, and bustled down the hall.

"That reminds me," Olli said. "You said you'd help me pick a blouse for today…" She looked at Olli with apprehension in her gaze. "I've got them in the front room."

"Let's go," Ginny said, as she loved to dress Olli, who really had the worst fashion sense on the planet. It was something Ginny adored about her, and as she considered the two choices Olli had brought, Ginny prayed her best friend would always have room in her life for a spinster.

"The emerald one," she said. "It'll be gorgeous with your hair."

"Emerald," Olli said with a scoff. "It's *green*, Ginny. Just green." She grinned at Ginny, and the two of them laughed together. Ginny sure did love Olli, but she couldn't quite remember a time when that friendship love was enough.

She knew now what it felt like to have a man like Cayden, and she wanted to share her life, the inside jokes, the good news, and the bad, with *him*.

Later, Ginny snuck out of the party before it was quite over. Lawrence and Duke had said they'd take down the tiers and clean up the table, and Ginny saw no reason to torture herself by staying in the same room with Cayden when they weren't speaking to each other.

Beth and Trey had renewed their vows at the ranch where they lived, and that was only a twenty-minute drive from the country house. Exhaustion pulled through Ginny's muscles and neck as she drove home. She simply wanted a chocolate-shell ice cream bar, a hot bath, and a pair of elastic-waist pants.

She wanted to lock all the doors and curtain all the windows. She'd turn off her phone and hunker down. If Cayden couldn't talk to her, he couldn't break up with her.

"That's not true," she muttered to herself. When they'd stopped talking at the beginning of the year, they were definitely not together.

She turned off the highway and onto the dirt lane that led back to the house. Once around the bend and past the trees, she slammed on the brakes, bringing her SUV to a sudden and complete stop.

A shiny red sedan sat in front of the country house, and it didn't belong to Drake.

It belonged to Sydney, Mother's assistant.

"She's here," Ginny said, her voice hollow and her fingers strangling the steering wheel.

19

Cayden wiped down the counter next to the fridge, glad the festivities for the day had ended. The work he needed to do that day wasn't, but he'd learned to compartmentalize as an early teenager once his father had really started laying on the chores.

With school, family, friends, and all the responsibilities heaped on him, Cayden made methods and systems for himself that he'd been using for three decades.

He tossed the rag into the sink just as Trey and Beth, along with Blaine and Tam, came into the farmhouse through the back door. They were all talking at the same time, and that was Cayden's cue to get out of there.

"This is all clean," he said as Trey set a stack of dirty cake plates in the sink Cayden had just emptied. If he'd have done that at the homestead after Cayden had spent twenty minutes cleaning, he'd have said something. As it was, this wasn't his house, and he'd just been trying to help. A healthy pounding of annoyance ran through him, though.

He could've left twenty minutes ago. Heaven knew he had plenty to do that afternoon.

"Thanks," Trey said, his smile fading. "Are you taking off?"

"Yes," Cayden said. "I have to go over the menus for the Smash. I'm meeting with Bryson on Monday morning."

"We wanted to talk to you," Blaine said, closing in on Cayden's other side.

He flinched away from the voice and the proximity of his brother. "I don't think that's going to work for me," Cayden said.

"Seems like nothing's working for you these days," Trey said.

Cayden wasn't going to do this. The kitchen in the farmhouse was huge, and all he had to do to get away from Trey and Blaine was back up. He did, going all the way until his back met the island behind him. "It was a great party."

"Especially that cake display," Beth said.

Cayden dang near rolled his eyes. Did they think ending things with Ginny was easy for him? He didn't see how it was any of their business. When Blaine had finally broken off his engagement with his ex-fiancée, Cayden hadn't asked him a single question. He'd waited for his brother to come to him.

Even then, Blaine's pain had been heart-wrenching.

Cayden took a breath, his lungs shuddering with the effort. "I have to end things with her," he said quietly, his eyes stuck on the glowing digital clock on the stove. "If she stays with me, she'll lose Sweet Rose Whiskey."

"She's a grown woman," Trey said. "I think she knows what she's doing."

"She knows what she wants," Blaine added, smartly keeping his back to Cayden as he started rinsing plates.

"It makes no sense," Cayden said, realizing they'd somehow gotten him to start talking. Sneaky. "It doesn't matter. I don't have time to talk right now." He sidestepped Trey, who wouldn't stop glaring at him, and strode along the length of the island and toward the wide, arched doorway that led into the front of the house.

As if Trey had any room to talk at all. He'd moved back to the homestead for a little while when he and Beth weren't getting along. Everyone had hard times; the difference here was that Cayden couldn't see a way for him to be with Ginny that didn't require her to sacrifice everything.

Surprisingly, no one tried to stop him. Beth kept quiet, though Cayden saw something in her eye that suggested she had plenty to say. He was sure she did. She adored Ginny, as did everyone, himself included.

A great sigh filled his chest as he left the farmhouse,

and his boots clunked down the front steps at a fast clip as he almost ran away from his family. Once inside the safety of his truck, he took another deep breath.

The scent of Ginny's perfume came with the air, and he wished he could expel all the air right back out. Instead, he breathed in again, getting that bright citrusy flavor of her shampoo, with the undertones of flowers and soap.

"I don't know what to do," he said aloud as he backed out of the spot where he'd parked. "If someone would tell me how she can be with me and still keep her company, I'd do it." Deep desperation lodged in his throat, and it wouldn't budge no matter how he tried to clear it away.

Back at Bluegrass Ranch, he opened the mini-fridge they kept in the conference room and took out two bottles of ice-cold water. He drank half of one before he realized swallowing wouldn't rid him of the panic and desperation either.

Perhaps work would. Cayden had drowned out other unpleasant things in his life by simply working hard enough for long enough. He entered his office, closed the door behind him, and locked it. He made sure all the lights were off before stepping over to the blinds and closing those too.

Completely sequestered in his office, he finally started to relax a little bit. If he didn't go home tonight, though, Lawrence would know right where to find him. Everyone would.

"Doesn't matter," he said, pushing everything out of his mind. "You need to get the menus tallied. Do that. Then you can do something else."

He sat down behind his desk and swiveled in his big executive chair to get the expandable files from the counter behind him. With all the printed menus in his hand, he turned back to his computer. He loved doing things digitally, but with something this large, that needed to be done absolutely right, he set about printing any menus that had been emailed to him.

He printed the master list of who'd rented the suites that had optional catering, and he systematically checked off each one as he looked at their menu to make sure he had every single one.

Mariah and Lawrence had come through, and all the menus were accounted for.

Next, he printed the master list of meals, drinks, sides, and à la carte items that had been offered to their guests. With a pen in his hand, and his concentration only on the menu in front of him, he began marking each item that had been ordered.

When he finished a menu, he put down his black pen and picked up a red one. A check-mark went at the top of the paper, and it got put face-down in a separate pile.

He worked steadily, his mind wandering from time to time. He had enough mental strength to rein it in every time it did, though, and he got up from his desk after an hour had passed.

He stretched his arms above his head, left and right, and bent over to touch the floor. He'd been working behind a desk for long enough to know he couldn't sit in one spot for much longer than an hour. His attention-span wouldn't allow it either.

Stretched and hydrated, he sat back down and finished the menus. Chef Bryson would have a list of individual ingredients needed for each item on Cayden's sheet, and he'd put in the food order on Monday afternoon once they'd met.

"What else?" Cayden asked, refiling the menus with his tally sheet. "Income from that." He pulled the tally sheet back out and swung back around to his desk.

On and on he worked. When one task got completed, he immediately found another one that needed doing. He simply couldn't have a single moment where he allowed himself to think too hard about Ginny Winters.

He hadn't explicitly broken up with her, but he'd be shocked if she called or texted him in the future. "Other than business," he muttered to himself. She was sponsoring the Smash, and Sweet Rose Whiskey had bought the corporate suite attached to the Bonfire Room on the second floor.

"Doesn't matter," he said, lifting his shoulders up tall. He wouldn't have to see her on race day. They'd already planned on him being extraordinarily busy, which was why she'd bought the suite and invited her family, friends, and employees.

She'd be welcome in the Chappell's corner of the arena too, and Cayden found himself smiling when he realized how much everyone loved Ginny.

He froze, realizing he'd been thinking about her, and he cleared his throat and tried to push her out of his head.

She refused to go, though, and while he could get ten or fifteen seconds of Ginny-free thoughts, she kept showing up.

He finally leaned away from his computer, a growl for himself in the back of his throat.

When he flipped over his phone, he saw half a dozen notifications, from calls to texts to social media icons.

Spur had called three times, and the voicemail notification winked up at Cayden.

"I don't want to talk," he said. "Isn't that obvious?"

Sometimes he really hated being a Chappell. Like a bolt of lightning, he realized now why Blaine had simply loaded up in his truck and crossed state lines. The urge for Cayden to do the same had him standing up and tucking his phone in his pocket like he'd go right now.

As his brain caught up to reality, he sat back down. He had more responsibilities here than Blaine had had at the time. The Summer Smash was in just three weeks, and Cayden couldn't just skip town because he'd broken up with his girlfriend.

None of the owners he'd booked would care. None of the twelve thousand people who'd bought tickets for the race would care. Heck, when it came right down to it,

Spur wouldn't care. The Smash was meant to bring awareness to Bluegrass Ranch, produce profit—a healthy six-figure profit, though Cayden wanted seven-figure profit—and get more people onto the ranch for future events.

He'd been working toward the Smash for six months; he didn't get to stop because he'd fallen in love with Ginny Winters and had an extremely hard decision to make.

"You made it," he said, getting up from his chair. He just needed a break, and he moved over to the couch and stretched out on it, holding his phone up above his head as he read the texts.

Spur wanted to know where he'd gone. He'd invited everyone over to Olli's for games and pizza that night on the brother's group text, and then he'd invited Cayden specifically.

The words, *Ginny won't be there*, stood out to Cayden, and he pressed his eyes closed. They burned with his exhaustion, and he put his phone against his chest and just focused on breathing in and out. If he could just do that over and over, maybe the complete agony streaming through him would eventually go away.

～

CAYDEN WOKE ALL AT ONCE, SOMETHING LOUD BRINGING HIM out of unconsciousness. His neck ached, and a pinch of pain radiated through his back.

Pounding on his door told him that was what had

awakened him, and he sat up slowly so as to not further aggravate his back. He leaned over his knees, trying to get the ache out and his heartbeat to calm down.

"Cayden," Lawrence called, but Cayden didn't get up to open the door. Darkness drenched the whole office, and if he didn't make any noise, Lawrence would have no reason to think he was there.

He wasn't sure why he wanted to be alone, only that he did.

More than one voice came through the door, muted and low so Cayden didn't know what his brothers were saying.

Doesn't matter, he thought, and he decided to adopt it as his new life motto. He'd said it enough that day alone to make it one.

He'd have to face everyone soon enough, but it didn't have to be today.

No one knocked again, and the voices retreated. He knew they'd be worried about him, and he should appreciate that. He didn't need one of them calling the cops, so he quickly navigated back to Spur's individual text string and started typing a response.

After he'd sent the apology and excuse that he'd fallen asleep, he watched the text pop up with the time above it.

He pulled in a breath. It was almost midnight. No wonder his brothers were worried about him. Spur wasn't one to stay up late, and Cayden put the same message in the brothers' string, knowing at least Lawrence was awake.

Messages started pouring in through that group text, from Lawrence, Conrad, Duke, and Blaine. Spur said nothing, which meant the man had gone to bed.

"Guess not everyone is all that worried," Cayden said. As soon as he said it, the phone rang, and Spur's name sat there.

Cayden couldn't ignore it; he'd literally just texted. With a sigh, he swiped on the call. "Hey."

"Where are you? Are you okay?"

"I'm perfectly fine," Cayden said. "I just fell asleep, that's all."

"He's fine," Spur said, clearly not to him. "I mean, I'm sure he's not fine. I'm sure he's absolutely devastated, but he's alive."

Cayden allowed a small smile to touch his lips. "I'm not on speaker, am I?"

"No," Spur said.

"You're relaying everything to Olli, though."

Scuffling came through the line, and Spur said, "Give me a sec." He clearly covered the speaker and said something to his wife, and then he was on the move. "It's a good thing you didn't come tonight," he whispered. "Ginny did end up coming after Olli told her you weren't there, and she is a mess."

"I don't want to hear about it." Cayden was surprised

at the strength in his words, but they were true. "I know exactly how she probably is, and I've made my choice."

"I respect that," Spur said. "I do. We all do, but Cayden... did you really tell her no when she said she loved you?"

"She told you that?"

"Oh, I was pressurin' her about the two of you, and she got in my face." He sighed, and Cayden didn't want to keep him up. Tomorrow was Sunday, but the ranch needed care every single day of the week. "It was my fault. I don't think she'd have said anything otherwise."

"I don't know how to explain it," Cayden said. "I really don't. It's a very difficult situation, and I am not going to allow her to give up something that is her birthright and something she's literally worked on and for over the past thirty years of her life." He shook his head, his determination hardening as he spoke. "I'm not. Not for me."

"Even if she wants to?"

"How could a person really want that?" he demanded. "That's just stupid."

"So you think she's stupid?"

"No," Cayden said, his anger calming after the flare. "No, of course not."

"That's the message you're giving her."

Cayden couldn't control how Ginny felt. He sighed and hung his head. "Why did she come over?"

"Her mother was at the country house when she showed up after the vow renewal."

Cayden got to his feet. "Really?" In his mind, when Ginny admitted to their relationship, he stood at her side, his hand steady and strong in hers. They'd face Wendy Winters—and their future—together, because they *belonged* together, and if her mother couldn't see it, that was her problem.

I belong with her, he thought. *I love her.*

Horror filled him and he sank back to the couch, Spur saying something he didn't hear. All he could hear was a shrieking sound in his ears that made his chest tighten with every passing second.

"I have to go," he blurted, and he pulled the phone from his ear while Spur said, "Check in tomorrow. You're in the state, right?"

"Yes," Cayden said. "I'll check in." He hung up and got to his feet again. A couple of steps got him to the desk, and he snapped on the lamp there. It was far too late to go to Ginny's house. He wasn't even sure where she'd be.

He pressed one of his hands to his eyes, trying to think of what he could do right now.

"You need a plan," he said. "But do you really?" He paced to the locked door and touched it. "Maybe you just get in the truck and go find her." He had no idea what he'd even say to her, and the way his mind circled without grabbing onto any one thought wasn't comforting.

"It's too late to go find her," he said. "You'll scare her, and that's the last thing she needs." He paced back and forth. "Okay, plan."

All he could come up with was a Swiss cheese and spinach quiche, which was one of Ginny's favorite foods. He'd brought her the treat once or twice when she had to go into the office early.

He could take her that tomorrow and beg her to forgive him for being so stupid. Technically, they hadn't broken up yet. She'd asked him to wait until today, and he hadn't done it. He had watched her sneak out of the farmhouse without going after her. Maybe that was as good as a break-up.

Cayden sat at his desk again, waking his computer with a couple of clicks on the mouse. Then he started to plan.

~

"And that's where I am," he said the next morning, the cheese and spinach quiche on the table between him and his parents. "She wasn't at the country house or the mansion on Virginia Lane." He hung his head and picked at the blueberry muffin his mother had put on a plate for him. Daddy was eating the quiche, because someone should. "I didn't dare go to her mother's house."

Neither his father nor mother said anything, and Cayden looked up. "Tell me what to do."

"Oh, baby, we can't tell you that," Mom said. "I can see why you felt the way you did though. She shouldn't have to give up her company to be with you."

"It's crazy," he said. "Do I go ask Olli where she is? Call her brothers?" How desperate did he want to be? The truth was, he *was* desperate, and maybe Ginny needed to know. He took out his phone. "I'm going to call Olli."

"That's right," Mom said with a smile. "You go find her, son. Tell her how you feel. That's what she wants."

"Probably *all* she wants," Daddy said, forking up another bite of quiche.

Cayden nodded, his hard feelings of refusal from the past few days melting into foolishness once again.

"Cayden," Olli said. "Hey. You realize I'm in church, right?"

"Sorry," he said, getting up from the table. His nervous energy wouldn't allow him to sit still for very long. "I actually have no idea what time it is. I'm trying to find Ginny." He moved into the kitchen and looked out the window. "Do you know where she is?"

"I'm sorry," she whispered. "I don't. She left my house this morning before dawn. I wasn't even up."

Cayden sighed and nodded. He hadn't known she'd stayed at Olli's last night, but that made sense. She'd told him once that she always called Olli in times of emergency. "Okay, thanks."

"Spur might have seen her. I'll have him text you."

"Okay." Cayden hung up and immediately started thumbing through his contacts. Ginny had given him Elliot's number when she'd said he might be interested in having the Whiskey Cakes food truck at the Smash.

"Please, Lord," he whispered as he found the name and tapped on it. "I know I messed up. I acknowledge what I did wrong. I need to fix it, but I can't do that if I can't find Virginia Winters."

"Amen," Mom said as she joined him at the counter to refill her coffee mug.

The line started to ring, and Cayden kept praying. He'd buy a thousand quiches and drive any number of miles to get to Ginny. He just needed to know where she was.

20

Ginny turned to stir the crisping bacon, moving from one task to the other easily. She loved having time and energy to cook. After she'd left Olli's house that morning, Ginny had called one of her real estate acquaintances and said only a few words, "I need a rental I can be in today. What have you got?"

Mother had frozen her business accounts, but Ginny had plenty of money in her personal accounts that Mother couldn't touch. She didn't even know about them, and she'd thought she'd cut Ginny off from everything. When she'd run from Drake's country house yesterday, Ginny let her believe that.

She'd let her tower over her and lecture her. She'd let her say harsh and cruel things. None of it mattered. Nothing hurt more than Cayden's departure from her life, and Ginny was done caring what her mother thought of her.

Thankfully, Karyn had three houses that were available for immediate lease, and Ginny had chosen the one with the biggest gardens, the largest kitchen, and that sat the furthest from Dreamsville.

She could still get back to Olli's in half an hour, but she had no plans to do that. Her plans only included this baked potato salad she was currently putting together, a romantic comedy she hadn't watched yet, and staying in the silk pajamas she'd bought on her way to sign the rental agreement for the house.

She'd left the country house with only the clothes on her back, her purse, and her dogs. "Yes, I couldn't leave you three behind, could I?" she cooed at the pups. Uncle Joe was the bravest of them, and he got to his feet and dared to come into the kitchen.

"Out," she said with a smile, though she understood the siren's call of bacon. She loved it herself, and she couldn't wait for it to be brown and crisp so she could taste the salty bits.

After signing the lease, she'd stopped at a big department store and grocery in Jeffersonville, and she hadn't seen a single person she knew. She had dog food now, and new bowls, fresh towels, her favorite shampoo and conditioner, plenty of toothpaste, and more carbs in the house than she'd eaten in a year.

She hummed to herself as she turned back to the

cutting board and kept dicing the potatoes into half-inch chunks. The tune was melancholy, and it took her a few seconds to realize it was one of the hymns she'd learned over the months as she'd attended church with Cayden.

Instant tears pressed behind her eyes, and she fought against them. She'd felt like this before, but she wasn't sure she'd recover this time.

She'd loved Darrel Brown, and Mother had deemed him inadequate. Ginny had let her, as satisfying her mother was far more important than love at age thirty-five. She'd done it again when she'd fallen for Oliver Hansen.

With two broken hearts in her thirties, Ginny had taken a break from dating for a few years. As time wore on and she continued to heal, she'd started to think she'd never find someone who would want her as she was and that who could meet Mother's expectations.

She'd learned that no one could meet Mother's expectations, not even her.

"Tell me what to do," she said as she scooped up the last of the potatoes and put them in the huge glass measuring bowl with the others. "I will do it. My time is yours, Lord. I have nothing to offer but that."

She turned to the stove and poured the potatoes into the boiling water. She stirred the bacon. She got out the broccoli and began tearing it into tiny trees. The Lord did not tell her what to do with her time, and Ginny's frustration grew as she continued working in the kitchen.

Surely God wanted her to do more than spend her time and money cooking in someone else's house. Alone.

With the potato salad finished and in the fridge to chill, Ginny went into the master bedroom, which was a cozy room with big, muted watercolor paintings on the wall above the bed. She smiled at them, the crazy idea that she should learn to paint with watercolors moving through her thoughts.

As she climbed into bed, she asked, "Is that what I'm supposed to do? Take a watercolor class?"

She started a movie on her tablet but used her new phone to search for watercolor classes in Jeffersonville. There weren't any—but there was one in Dreamsville, with a woman named Barbara Delaney.

"Barb, of course," Ginny said, exiting from her Internet browser. She knew Barb, because she had a son who had two children with special needs. They'd come to the private children's event last July at Ginny's personal request.

She didn't have any of her old numbers in this new phone, so she had to go into her email client and the contacts there to find Barb's number. She dialed, ready to charm her way into whatever class she could. She had no idea why, but it was literally the only thought that had come to her since she'd asked the Lord for help.

"Hello?" Barb answered.

"Barb," she said. "It's Ginny Winters." She felt herself slipping into her fake persona, and she yanked herself right back out. She wasn't going to talk in that false tone, and she wasn't going to act like everything was peachy when it wasn't.

"Ginny, dear," Barb said in such a pleasant tone that relief rushed through Ginny. At the same time, tears flowed down her face. Barbara Delaney was the picture-perfect grandmother. She could be Ginny's mother, and Ginny wished she was with the power of gravity.

What would it be like to have a kind parent? One she could turn to when life got hard and she needed somewhere soft to fall?

As it was, she had only one place to go when that happened: Olivia Hudson.

"Are you there?" Barb asked, and Ginny sobbed.

"Yes," she said, her voice broken. "I'm here."

"Ginny, my dear, what's the matter?"

She drew in a shuddering breath, feeling some strength come back to her. Her mind slowed enough to remember the things the pastor had said all these weeks. She wasn't worthless. No matter where she existed in the journey, the Lord wanted her to come to Him.

She would always be enough for Him.

"I wondered if you'd give me some painting lessons," she said, smoothing her voice out by the end of the sentence.

Barb remained quiet, and Ginny thought she'd probably scared her with the sobbing and now she didn't know how to respond. She finally said, "I'm sure I can, dear. Do you want private lessons or a group class?"

"Group is probably fine," she said, not wanting to be a burden. "How many are in a group?"

"Six, and I have a new group starting on Thursday that has a spot, if you'd like it."

"I would," Ginny said, smiling through her tears. "Thank you, Barb."

They continued to chat about the details of the class, and then a pause filled the line. "I just made two apple pies," Barb said. "I'd love to bring you one."

"I'd like that too," Ginny said. "However, I'm not home right now. I'm...out of town for a few more days."

"Okay," Barb said. "You're sure you're okay?"

"I am," she said. "Really. Thanks, Barb." She ended the call as quickly as she could after that and laid back on her pile of pillows.

The romantic comedy played in front of her, but she focused on the rough texture of the ceiling above her. "Really, Lord? Watercolor classes? What is that supposed to do for me?"

She amended the question quickly—the class wasn't for her. It was for the Lord.

She also couldn't leave Olli and her family in the dark. She'd promised them all that she'd let them know she was okay, and she quickly tapped out two messages. One for Olli, saying, *Here's my new number. I'm doing good today, and I've made a delicious potato salad I'm going to eat for breakfast, lunch, and dinner for the foreseeable future.*

As she waited for her best friend to respond, she put all three of her brothers into one text and sent them a similar message, minus the reference to potato salad. They responded quicker, as no one in the Winters family ever did much without their phone surgically attached to their hands.

She could feel their love coming through in the messages, and Ginny closed her eyes and said, "Thank you, Lord,"

∼

By Thursday, Ginny had gained at least five pounds, cried herself to sleep each night, and watched more movies than any woman should in only four days' time. She'd spent hours cooking each day too, usually some rich dish with pasta, potatoes, bread, or a lot of cream cheese. She'd taken a nap every day, did not bathe every day, and she'd only spoken on the phone to one person —Olli.

She'd seemed a little bit off—distracted—but Ginny understood that better than most. She was used to having so many tasks on her to-do list she couldn't see straight, but Olli's business was growing by leaps and bounds right now, and she was overwhelmed.

She hadn't said so to Ginny, but she was worried about

what would happen with her perfumery once she had the baby. As Ginny drove along the quiet country road connecting her rental house to Dreamsville, another idea struck her right between the eyes.

"*I* can run Olli's perfumery." She'd never be able to come up with the scents; that was what made Olli special. She paired things no one else ever would. Ginny could oversee production, though. She could label boxes. She could update a website in her sleep.

"Call Olli," she barked to the car, and the cool female voice confirmed the action a moment later.

"Heya, Ginny, I have a meeting in three minutes."

"I only need one," Ginny said, her mind blitzing now. "I need a job, and you need a manager for your perfumery. I know you're worried about running it and expanding and doing all you do now, and you're stressed about what will happen when the baby comes. I can do it, Olli. I'd literally *die* to do it."

Olli scoffed and started to laugh but cut the sound off halfway through. "Wait. What?"

Ginny just waited, because Olli always needed a few extra seconds to string everything together.

"I can't afford you," Olli said. "Even if everything you said is true—and I'm not saying it is—I can't—"

"It *is* true," Ginny said. "And you *can* afford me, because I don't need a salary. At least for the first year. Then, after you see how amazing I am, and when I've taken what you've started and finished it, you'll love me so much and offer me a full-time job—with benefits."

She smiled, though she'd also realized something horribly powerful. She thought she had to work herself to the bone and put on the biggest, best event Dreamsville had ever seen in order to be loved. She had to dress the part, act the part, speak the part, and become a cardboard cutout of herself in order to be loved. She had to achieve perfection in order for her mother to love her, and that was just impossible. No one was perfect. No one.

"Ginny, I already love you," Olli said with a light laugh that told Ginny she didn't understand what Ginny had just discovered. "You don't want to work for me."

"Yes, I do."

A male voice came through the line, and Olli said, "I'm so sorry, babe, but I have to go. Call me later."

"Okay," Ginny said, but the call ended before she could even get the second syllable out. She frowned, because it certainly felt like Olli didn't need her anymore. In the past, she'd have said, "I'll call you later," but now Ginny had to call her.

"You're making stuff up," she said, straightening in her seat. "You can call her; she can call you. It's not a contest to see who does more." She turned up the radio to help drive her poisonous thoughts away, and she finished the drive to Barb's art studio.

She pulled up to the little yellow cottage, frowning at the lack of cars out front. There should be six people in the class, and she certainly wasn't so early that she'd be the only one there. Perhaps she'd gotten the time wrong.

She sat in her SUV and pulled up the website she'd looked at. "Seven o'clock," she said, looking at the dashboard clock. She literally had three minutes to get inside or she'd be late, and yet there wasn't another car in this part of the lot.

She glanced left and right, almost afraid to get out. This was a nice part of town, though, with a coffee shop just down the sidewalk a bit, and a nail salon right next door to that which had plenty of cars out front.

"If there's no class tonight," she told herself as she unbuckled. "You'll go get a pedicure." The drive wouldn't be a loss.

Glancing around as she got out, Ginny didn't see anything nefarious. She crossed to the entrance quickly, and a little bell rang as the door opened under her touch. She stepped inside the art studio, the scent of paint and paper filling her nose.

No one waited to greet her, and Ginny's frown deepened. "Hello?" she called. "Barb?"

The space looked like it was set up for a painting class. Two tables had been pushed end-to-end and covered with white paper. A stack of blank canvases sat on one end, and an easel held another one.

Footsteps came down a hall somewhere, and Ginny looked to the right, where an open door led further into the building. She expected to see Barb Delaney appear, perhaps wearing a brightly colored smock and a smile.

Instead, the clunky footsteps that came closer finally revealed Cayden Chappell. He paused in the doorway, his eyes wide and afraid. When he smiled, everything relaxed, from his shoulders to his expression.

Ginny stumbled backward a step, because seeing him so soon was like reopening the wounds in her soul and pouring acid on them. She had to get out of there right now.

"You are a very hard woman to find when you don't want to be found," he said.

The smooth cadence of his voice calmed her, and she stopped searching for the doorknob behind her.

She drank in the sight of him, and he was cool, soothing water to everything inside her that was overheated and wrong. He still had some questions to answer though, starting with, "What are you doing here?"

21

Cayden swallowed, the sight of Ginny in front of him almost too much for his brain to handle. "I came to ask you if you think you could forgive me."

"I have a painting class tonight," she said.

"Yes," he said. "I've had calls out to literally everyone I know. Everyone Spur knows, and everyone Blaine knows. Oh, and Beth too." He smiled, though she still hadn't yet, and he felt like the ground might disappear beneath his feet at any moment. He straightened his lips. "Once I finally heard that you would be here tonight, I called Barbara Delaney and begged her for thirty minutes alone with you. The class is still happening, but it starts at seven-thirty now."

Ginny's mouth dropped open slightly, and she didn't look thrilled as she shook her head. This so wasn't going how Cayden had pictured it would.

She'd told him she loved him one week ago. Had her feelings changed so fast?

"I'm sorry I hurt you," he said, deciding he better get the most important words out first. "I was an idiot, and you were right, and we belong together."

Ginny folded her arms, her expression masked off.

"I'm in love with you," he said. "I have been for a long time. I hate that I wasn't there at your side when you spoke to your mother. When I heard she was at the country house after the vow renewal, I saw this vision in my head. It was me and you, side-by-side, a united front. Even if she couldn't see it and she didn't allow you to keep Sweet Rose, we'd know how we felt about one another." He gestured between the two of them, even taking a step toward her.

"I messed up. I should've been there. I shouldn't have said no when you said you loved me." He wanted to duck his head in shame, but Trey's voice told him to maintain eye contact and to be strong. "I guess I just...I was worried that you'd wake up one day and realize that I am not worth everything you have to lose to be with me."

"You're not still worried about that?" she asked.

"Honestly? Yeah, I am," he said. "I'm going to try every day, though, Ginny, to be the man you need and want. Every single day." He continued to close the gap between them until he stood right in front of her.

"I love you, Ginny, and you'd make me the happiest man in the world if I could just take you to dinner."

She looked up at him, searching for something. "How'd you find out I signed up for this class?"

"Barbara lives in the same neighborhood as Hugh, Beth's brother. He was just casually talking to her about her art, and she mentioned that she'd finally filled one of her classes, and hey, it was an old friend she hadn't seen for a while who's registered last."

He wanted to reach out and touch her, but he didn't quite dare. "Hugh asked who it was, and she said you, and he called Beth, who told me, and here I am."

Ginny reached out and touched one of the buttons on his shirt. Pure fire licked through him as she said, "Here you are."

"Will you please go to dinner with me sometime?" He carefully and slowly slipped one hand along her hip and around to her back. She definitely lit him up, and Cayden couldn't believe the difference in how he felt right now compared to the dark cloud he'd been operating under for a week now.

Everything was brighter with Ginny in his life. Everything was better. He had so much to live for.

She put her hands on his chest and slid them up to his shoulders. "You don't need to ask me. Just tell me when and where, and I'll be there."

He grinned at her, recognizing those words as ones he'd said to her at the Gems & Gin event. "How set are you on taking this class?" he whispered.

"Well, I'll feel bad if I skip it now," she said. "Barb obviously seemed excited that she'd finally filled a class."

Cayden chuckled, ducking his head to get closer to the scent of Ginny's skin. "I love you," he said. "These past several days have been torture without you. I love you, I love you, I love you." He pressed his lips to her neck, glad when she sighed and leaned into the touch.

"I love you, too, Cayden."

He moved his mouth to hers, the pure heat of love pouring through him.

∼

Cayden was the first one to arrive at the arena on Saturday morning, the day of the Summer Smash finally here. That wasn't that hard to do, because he'd slept in his office. The past couple of weeks had felt like a whirlwind in every respect, from his personal relationships with his brothers, to his improved friendship with his parents, to his love life.

Ginny had been working with him exclusively on the Smash, and they'd started talking about what she might do now that Sweet Rose Whiskey didn't consume her every moment. She'd told him she wanted to work with Olli, and she'd been going over there some mornings.

Olli was resistant for some reason Ginny didn't know, but she'd told Cayden she was working on finding out what the hang-up was.

He'd just put on fresh deodorant and his bright blue shirt and a dark brown checkered tie when someone knocked on his door. "Yep," he said as an indication they could come in. He expected to see Ginny or Mariah, as the knock had been light and feminine.

Instead, a woman he'd never seen before stood there, her long, blonde hair tumbling over her shoulders in precise ways. Cayden stopped fiddling with his belt and adopted his professional demeanor. "Can I help you? The gates for the race don't open until eleven."

"We're not here for the race," she said, her voice quiet but her face fierce. "Well, we are, but not until later. We're aware of what time the gates open." She stepped into his office slightly. "I'm Sydney Terfel, Miss Wendy's assistant. She's asked me to bring her here to speak with you." She glanced around, and Cayden was suddenly embarrassed by the blanket on the couch and the state of his desk. He'd laid everything out again last night, and he, Lawrence, Mariah, and Ginny had tried to find any holes that could cause a leak and sink the ship.

They hadn't been able to find any, and he hadn't cleaned up before joining everyone for dinner in the conference room.

"Is now a good time?" Sydney asked, almost adopting a British accent.

"Sure, okay," Cayden said, though his heart was actually trying to flee from his body. "Let me clean up a little."

"I have to return to the car to get her," Sydney said

with a smile. "She's not a fast walker, either, so you should have a few minutes."

"Great." He reached for the plans he'd spent hours preparing and stacked them neatly while Sydney glided from the room. "Yikes," he said under his breath. How she could work alongside Wendy Winters every day was a mystery to him. Cayden had only met the woman a few times, and she was utterly terrifying.

His hands stuck to the papers as he tried to shove them in the file folder. Sweat ran down the side of his face as he folded the blanket and shoved it in the coat closet. He paused and looked out the window, taking a moment to wipe his face and take a breath.

Ginny had faced her mother alone. Cayden could do it too.

He wasn't sure where Ginny was at the moment, as she'd been renting a house clear up by Jeffersonville. He was the only one who knew that, and he'd promised not to tell anyone, even Olli.

He hadn't been there, because Ginny had been coming to Bluegrass. They lounged on the couch in the living room at the homestead, and Duke had taken control of the kitchen since Blaine's departure. He put out good food too, and Cayden had just started to think about how and when he should propose to Ginny.

Turning back to his desk, a keen sense of calmness and peace descended on him. It didn't matter if his office wasn't spotless. He worked here every day. He'd seen

Ginny's office, and she definitely had papers and piles and products everywhere.

He picked up the clipboard he and Lawrence had put together for today's event, and he flipped to the blue tab which listed all of their top tier guests. He reminded himself that he dealt with rich people every day of the week. Heck, *he* was a rich person; he could handle Wendy Winters.

He heard footsteps coming down the hall, and he set down the clipboard and walked toward the doorway, remembering his not-quite-finished belt buckle. He quickly put that piece in place before stepping into the hallway.

Sydney had her arm laced through Wendy's, and they shuffled down the hallway together. She looked like half the woman she'd been at the New Year's Eve party, and Cayden had the urge to hurry across the distance between them and support Wendy on her left side.

He did just that, saying, "Good morning, ma'am," as he approached. Wendy looked at him with those same powerful eyes Ginny had, but hers were more black than dark blue. She carried more emotion there than Ginny normally did as well, and Cayden could only imagine what she'd experienced in her life to put those feelings there.

She didn't say good morning back, but she did allow him to hook his hand through her elbow. "Ginny says your suite is beautiful," he said, not quite sure where the words had come from. "She showed me all the pictures. I hope I can see it someday."

He looked at Sydney, who simply stared at him as if he'd turned a bright shade of purple and needed immediate medical attention. Her eyes widened and she gave an almost imperceptible shake of her head.

Cayden didn't care. Ginny had already lost Sweet Rose. Wendy had come to him. He wasn't going to apologize for loving her daughter, and he wasn't going to back down from it either.

"Here you go, ma'am," he said, leading her straight to the chair in front of his desk.

"You can go, Sydney," Wendy said as she settled into the chair. She put her oversized purse on her lap as Sydney left the room, pulling the door closed behind her and everything.

Cayden took in the situation for a moment and then he sat behind his desk. He put his forearms flat on it and folded his hands. "What brings you to Bluegrass this morning?"

Wendy looked at him with those dark, deep, dangerous eyes. He had the urge to clear his throat and shift in his seat, but he did neither. He'd sat at this desk and had difficult conversations before, with men and women who meant more to him than Wendy Winters did.

"I would like to speak to my daughter," she said. "No one knows where she is except for you. So I came to see you."

Cayden smiled at her in such a way that said he'd really like to help, but...

"I'm afraid I can't help you," he said.

"You don't know where she is?"

"At the moment? No. She'll be at the Smash today, though, and Sydney said you would be too. I'm sure you can talk to her then."

"Is she living here?"

"No, ma'am," he said pleasantly.

Wendy glanced around the office, her mouth actually turned down. He wondered if she'd practiced that frown before using it in public. "Do you know where she's living?"

"Yes, ma'am."

"You're not going to tell me." She pinned him with a glare, and Cayden's heartbeat stuttered.

"I'd like to," he said. "I would. I want nothing more than for you and Ginny to be on speaking terms. You're her mother, and she loves you. She's just...hurting right now." *Grieving* might be a better word, but Cayden didn't want to give Wendy that much power.

She dropped her eyes to her purse, and Cayden had the sudden flash of thought that she was hurting too.

"Seems like you might be hurting yourself," he said gently.

Wendy's dark eyes flew back to his, and she wasn't happy with his assessment. "I'm fine."

"I'm sure you are," he said crisply. "You always seem

to be, no matter what." He leaned back into his chair. "Kind of like a robot. Uncaring. Cold." He gave her another smile that didn't hold nearly the happiness it had before. "I know exactly the part you play, Miss Winters. Ma'am. I've seen Ginny do it too. It's all fake. You're pretending to be something and someone you're not."

"You don't know me."

"No, I do not," he said. "Though I would like to."

She held his gaze for only another moment before dropping her attention back to her purse. Victory sang through Cayden, but he held back his smile. "I know you're not really cold and uncaring," he said. "I also know you're not okay, but you don't have to admit anything to me."

"I worked for decades to make Sweet Rose and Ginny into what they needed to be." She extracted a plain, white envelope from her bag.

"Sure," Cayden said. "You just forgot one of them is a human being and not a piece of clay."

Wendy looked at him with complete shock covering every inch of her face. "How dare you?"

"I have *eyes*, Miss Winters," he said dryly, realizing he'd gone down a path he shouldn't have. "Are you going to give that to me to give to her?"

Wendy pressed the envelope to her chest, her eye searching his face. She seemed almost wild, but he watched her reel it all back together and cover everything with a perfect mask. How he hated that, but he could see where Ginny got it from.

"Do you really love my daughter?"

"Yes, ma'am," he said quietly, allowing his chin to drop slightly for only a moment. "I sure do, with everything inside me."

Wendy seemed to soften slightly. "Have you been married before?"

"I don't believe you don't already know the answer to any question about me," he said just as quietly and just as powerfully as when he'd declared his love for Ginny. "But no, I haven't been married before. Yes, I have a degree from Tulane. I'm the fourth of eight brothers, and we all live here and run this ranch."

He leaned forward again, something fiery crackling through him. "I spoke to my mother about her relationship with Harvey, and they did *not* have an affair after you two were married. She did *nothing* wrong. *He* pursued *her*, and while that might hurt you, and I sincerely apologize about that, your grudge and cruel behavior because of it is completely unwarranted."

Wendy's eyes widened with every word he spoke, and when he finished, he stood. "I'm so sorry, Miss Winters, but I have a *very* busy day ahead, and I need to get out to the stables to make sure my owners are happy."

Before he could offer to help her stand, another light knock sounded on the door, and this time it opened before he could say anything.

"Cay," Ginny said as she entered. "I've called you twice, and we need you out in the—" She cut off when she finally saw her mother sitting in the chair. "Mother."

Wendy got to her feet, and Cayden reached for Ginny. She didn't have to face her alone this time. Cayden would be right there at her side, the way he'd always envisioned he would be.

22

Ginny quickly crossed the room to Cayden and took his hand. Their eyes met, and he smiled at her as if to say, *No big deal, sweetheart. I'm fine. You're fine. This is fine.*

She swallowed and looked back at her mother. The first thing that came to her mind was to pay her a compliment. Mother loved compliments, and that usually started them off on the right foot.

Ginny held back, because she wasn't the one who'd caused this massive divide between them.

"Your mother was just leaving," Cayden said smoothly, his voice as melodic and perfect as always. "I think she brought something for you, though."

Ginny noticed the envelope in her mother's hand, and her heartbeat started to crash. It was a plain, white envelope, the kind used to mail simple letters and folded bills.

There was no writing that Ginny could see, and it couldn't hold very much as it was very thin.

So not a revised will, Ginny thought. Honestly, at this point, she wasn't sure she'd go back to Sweet Rose, at least not in the same capacity. She'd been enjoying her time in the kitchen and the garden, at Bluegrass Ranch riding Raven, and spending relaxing evenings with the man she loved.

"Do you love him?" Wendy asked.

"Of course," Ginny said instantly as a smile touched her soul. She looked up at Cayden, who had everything put together and ready for the day, right down to his big, shiny belt buckle, and his perfectly perched cowboy hat. The only thing he was missing was the cologne, and surely Mother had just interrupted him a little bit too soon.

"I'm madly in love with him." She smiled as he did, and together, they looked at Mother again. Ginny took a breath and held it for a moment. Then she said, "You don't get to dictate my life to me anymore, Mother. I love him, and he loves me, and just as soon as this Smash is over, we're going to start planning our wedding."

"Is that so?" Cayden whispered, and Ginny bumped into him with her hip.

"That's so, cowboy," she murmured, her mouth barely moving. "I figure with the two of us on the job, it'll be the most spectacular wedding anyone has ever seen in the Bluegrass region."

"No doubt," Cayden said, chuckling.

Ginny basked in the love she felt from him, and such happiness flowed through her that she'd almost forgotten about her mother standing there. She focused on her again, her phone buzzing against her thigh. "My phone is ringing, and we really are terribly busy this morning, Mother. What do you need?"

She took her phone out of her pocket and handed it to Cayden.

He stepped away from her and answered the call with, "Lawrence, we're five minutes out."

Ginny took the few steps to her mother and embraced her, surprised by her actions. There was something healing about the hug, though, and something powerful moved through her. She could only identify it as forgiveness, and she wanted to give that to her mother as freely as she could.

"It's good to see you. Drake said you'd be here today. You know which suite we're in?"

"Sydney has all the details," Mother said, her voice scratchy and low. She hugged Ginny in response, and Ginny hoped she could feel some measure of healing too. Mother broke the embrace and handed Ginny the envelope. "I wanted you to have this."

"What is it?" Ginny started to open the envelope, but her mother's weathered hand came down over her fingers.

"Open it after the race," she said. With that, she turned

and left, calling for Sydney the moment she got to the doorway.

Ginny watched her go, one ear on the conversation Cayden was having with his brother behind her. He finished and came to her side. "What did she say?"

"Nothing," Ginny said, handing him the envelope. "Well, she did say to open this after the race."

"Okay," he said, ripping the flap open. Ginny stared at him, mildly horrified. He didn't seem to notice as he took the single sheet of paper out of the envelope. His eyes moved side to side, and Ginny's nerves, excitement, and fear increased with every second he stayed silent.

"It's the deed to Sweet Rose," he said quietly.

"What?"

"The land deed," he said, tilting the paper for her to see. It was a thicker piece of paper, and definitely colored as if it had been soaking in the amber whiskey Sweet Rose produced. "It has your name on it."

She could see that, right there at the top. "I own it?"

"You own it all," he said. "The entire square where all of your family's houses are. The fields. The distillery." He read from the paper. "The event center located adjacent to the fields, and the one downtown." He looked up. "Sweet Rose has an event center downtown?"

Ginny couldn't get her mind to work fast enough to answer his question. Owning the land wasn't the same as having authority to run the company. Mother had to give that, because Mother…owned the land.

She took the piece of paper from Cayden and studied it. "Yes," she finally said when she got to the line about the downtown event center. "We own the Palisades Theater." She looked up. "I'm so confused."

"We need to talk to Harvey, Elliot, and Drake," Cayden said. "But I'm afraid Lawrence is going to lose his mind if we don't get out to the stables in the next, oh, two minutes."

"Let's go," Ginny quickly refolded the deed and slipped it back into the envelope. She tossed that onto Cayden's desk and turned to leave the office.

"You're just going to leave it there?" he asked.

"Yes," she said, turning back. "What would you like me to do with it?"

"It's your entire family fortune," he said. "I don't think it should just sit on the desk like a piece of trash." He picked it up and put it in a drawer. "I'll put it in this locked drawer."

He approached and took her hand, and Ginny didn't know how to say what was revolving through her mind. "Cayden," she said as they exited the building. "What if I don't want it? What if I do want to just toss that deed in the trash and put Sweet Rose behind me?"

"I don't get it," he said.

"I don't either," she murmured. "I just need more time to work through everything."

"Text your brothers," he said. "You guys could have a meeting tonight. Old Ember's. Figure things out."

"No," she said. "You and I have plans for tonight." She took his hand and squeezed it. "Our celebratory plans, remember?"

"I think I said I wanted to collapse on the couch, eat a whole pan of brownies, and deal with final numbers next weekend."

"Exactly," she said. "What do you think I've been whipping up in the kitchen for the past week?" If he'd slept at the homestead, he'd have already seen the eight pans of brownies she'd unloaded onto the kitchen counter a half an hour ago.

She looked at him, and he gazed down at her, a slip of confusion in those handsome eyes. "Brownies," she finally said, swatting at his chest. "I made *brownies*, Cay."

He laughed, stepped in front of her, and stopped walking.

"We're going to be late," she said. "We're already late."

"I don't care," he said, taking her into his arms and leaning down. "I love you, and I need to kiss you right now." He did, and Ginny could barely hang on as the passion and love from his kiss flowed from him and into her.

They'd shared some pretty spectacular kisses in the past, but this one blew them all out of the water. He was rough and insistent, slowing to calm and gentle yet still so intense as to convey how he really felt about her. He knew how to rev her up and pull her back down again, and Ginny loved him for that.

She loved him for his kind heart.
She loved him for his brave spirit.
She loved him for his calm demeanor.
She simply loved him.

∼

"No," Ginny said hours later. "I don't think you should get that roan." She looked at Drake, who hadn't been out of the program for longer than it took to watch a race all afternoon. "He's going to go for too much," she added. "He's not that great."

"He won," Drake said.

"He almost fell out of the starting gate."

"And then *won*." Drake shook his head and looked back at the program. "What about the gray one?"

"There were three gray ones," Ginny said in a deadpan as she got to her feet. "What are you going to do with a racehorse anyway?"

"Race him," Drake called as Ginny went to check on the chips and dips she'd ordered. She found she could hardly sit still during the breaks between races. She wasn't sure why. Mother and Sydney had not come to the Bonfire Room despite the advertisement for lunch.

She could host sixty people between the suite and the dining room, and Sweet Rose employees and friends and family had been in and out all day. She'd paid for a personal host, and it was actually Marcus's job to make sure the chips and dips stayed full and fresh, all the fruit salad got replenished, and any special requests for the buffet got communicated with the kitchen.

Yet Ginny found herself stirring the mandarin oranges, pineapple, and strawberries, her nervous energy too much to be contained. She had not texted her brothers about the deed yet, and as she moved down and picked up a bowl to get herself yet another serving of the banana pudding that had set her taste buds rejoicing, she decided she better.

They'd brought their ideas to her, and she'd listened. They'd do the same for her.

If only you knew what your idea is, she thought. She had an inkling, a very core, but nothing had manifested itself to her quite yet.

With a full bowl of pudding sitting on the table in front of her, she texted her three brothers in one text.

Would love an emergency meeting at your earliest, she said. *I have a new business idea I need help with, and Mother stopped by Cayden's office this morning and gave me the land deed to Sweet Rose. Need help with that, obviously.*

She read over the text and then sent it. Her phone had barely bleeped to indicate that the message had gone through before Drake entered the dining room. "You have the deed?"

Not five seconds later, Elliot rose from his chair overlooking the track. He leaned down as he said something to his wife, kissed her forehead, and came toward her.

Coats and jackets were required in this suite, and he buttoned his as he walked inside.

"I didn't mean right now," Ginny said as she took another bite of her pudding. "Have you guys had this? It's *amazing*."

"Where's Harvey?" Elliot asked, ignoring her question about the pudding.

Drake said, "I'll get a snack and be right back." He went straight to the pudding, and Ginny smiled as her oldest brother came in from the hallway. He brought Sullivan, his fifteen-year-old son with him, and neither of them looked very happy.

As soon as Drake returned with his banana pudding and a plate overflowing with oversized cookies, Harvey asked, "Where's the deed?"

"In Cayden's office," she said, thinking of how she'd just walked away from it. She quickly relayed the story of Mother being in his office and the hug and then the envelope. "I don't know what to do with it."

"You own it now," Harvey said. "There's nothing to do. She not only gave you control of Sweet Rose, but she gave the whole thing to you."

Ginny swirled the spoon through her pudding. "Is that what the estate lawyers will say?"

"It doesn't matter what they say," Harvey said. "They won't have anything to do with it, because your name is on the deed. It's not part of Mother's estate anymore at all."

"The part about who Sweet Rose goes to in the will is null," Drake said. "Right?"

Everyone looked at Harvey, because he'd been a lawyer for the company forever. "Right," he said. "That's right." A slow smile started to seep across his face. "Congratulations, Ginny. I don't think I've ever known someone who beat Mother."

Elliot chuckled, but Ginny didn't feel an ounce of happiness in her soul. She couldn't even put another bite of pudding in her mouth. "What if I don't want it?" She looked up then, employing her bravery and remembering the countless times she'd stared down men just like her brothers. Suited, polished, and smart, her brothers were the businessmen Ginny had been working with for years.

"What?" Elliot asked. "Why wouldn't you want it?"

"I've been thinking about something else," she said. "Though maybe without Mother's constant picking, I'd enjoy my time at Sweet Rose more."

"What's the something else?" Harvey asked.

"Events," Ginny said. "I've loved planning a few simple things in the past couple of months, and I'm really, *really* good at event-planning." She tapped on her phone and swiped to her gallery. "Here's a cake I made for Cayden's brother's vow renewal." She turned the phone so they could see the entire table that had transformed into the cake.

"I want to do that kind of stuff. I want to plan elite events, with spectacular showcases no one has ever seen before." As she spoke, the ideas came, as she'd hoped they would. "I've been helping Cayden with the Smash a lot the past couple of weeks, and I really enjoyed it."

"Because of the event or because of him?" Harvey asked, no trace of teasing in his voice or face.

"Both," Ginny admitted. "I've been thinking about asking him about doing events here at the ranch. I'm going to live here, you know."

"You won't come back to the Avenue?" Elliot asked, and he did look very surprised by that.

"No," Ginny said. She ducked her head, though she didn't need to hide from her brothers. "I belong here."

The bell sounded, and Drake jerked his attention toward the wall of windows showing the track. That bell signaled five minutes until bets had to be placed, and then the next race would start immediately after that.

"I've been thinking about partnering with Olli," Ginny said. "For when she has her baby. There's so much more I can do than run Sweet Rose." She'd pledged her time and talent to the Lord, and she wanted to do what He wanted her to do. Somehow, she felt Him gently leading her away from the distillery.

"We can talk more about it on Tuesday," she said, smiling around at the lot of them. "Go get your bets in, Drake."

"I can do it from right here," he said. "I just left my program out there…"

"I think I'm going to bet on this one too," Ginny said,

standing up. "Let's go." She led the way outside, retaking her seat on the front row of the balcony. She tapped on her phone to get to the current race, seeing there was only one more after this one.

Then the Smash would be over. Done.

It had been a roaring success, and if there had been any problems, Ginny didn't know about them. That was always a good sign, because things could be falling apart but as long as the customers didn't know, it was fine.

She looked at the names of the horses, having no idea which one to bet on. She picked Luck and Lace, because she liked the alliteration and entered a bet of fifty dollars.

"Done," she said, and Drake shook his head, still studying his phone.

"It's not a race, Ginny," he said.

"Actually, that's exactly what it is." She laughed, and Drake joined in as he kept tapping.

He finished his betting with thirty seconds to go and stood up to watch the horses come out, just like he had before every other race.

"Hey, look at that."

"What?" Ginny asked, but she was using his program to fan herself. She didn't really care who won the races or about what Drake had seen.

"Look at this," he said, turning back to her. With the new animation in his voice, Ginny's attention piqued. She stood too and looked to the left where he was pointing.

Two men rode two horses out on the track, but they weren't racers and they weren't jockeys.

Ginny knew exactly who they were.

Lawrence and Cayden, riding Honeyduke and Raven. The two horses next to each other looked so different, and Ginny sucked in a breath at the sight of her cowboy on his horse.

"Ladies and gentlemen," the announcer came over the speaker system. "Bets are now closed, and we have one item to take care of before the horses come out. Will you please direct your attention to the track, where your owners and organizers of the Summer Smash are? Cayden and Lawrence Chappell!" He said their names like they were celebrities, and as the crowd roared for them, Ginny went right along with the tide of applause.

Cayden lifted a microphone to his mouth and said, "Thank you. Thank you all for coming." Honey started walking, but Raven didn't, and a banner started unrolling with every step Honey took.

"Ginny," Duke said with plenty of warning in his voice.

"This is not happening," Ginny whispered as the crowd started to die down.

"We sure hope y'all have enjoyed your day at the races with us," Cayden said. "We hope you'll come back for many more. There's just one quick question I need everyone to answer, and you can find a notification in your app to do that right about..." He looked behind him at the banner and let Honey take four or five more steps. "Now."

Ginny pressed both hands to her mouth so she wouldn't scream.

"My girlfriend is in one of our corporate suites on the second floor," Cayden said. "I love her with my whole heart, and this is an important question I'm going to need her to answer." He nodded at the banner, lowered the mic, and looked directly at Ginny with a huge smile on his face.

The banner read *Should Ginny Winters marry me?*

Her hands shook as she tried to get her phone out to vote. She fumbled the device and it went tumbling right over the railing. A choked cry came out of her mouth, and then she started laughing.

"I voted yes," Drake said beside her. "You should go, Ginny. Go find him right now and tell him yes."

The crowd started chanting, "Yes, yes, yes!" and Ginny spun away from the railing.

Her brothers cheered, and her employees clapped, and Ginny exploded into the empty hallway outside the Bonfire Room, almost panicked in her need to get to Cayden.

Olli stood there as if waiting for her, and Ginny burst into tears.

"Come on," Olli said, gathering her into a tight, tight hug the way a best friend should. "Let's go get your cowboy." She led Ginny down the hallway and around a corner to some steps. Down they went, and Ginny was suddenly grateful she'd booked a suite on only the second floor.

Someone said something over the speaker system, but Ginny's senses were one-hundred percent overwhelmed, and she couldn't make out the words.

She did see all the people smiling and clapping as Olli kept a tight grip on her hand and kept moving forward. The crowd seemed to part for her, as they should, because Olli was powerful and fierce.

"Go with Spur now," she said, passing Ginny's hand from her soft one to Spur's more calloused one.

Spur grinned at her, and Ginny swiped at her face. "I'm going to be on camera, aren't I?"

"That's a definite yes," he said. It was more a yell, as some parts of the crowd were still chanting "Yes, yes, yes!"

He looked at her and raised his eyebrows. "You ready?"

"I dropped my phone over the side of the balcony," she said.

"Lawrence has it," he said, grinning. "I told him you were going to hate this."

"I don't hate it," Ginny said. "I just—a heads-up would've been nice." She put a smile on her face, though, and nodded. "I'm ready."

Spur turned, keeping her hand in his and started through the crowd gathered in front of the stands. Then on the lawn before the track. A roar swelled with every step Ginny took, and he finally burst through all the people.

Only the rail separated her from Cayden, who swung down off his horse and jogged toward her.

She ducked under the railing and stepped onto the track, which was so not as hard as she'd expected it to be. Her feet squished all over, and dirt filled her sandals. She laughed as she cried, and she kicked her shoes off just before Cayden swooped her into his arms.

They laughed together as he lifted her right up off her feet. She squealed and braced herself against his shoulders.

"They think you should say yes," he said, pointing to the scoreboard where the poll results sat.

"All right, then," she said. "Yes."

Cayden's eyes sparkled at her like dark diamonds. He filled her with joy, and she couldn't believe she'd get to be his, and that he was willing to be hers.

Lawrence arrived, and he passed the mic down to Cayden, who turned toward the crowd and backed up. Ginny went with him, and he lifted the mic to his lips and said, "She said yes!"

Ginny didn't know what fifteen thousand people screaming and whistling and clapping sounded like and looked like until that moment. She gazed up at all of them, her smile the realest one she'd ever worn.

Cayden lifted their joined hands, and Ginny laughed again.

"All right," Cayden said into the mic, but a new chant started in the crowd, and he cupped his hand around his ear as if he really wanted to hear what they were saying. The words increased in volume, and Ginny recognized them before Cayden did.

"...kiss her, kiss her, kiss her!"

Cayden figured it out a few seconds later, and he turned toward Ginny, questions in his eyes.

She grabbed onto his face and drew him to her for a kiss, sending the crowd into another rousing round of yelling, this time with plenty of cat-calling.

"I love you," Cayden said, somehow making the moment intimate though they literally stood in front of thousands and thousands of people.

"I love you too," she whispered, her lips catching on his enough to warrant kissing him again.

~

Keep reading for a bonus sneak peek of the next book in the Bluegrass Ranch series, PROMOTING THE COWBOY BILLIONAIRE.

PROMOTING THE COWBOY BILLIONAIRE CHAPTER ONE:

*L*awrence Chappell sighed as he stepped up to the mirror in the bathroom on the second floor at the homestead. He'd just showered for the second time that day, and he wished it was so he could go to bed clean.

Instead, he'd trim up his beard, splash on plenty of the cologne Olli had made for Spur, and get dressed in his best pair of jeans.

As he looked into his own pair of dark eyes, he could see the text from Mariah Barker. He wasn't sure how to label her, though he'd like to say she was his girlfriend. They'd been out several times this summer, but he'd never kissed her.

They went to her work events and held hands, talked, and laughed. He knew the women she sat by at work, and they knew him. To everyone outside the relationship,

Lawrence and Mariah were a couple, and they'd been dating since June.

To Lawrence, though, who lived inside the relationship, he knew they were one-hundred percent *not* dating.

Though Mariah acted interested, Lawrence could no longer decide what was pretend for her and what wasn't.

Thus, he sighed again as he picked up his razor. He trimmed his beard, his unrest growing by the second. When he finished, he rinsed his face and splashed on aftershave so his skin wouldn't break out in tiny bumps. He seemed to be just one shade below the rest of his brothers.

His skin was fairer, and he had to wear sunscreen when he went outside. He'd learned through some recent painful encounters to spray it on every time, no matter what.

He still had the dark hair, though his wasn't nearly black like Spur's or Duke's. He'd definitely inherited more of the feminine qualities from his mother, and he turned away from his reflection at the thought of her.

Lawrence had struggled the most out of all the brothers to talk to women. Even in high school, girls had scared him, and somewhere along the line, Mom had decided it was her life's mission to set Lawrence up with every woman she deemed pretty—and Mom literally thought every woman was pretty.

He'd gone on several of her blind dates, but she wanted to dish with him afterward. She wanted all the details, down to exact lines said during conversations. If Lawrence didn't like one of her choices, she'd demand to know why.

After a while, Lawrence's embarrassment over being set up by his mother became too much, and he'd told her he didn't want her to keep doing so. They'd argued, of course. Everything with Mom was an argument.

As Lawrence went back across the hall to his bedroom, he told himself he wasn't being fair. Mom had come a long way this year, and he knew he needed to get down the lane and make his peace with her. She'd been trying hard, sending out memes and links to articles she thought he'd like. She had not invited him to come to the house where she and Daddy now lived out their retirement from full-time work at Bluegrass Ranch.

Daddy had recovered well from his hip replacement surgery last year, and he came out into the Chappell stables almost every day. He cleaned equipment and brushed down horses for anyone who wanted him to. He'd been back on a horse in the past month, and only Lawrence knew.

If Mom knew... Lawrence chuckled as he shook his head. He dressed in his pressed and clean clothes, his mind moving forward too fast for him to keep up. No matter what else was in his head, he kept coming back to one thing: He needed to end things with Mariah.

The Summer Smash had concluded three weeks ago, and once upon a time, they'd agreed to keep their relationship "professional" until the inaugural race at Bluegrass had finished. She'd been the marketing executive assigned to the ranch, and Lawrence could admit she'd done an amazing job. Everyone thought so, and even Cayden—perfect, polished, and expects-perfection-and-polish-in-return—said he'd definitely use her again.

"I'm tired of being used, though," he muttered as he bent to put on the pair of cowboy boots Mariah had actually bought for him. A rush of humiliation pulled through him, and he stalled in the movement to dress himself the way she wanted him to.

"You're such an idiot." He stood up, bootless, and strode out of the bedroom. Duke had finally moved into the homestead too, and his bedroom sat just down the hall from Lawrence's. He went that way and banged on the door. "Duke," he called. "I need your help."

"Comin'." A few seconds later, Duke opened the door, his headset still on. "Sorry." He reached up and took it off. "They're in the middle of a share," he said. "I have to be muted and off-camera, but the professor could come back on any second." He'd started taking some classes in ranch management just about a week ago, and Lawrence did like listening to him talk about it.

Duke was always so animated. He did tend to talk too much, but he also had the ability to know when he'd let his mouth run away from him, something Conrad and Ian didn't possess.

"It won't take long," Lawrence said. "I just need a yes

or no answer."

"Okay, shoot." Duke glanced over his shoulder and then focused his full attention on Lawrence.

"Say the woman you've been going out with starts making excuses for why she can't see you if the two of you aren't going to a work party. For her. A work party for *her*." He cleared his throat. "Then she's available, and by the stars in heaven, you better be available too."

Duke started to narrow his eyes, but Lawrence plowed forward. "She says your boots make you look dirty, and she actually buys you a new pair. She texts you what she's wearing and makes suggestions for what you should wear. She doesn't let you come pick her up, but she arranges a meeting place so you can arrive at the party together. You haven't kissed her, but it's been months of this."

"I know where this is going."

Lawrence was sure he did. Duke went out with a lot of women, and he had no problem getting random strangers to come sit by him at weddings, dance with him, or attend any number of family parties and events with a simple smile and a cocked eyebrow.

"Should you break up with her?" Lawrence asked.

"The real question is: Are you even dating this woman?" Duke put both eyebrows up, the question clear.

"Let's say you thought you were. She might even think you are."

"Yes," Duke said. "If it's yes or no, Larry, it's yes."

Despite the nickname he hated, Lawrence nodded, his

gaze suddenly finding something so much more interesting to look at over Duke's shoulder. "Yeah, I think so too. Thanks." He turned and started back to his bedroom, his heart heavy and his feet feeling like wooden blocks he could barely lift.

"And don't wear those boots," Duke said. "Be who you are, Lawrence."

Lawrence waited until he was back in his room, the door closed, before he said, "Easy for you to say, Duke. You went out with one blonde last night and have a date with a different one tonight."

He paused in the middle of the room and looked at the boots lying beside the bed. Nope, he wasn't going to wear those. He kicked them under the bed and went to his closet to get out a pair of sneakers. Mariah would hate these, and he put them on anyway.

She'd texted to say she'd be wearing a flowered sundress in navy and white, and wouldn't they look so cute if he wore a red shirt? *Like the flag*, she'd said with a smiley face.

"So cute," he muttered, stripping off the red shirt he'd already put on. He didn't even like the color red, because it made his skin look pinker than it really needed to look, ever.

He pulled on a black plaid shirt that had big boxes of white in between the black ones. Faint yellow pinstripes ran down and across in the white parts, and he felt more like himself instantly.

He skipped brushing his teeth, because he wasn't going to kiss Mariah anyway, and he went downstairs to find Ginny standing in the kitchen, a wooden spoon in one hand while she licked something off her fingers on the other.

She grinned at him, a bit of color coming into her face. "Heya, Lawrence."

"Evening, ma'am," he said. He was used to seeing Ginny Winters in the homestead. She and Cayden had been engaged since the Smash, and she loved to cook until he came in from the administration building.

Then whoever was around would eat, and she and Cayden would spread out their wedding plans on the dining room table and talk and talk and talk.

"Going out with Mariah again?"

"Again?" he asked. "We haven't been out in weeks."

Ginny lowered the wooden spoon. "Oh, I thought... You're right. You left last week, but then you came back." Her dark eyes fired questions at him, but Lawrence couldn't even answer the ones already swimming in his own mind.

"I'm sorry," she added, turning back to the bowl she'd been stirring.

"No, I'm sorry," he said with a sigh. "I'm just in a mood, because I'm going to break up with her tonight."

Ginny didn't turn back to him, and he appreciated that. "You are? Things aren't going well?"

"I think she's only using me to go to her company parties."

Ginny did face him again then, her eyes wide. "Have you asked her?"

"We sorta talked about it a while ago," he mumbled. "At Blaine's wedding, we *did* agree to use the relationship as a way for her to get to her boss's parties, but in my head, the agreement ended once the Smash did. Then we'd become a real couple, because she wouldn't be working for us anymore." He watched Ginny absorb the information, her mind obviously working much faster than his ever had.

"She had some sort of personal policy against dating clients," he finished.

"Now she doesn't want to go out," Ginny said.

"Doesn't seem like it."

"Maybe she's really busy?" Ginny guessed. "When Cayden first asked me out, I was so busy with the Harvest Festival at Sweet Rose, I put him off."

"I don't know," Lawrence said, but he seriously doubted it. Mariah seemed to have plenty of time to go for coffee with friends after work, or get her nails done, both things he'd seen on her social media this week.

He gave Ginny a small smile and reached up to touch his hat. Mariah had tried to get him to not wear it once, but he'd done it anyway. She hadn't said anything again, and Lawrence wondered how she'd react if the tables were turned.

He couldn't even imagine texting her and telling her what to wear for their fake date that night—to an apple-tasting party, of all things.

No wonder she wanted him to wear red. When they'd gone to an event over the summer, she'd known the theme was country chic, but he hadn't. She'd suggested he wear a red and white checkered shirt, and no less than twenty people had commented on how he and Mariah had really played up the theme.

In fact, she'd gotten the biggest case of the party because of it.

Guilt pulled through him as he left the homestead and walked over to his brand-new truck. None of his brothers had said anything, because he had his own money to spend, and if he wanted a two-ton truck, he could have a two-ton truck.

He didn't like thinking that he'd bought the huge truck to make up for how small he felt inside his own life.

Think about it he did as he navigated across town to the spot where he'd met Mariah several times in the past. A parking lot at an all-night doughnut shop. Lawrence didn't understand the point of Doughnuts After Dark, but they did have an amazing cake doughnut with maple frosting and a crumb topping.

Sometimes, if he was early, he went inside and got himself a tasty treat.

He wasn't early tonight. If anything, he was late. He tried to care, but he was having a hard time with all of it.

When he pulled into the parking lot, Mariah's white SUV was already parked on the outside row of spaces, and Lawrence eased his truck next to it. She always rode with him, and tonight was no different.

She smiled at him through the glass, and Lawrence started second-guessing himself. It honestly was probably a third- or fourth-guessing to be honest.

"Hey," she said.

"Hey," he responded. He had the urge to tell her he was sorry he was late, but he bit back the words. She did look amazing in the flirty sundress, and she'd paired the dark dress with white flowers all over it with a pair of bright pink sandals Lawrence really liked.

He really liked *her*, and he didn't understand what had turned cold between them since Blaine's wedding. He pulled out of the parking spot and eased back onto the highway to get to her boss's house.

They drove along, and Lawrence waited for her to ask him something. He often started the conversations with questions about her day, or a client, or a co-worker.

"How's the ranch?" she finally asked.

"Good," Lawrence said, hating the false quality in his voice. He sighed again, and added, "Listen, Mariah, we need to talk."

"About what?"

"About what we're doing," he said, glancing at her. "I thought we were going to become a real couple after the Smash, but every time I ask you out, you have something else to do." He swallowed, but he'd started and he couldn't stop now. "Which is fine. Maybe you're really busy at work right now. Ginny said she did that; she was so busy and she couldn't date Cayden."

He stopped to shake his thoughts back into some semblance of order. He also needed to breathe. "Anyway, that's neither here nor there. I just want to know what you want *this* to be." He gestured between the two of them, his frustration obvious.

She gaped at him with wide eyes, and Lawrence felt the same shock moving through him.

"I..." she said. "I don't know." She looked out her window, and Lawrence had his answer.

"I don't think we should see each other anymore," he said. "I'll go to this party, and I'll be exactly who I've been all the other times." He shifted in his seat, his mouth so dry. "Then that's that. Okay?"

She didn't answer, and when Lawrence looked over at her, he found her nodding.

"Okay, then," he said, and a cloud of awkward silence draped over the two of them. *Idiot*, he chastised himself. *You should've waited until after the party to break-up with her.*

Now he had to attend the party as her fake boyfriend when he was exactly that. At least before, he'd had some hope of a real relationship with her, which had made the pretending easier.

This was going to be torture.

PROMOTING THE COWBOY BILLIONAIRE CHAPTER TWO:

Mariah Barker woke up to the scent of pumpkin pie spice and cream, and she groaned as she rolled over. She fumbled for her phone to check the time, and it couldn't be too late yet, because hardly any light came through her blinds.

Someone making coffee down the hall in her kitchen meant her sister had come over, and Mariah rolled onto her back and stared up at the ceiling. She'd managed to find a reason why she hadn't been able to make the family brunches, but Dani had the nose of a bloodhound, and she'd been texting Mariah for over a week now.

She didn't want to tell Dani about Lawrence; she didn't want to tell anyone about Lawrence. She'd been cursing her luck, the stars, and any cracks in sidewalks she'd somehow stepped on since the middle of July.

With only a week until the Smash, Dr. Biggers had

called her into his office and said he thought she'd been using Lawrence to get better jobs. Her heart thumped harder in her chest even now.

She'd denied it, and thankfully, Dr. Biggers had thought she meant she'd been mining the Chappells for more clients. She hadn't been; she'd simply been able to network with a lot of people while she'd worked on their event. She'd met a lot of people at the event, and she'd learned to carry her business cards everywhere with her.

Dr. Biggers had cautioned her not to mix business and pleasure, and Mariah didn't know what to do with that. She didn't know how to separate Lawrence from her life when he was the reason she got to go to the events that kept her working with the clients she wanted to work with.

She'd tried explaining to Dr. Biggers, but he'd flat-out told her not to ask Lawrence for clients if she was going to date him. *If you break-up with him*, he'd said. *Well, that's a different story. Then he's not a personal contact, but a business one.*

Mariah felt trapped between two plates of steel, and she had no idea how to slip out. She'd made a mess of things by trying to put Lawrence off in a fun, flirty way, hoping he wouldn't notice that they weren't going out for real.

"I want to," she whispered. "I just don't know *how*."

That was the story of Mariah's life, and she'd endured the apple extravaganza a couple of weeks ago, and she'd told no one that she and Lawrence hadn't spoken since that night.

Dani would get the story out of her, but Mariah couldn't put her off forever. She finally got up and shimmied into a pair of leggings to give her sister the appearance that she was going to work out today.

She wasn't, because Saturdays simply weren't for working out. They were for sleeping in and sipping pumpkin spice lattes, and Dani understood that.

Mariah padded out into the kitchen, where she found Dani pouring raw scrambled eggs into a muffin tin.

"It's about time you got up," Dani said. "I was going to slide these in and come see what was going on."

"What's going on," Mariah said as she overturned a mug her older sister had put on the counter. "Is that it's Saturday and barely eight a.m." She smiled at her sister as she poured her coffee and reached for the container of pumpkin spice creamer. "You are a Godsend, though. I've had a horribly busy week, and next week is going to be worse."

"You shouldn't have—"

"I know," Mariah said, giving her a glare. "Okay? I know."

Dani held up one hand in acquiescence and slid the muffin tin into the oven. She leaned one hip into the counter and asked, "How does your boyfriend feel about your busy schedule?"

Mariah tucked her messy hair behind her ear and shrugged.

"You broke up with him." Dani's voice carried shock.

"He broke up with me," Mariah said, and Lawrence was right to do so. Mariah wouldn't want to only go out with him so he could have an in with his boss. The fact that he'd kept doing it for almost a month after the Smash was a testament to him, and Mariah wished the situation was different.

"What happened?" Dani asked.

"I don't want to talk about it," Mariah said. "That's why I didn't text you back or come to the last two brunches." She cocked her left eyebrow at Dani. "Can we not talk about it today?"

"You liked him so much," she said. "I could tell."

"This is the opposite of not talking about him."

"Hey, I came and made coffee and breakfast," she said.

"Yeah, because your husband is out of town, and you don't know what to do with yourself if you're not mothering someone."

A pinch of hurt crossed Dani's face, and Mariah added her pain to the guilt that had been collecting in her stomach for a while now. "Sorry," she murmured.

"It's okay," Dani said. "What are you doing for Halloween?"

"Halloween?" Mariah chuckled. "It's almost two months away still."

"You make elaborate costumes, though." Dani smiled at her. "I know you have a plan. Just tell me."

"I was thinking about, I don't know. A Smurf or something."

Dani laughed and shook her head. "You're impossible."

A dog barked, and she straightened before walking over to the back door to let in her dog. "You're not supposed to bark," she said. "You and that little dog next door need to learn to get along. Your relationship is dysfunctional."

Mariah laughed, because the idea of the two dogs having a dysfunctional relationship was hilarious. Dani's black dog with the big white patch on his chest caught sight of her and came running over.

"Whoa, whoa," she said, still giggling. "Not so fast." Phantom skidded to a stop just in time, his doggy face so happy to see her. "Yes, it's good to see you too. So good." Mariah scratched the dog's back and that white patch, his fur so soft. "You've been to the groomer recently, haven't you, bud? Yes, you have. You have."

"So, are you looking for a new boyfriend?" Dani asked, stepping over to the stove to check on the baked eggs.

"No," Mariah said. "I have plenty of clients right now. Let Dr. Biggers overwhelm someone else for a few months." She picked up her coffee and took it to the couch. Phantom followed her and jumped up beside her.

Mariah relaxed into the couch and closed her eyes.

She could get used to someone taking care of her while she relaxed, as that hadn't happened in a while now. She'd been gearing up to ask Lawrence to come to her house for dinner, as he'd never been here to pick her up or anything. She hadn't wanted him to cross into her personal space while he was her client.

Dr. Biggers didn't have a problem with that, only with her using him to get more clients. All at once, Mariah realized why she'd gotten in trouble with him. *He* liked to be the one to bring the heavy hitting clients to his people, and he did not like her bringing her own companies to The Gemini Group.

"I need to quit my job," she said.

"What?" Dani asked, spinning from the stove. "You love that job."

"I hate my job," Mariah said, finally speaking the truth. "I *need* the job, and it's far better than anything else I've ever had. There's a difference."

Dani came toward her, and Mariah knew what she was going to say. She held up her hand. "Don't. I don't want to live in your basement."

"What about Dad's—?"

"I can't believe you even said that," Mariah said, getting to her feet. "I'm not moving back in with Dad. I'm thirty-seven years old." She'd had quite the disastrous decade in her twenties, and she'd been paying for it for almost a decade. She crossed into the kitchen, ready to dump her sister's coffee down the drain.

She stalled though, because she was thirty-seven years old, and she didn't need to act like a petulant child. "I liked Lawrence. Like him. I *like* him."

"Then go out with him," Dani said, her voice coming from clear across the room. At least she was smart. "Who cares what your boss says?"

"I just don't want to give any of the wrong impressions," Mariah said. "To anyone."

"You worry too much about what other people think."

"Yes," Mariah said. She wondered when that would disappear. Dani was three years older than her, and she and her husband hadn't been able to have children. They had their dog, and they had each other, and most of the time, that was enough.

Mariah knew there was an ache deep down inside Dani's soul, though. It came to life when it wasn't enough to have a husband and a dog, but she'd stopped talking to Mariah about it after her miscarriage and divorce, the filed bankruptcy and the temporary protective order.

"I don't want Lawrence to know about my past," she whispered.

Somehow her sister heard her, and Dani joined her in front of the kitchen sink. "If he's the one, Mya, he won't care."

Mariah leaned into her sister, who put her arm around her. "How do you know if a man is the one?"

"You just do," Dani said. "Unless you won't go out with him."

Mariah's smile came quickly at the teasing in her sister's voice. "Thank you." She turned into her and hugged her. A few moments later, the timer on the eggs went off, and Dani cleared her throat. "Okay, let's eat. I have some news for you."

"Lay it on me, Short Stack."

Dani giggled as she got the muffin tin out of the oven. She'd hated Mariah's nickname for her growing up, but it seemed to endear them to each other now. They only had one another—and their father—and Mariah suddenly felt bad for canceling on the last two brunch dates her family went on every Sunday.

"Doug and I might be getting a baby," she said, her eyes filled with hope but her voice calm and casual. "I'm not saying we are. We've got a meeting tomorrow morning at the agency, and Isaac says he's had a birth mother ask about us several times. He's going to put us in touch with her."

Wonder and amazement filled Mariah, and she hurried around the counter to her sister. "I'm so glad."

The strength with which Dani clung to her told Mariah that she was glad too, and her hopes were has high as they could go. "No promises," Dani said. "We've had birth moms ask about us before."

"Right." Mariah cleared her throat. "It's still exciting. Congratulations." She stepped back and ignored Dani as she wiped her eyes. She served her sister a couple of the omelet muffins and took two for herself too.

"How do you think I can get Lawrence to go out with me?"

"Just call him and ask."

Mariah shook her head as she split open her muffin and steam came pouring out. "That's not how it's done these days."

"No? Women don't ask men out? You wait for him to ask you?"

"No, you don't just call and ask." Mariah shook her head as she sprinkled salt over the eggs. "I need to, I don't know, run into him somehow. Like it's a mistake."

"That's ridiculous," Dani said.

It might be, but that was what Mariah needed to do. "I don't think he leaves the ranch much," she mused.

"Then I guess you've got to get out to Bluegrass Ranch," Dani said.

She did... Now she just needed to figure out *how*.

∼

A WEEK WENT BY WHILE MARIAH PLANNED THE PERFECT staged attempt to run into Lawrence Chappell again. She'd driven along the road that ran in front of Bluegrass Ranch a dozen times, hoping her old SUV would break down and he'd conveniently happen by in his truck to help her.

The car just kept running and running, though, and all Mariah did was rack up a higher gas bill that week.

Still, she thought she'd give it one more try. Inspiration had struck her so many times out at Bluegrass that she was sure it would one more time.

"Just one more time," she begged as she got behind the wheel of her car and started the pilgrimage to Bluegrass. It was a long way for her, but the time passed quickly under the cogs and wheels of her mind.

She was no closer to a solution when she approached the curve in the road where Bluegrass sat, up on the hill to her right.

A sign now sat there that hadn't been there before. *You Pick Peaches and Apples.*

It had a giant arrow pointing left, and Mariah knew from working with the Chappells on the Summer Smash that one of them actually lived down the road at this other ranch.

She hit the brakes and put on her blinker, though there was no one behind her. After making the turn off the highway and onto the white gravel of a long driveway, Mariah took a deep breath. "This is crazy," she said. "You don't have time to pick fruit."

She did adore peaches, though, and if she could get even a half-dozen of those, she'd have breakfast for a week.

A man rose from a chair positioned underneath a portable and collapsible shade, and Mariah recognized him. Not Lawrence, or Cayden, or Spur, whom she'd actually worked face-to-face with.

But Conrad Chappell, the brother who'd brought a giggly blonde to the family table during Blaine's wedding.

He came out a few steps, a clipboard in his hand and a smile on his face. "Good morning," he said, simply grinning at her like she was the one person he'd wanted to meet. "Welcome to Triple T Ranch. Do you want to pick apples or peaches?"

"Is there a price difference?"

"Yes, ma'am," he said, flipping something on his clipboard. He took off a stiff piece of plastic and handed it to her. "The peaches are at their peak right now, but we've had a lot of people out here in the past couple of days, so you have to climb up to get them. They're a bit more expensive. The apples are Liberties, and some of them need a few more weeks. Again, we've had a fair bit of traffic out here recently, and you'll have to hunt for the apples."

"Hunting and climbing," Mariah said. "Sounds like hard work." That she was going to pay to do. It made no sense, and yet, she found herself studying the plastic sheet. *This is the closest you've been to Lawrence in three weeks. Don't blow it.*

"We've got guys out there that can help you," he said.

Mariah looked up, her hopes climbing too as an idea occurred to her. "Do you recognize me, Conrad?" She handed him the plastic sheet back, his eyebrows furrowing down as he took it and reattached it to his clipboard.

"Should I?"

"Yes," she said. "I ate with you at Blaine's wedding. I sat next to Lawrence."

"Oh, right," he said, but his eyes didn't light up. He still had no idea who she was, and her stomach clawed at itself. "I was one of the marketing execs for the Smash."

That got him to really glow. "Of course. Mariah...Barker." He snapped his fingers, obviously proud of himself. Lawrence obviously didn't talk about his private life with this particular brother, or he wouldn't be smiling at her like that.

"Yes." She returned the smile, wishing she wasn't quite so far into her professional voice. "Listen, I haven't heard from Lawrence for a while. Is he one of the guys out in the fields?"

"Yes, ma'am," Conrad said, looking at his clipboard. "He's on peaches this morning."

Perfect, Mariah thought. "I think I want to pick some peaches," she said.

"Great." He started telling her where to go, and where to park once she got there. He said he'd radio ahead to "the guys" in the peach orchard and let them know they had a customer coming in.

Mariah employed every ounce of patience she had while he went on and on, finally taking the tag with a peach printed on it and tossing it onto her dashboard like he'd told her to. She went down the lane he'd indicated, and she found the parking area easily.

Only one other car sat there, and Mariah prayed with all the sincerity of her heart that Lawrence wasn't out in the orchard with that customer. She wasn't exactly dressed for picking peaches, as she'd done her hair and makeup, put on a cute pair of khaki shorts and a bright pink camouflage-patterned blouse that morning.

"The goal is the same," she muttered. "Get Lawrence's attention." She'd wanted to look good should she happen to run into him, and that would still be achieved.

She got out of the car, pocketed her keys and phone, and started for the fruit stand where they'd give her a basket and then weigh her out when she picked all the peaches she wanted.

As she approached, she met Duke's eyes—another brother she'd met a few times as she worked with the Chappells on their big event several weeks ago now.

"You're up, Larry," he said, his eyes glued to Mariah.

"Fine," Lawrence's voice said from inside the stand. "Then I'm goin' home. I'm on mowing tonight, and—" He froze as his gaze moved from Duke to Mariah.

Keep going, she told herself. *Keep going. Don't stop. Dear Lord, don't let me stop.*

"Mariah," Lawrence said, his voice grinding through his throat in the next moment. He reached up and adjusted his cowboy hat. She smiled at him, because he was so sexy in that hat, and when he spoke in that Southern voice, she wanted to melt right into his arms.

He glanced at Duke, but Mariah only had eyes for him.

In what felt like a rush of time, Mariah closed the distance between them and put her palm against his chest. His heart beat steadily beneath that handsome blue paisley shirt, and she felt completely outside of her head as she said, "I'm so sorry, Lawrence. I got all inside my head, and my boss said some things that confused me, and I didn't want to hurt you."

He blinked at her, his surprise evident. "Okay," he said.

Mariah couldn't go back now, so she might as well keep going. "What does *mowing tonight* entail? Would you have time to go to dinner?"

He fell back a step as if she'd hit him with her words. "Uh..."

Mariah didn't like the sound of that. She looked at Duke, who stood there watching them without any embarrassment at all. Plenty of it heated her face, and she dropped her gaze to the dirt at her feet.

The silence hanging in the air felt like poison, and Mariah shuffled backward. "Never—"

"He can't take you to dinner," Duke blurted out. "The mowing means he works all night mowing the hay."

She looked up at him as he moved between her and Lawrence.

"Duke," Lawrence said.

"He can take you to lunch, though," Duke said with a bright smile. "Right after y'all finish picking your peaches." He turned sideways and looked from Mariah to Lawrence and back, nodded, and went back inside the fruit stand.

Lawrence stared at her for another moment, a smile finally touching his face. He took a step toward her. "Are you free for lunch, Mariah?"

She grinned at him, nodded, and took his hand when he extended it toward her.

～

I can't wait to see if Mariah and Lawrence can navigate a difficult work situation and their feelings in
PROMOTING THE COWBOY BILLIONAIRE.

BLUEGRASS RANCH ROMANCE

Book 1: Winning the Cowboy Billionaire: She'll do anything to secure the funding she needs to take her perfumery to the next level...even date the boy next door.

Book 2: Roping the Cowboy Billionaire: She'll do anything to show her ex she's not still hung up on him...even date her best friend.

Book 3: Training the Cowboy Billionaire: She'll do anything to save her ranch...even marry a cowboy just so they can enter a race together.

Book 4: Parading the Cowboy Billionaire: She'll do anything to spite her mother and find her own happiness...even keep her cowboy billionaire boyfriend a secret.

Book 5: Promoting the Cowboy Billionaire: She'll do anything to keep her job...even date a client to stay on her boss's good side.

Book 6: Acquiring the Cowboy Billionaire: She'll do anything to keep her father's stud farm in the family...even marry the maddening cowboy billionaire she's never gotten along with.

Book 7: Saving the Cowboy Billionaire: She'll do anything to prove to her friends that she's over her ex...even date the cowboy she once went with in high school.

Book 8: Convincing the Cowboy Billionaire: She'll do anything to keep her dignity...even convincing the saltiest cowboy billionaire at the ranch to be her boyfriend.

CHESTNUT RANCH ROMANCE

Book 1: A Cowboy and his Neighbor: Best friends and neighbors shouldn't share a kiss...

Book 2: A Cowboy and his Mistletoe Kiss: He wasn't supposed to kiss her. Can Travis and Millie find a way to turn their mistletoe kiss into true love?

Book 3: A Cowboy and his Christmas Crush: Can a Christmas crush and their mutual love of rescuing dogs bring them back together?

Book 4: A Cowboy and his Daughter: They were married for a few months. She lost their baby...or so he thought.

Book 5: A Cowboy and his Boss: She's his boss. He's had a crush on her for a couple of summers now. Can Toni and Griffin mix business and pleasure while making sure the teens they're in charge of stay in line?

Book 6: A Cowboy and his Fake Marriage: She needs a husband to keep her ranch...can she convince the cowboy next-door to marry her?

Book 7: A Cowboy and his Secret Kiss: He likes the pretty adventure guide next door, but she wants to keep their relationship off the grid. Can he kiss her in secret and keep his heart intact?

Book 8: A Cowboy and his Skipped Christmas: He's been in love with her forever. She's told him no more times than either of them can count. Can Theo and Sorrell find their way through past pain to a happy future together?

ABOUT EMMY

Emmy is a Midwest mom who loves dogs, cowboys, and Texas. She's been writing for years and loves weaving stories of love, hope, and second chances. Learn more about her and her books at www.emmyeugene.com.